The Seaside Strategy

SWEET ROMANCE & WOMEN'S FRIENDSHIP FICTION

HILTON HEAD ISLAND
BOOK THREE

ELANA JOHNSON

ISBN-13: 978-1-63876-155-6

Chapter One

Lauren Keller used the remote on the larger of her two monitors to turn it off. She still had work to do, but she had to draw a line somewhere. Otherwise, she'd work twenty-four hours a day. She'd allowed herself to go down that path before, but not this summer.

No, this summer was about finding balance. Accepting things as they stood. Being more patient with herself—and those around her.

She sighed as she stretched both hands high above her head and held the position. Sitting at a desk wasn't the best for her shoulders and back, and Lauren stood and went through a few simple exercises that should help the knot in the back of her neck.

What she really needed was a good masseuse, and she'd ask Cass who to go to here on Hilton Head when she made it downstairs.

She left her bedroom-slash-office on the second floor of

Cass's beach house and went down the hallway. She'd be moving out next weekend, but she wouldn't be going far. When she'd first decided to come to the island for the summer—as she had last year—she'd secured a rental.

Cass had thrown a fit. A major, royal fit, and she'd insisted that Lauren take the bedroom where she'd stayed last year. Cass had wanted help with the wedding, and Lauren didn't need bad Supper Club mojo on her hands. So she'd been living with Cass and Conrad for about seven weeks, and the three of them got along splendidly.

Conrad once again worked for the outdoor tour company he'd been with last year, and Cass had plenty to keep her busy with her interior design clients. The house was cool and quiet, and Lauren loved everything about it.

So much so, that she'd started looking at properties here on Hilton Head too. If she was going to live here for five or six months out of the year, she figured she should have her own place.

Everything she did came with a strategy; she couldn't help it. Her job as a marketing analyst, team leader, and corporate strategist had the label in the title. She barely got dressed without a routine, a strategy to get the most done in the least amount of time.

Right now, however, she set aside her strategies and went into the kitchen. No one else lingered, and she reasoned that it was five o'clock somewhere. Almost here, as a glance at the clock told her. So she popped the top on her Diet Coke and emptied the can into a tall glass.

Cass didn't own any dishware that was plastic, and

Lauren actually liked that about her. It made Lauren feel less like a diva for the nice things she enjoyed. She splashed in an ounce of rum, stirred her drink, and took a healthy sip.

The alcohol warmed her mouth and throat, almost burning as she swallowed. She sighed and relaxed her hip against the countertop, then put away the bottle and took her drink out to the patio.

She sat in the rocking bench and looked out to the ocean, letting her mind come and go the way the waves did as they washed ashore. She could hear them chattering, even as far away as she was, and she wondered what they said to each other. She wondered why she found them so soothing to her soul. She wondered how she could make them part of her permanent reality.

Coming downstairs or out of an office to a drink and the sound of the ocean? That was heaven to Lauren, and she flicked on her phone and started a familiar search for property here on the island.

Her biggest obstacle was price. Oceanfront property wasn't exactly inexpensive, and it wasn't infinite. She earned a good salary, and she didn't really have anything or anyone keeping her in Texas.

Yes, her corporate headquarters were there, but they had branches and offices all over the country. All over the world. She was, in fact, assigned to the Miami office right now, and Lauren traveled for about a third of her working hours anyway.

She thought of Joy, Bessie, and Sage back in Sweet Water Falls. Cherry Forrester too, now that the woman had joined their Supper Club. Joy would especially be upset if Lauren made the move to Hilton Head permanent.

"It's not permanent," she murmured to herself. "It's a few months out of the year."

Her phone chimed, nearly deafening her, as she'd forgotten to turn down the notification volume when she'd turned off her computer screen. Thankfully, it wasn't from anyone on her team. No one needed help. There was no crisis.

This text had come from Harrison Tate, Cass's fiancée. The man she'd marry in just another week's time.

Lauren's heart bobbed around inside her body, nearly bursting through her ribs when she finished reading. *MaryLou just called*, Harrison had said. *They approved your rental. You can move into my place while Cass and I are on our honeymoon.*

"Thank you, Dear Lord." Lauren pressed her phone to her chest and smiled up to heaven. She'd always anticipated finding somewhere else to live once Cass and Harrison tied the knot. She'd secured two other rentals—and they'd both canceled on her. She'd been scrambling for a week now, and Harrison hadn't put his house up for sale yet.

He too was scrambling to finish the last building in a huge construction project he'd been working on for over a year. He wanted it done and signed off before the nuptials got said, and he hadn't had time to call a realtor, clean up his place, and get it listed.

Cass had put a lot of time and energy into her house, and she was quite particular about the yard, the house, the textiles, all of it. Harrison had readily agreed to move in to her house once they were married, and he'd have his outdoor kitchen transplanted over here once they returned from Bora Bora.

Lauren took another sip of her drink and looked at her phone again. She'd been about to search for property here on the island, and she decided to go ahead and do that. Not rentals, though.

Something to buy.

She swiped and tapped, read about floor plans, and leafed through pictures. There were some really gorgeous homes here on Hilton Head, but nothing that truly spoke to her soul. Her eyes started to blur, and she lowered the phone once again.

"There you are," Joy said, bringing up Lauren's head.

"Hey." She smiled up at her friend. "How was work?"

"Great." Joy exhaled as she sat down next to Lauren, the bench swaying wildly as it accommodated for the extra weight. "I called you. Harrison said the HOA approved his rental. We can move in there."

"I got his text," she said. Her tongue felt a little thick, and her brain a tiny bit fuzzy. Maybe she'd splashed in a little too much rum. Or maybe it was just so warm and gorgeous here on this patio. The swaying of the bench. Something.

"I'm relieved," Joy said. "I actually looked at a long-term hotel this morning." She shook her head and bent to take off her shoes. She worked as a classroom aide in an elementary school back in Texas, but she'd come to Hilton Head this summer too. She'd been here for almost a month now, and she'd gotten a job at the library. She got to wear her cute work clothes and she seemed to like the people and patrons on Hilton Head. So much so, that she volunteered at the library when she wasn't scheduled to work.

"Can you imagine?" Lauren asked. They laughed together, and then Lauren looked at her phone again. "Oh, I missed a call from my boss." She got to her feet, and she didn't wobble too much. She also had no idea how she'd missed a call from Mark. Had she fallen asleep after looking at real estate?

Probably.

She walked to the edge of the patio and tapped to call Mark Apgood, the man who'd been her boss for about a decade now. She worked directly beneath him, and there wasn't really anywhere else for her to go. Another company, perhaps, but she enjoyed the work she did now, as well as the people she worked with. Most of the time, anyway.

"Lauren," he said crisply when he picked up.

"Mark," she said back. No excuses. She missed calls sometimes, and it was after working hours. She didn't have to call him back until tomorrow if she didn't want to.

"Can you be on a plane to Texas tonight?"

"Wha—? I—" Lauren turned around and looked at Joy. She'd leaned back in the swinging bench and closed her eyes. "Why?"

"There's some serious stuff going down, and I need you here."

"How long?" Lauren asked, already moving back to the house. She could pack and be on the road to the airport in twenty minutes. Whether they had a flight or not, that was a different story. "Cass is getting married in six days, Mark."

"Not that long." Something banged on his end of the line. "I can guarantee you won't miss her wedding."

"I can't," Lauren said. "I won't."

"You won't," he assured her. "I'll see you when you get here."

"Your office?" True surprise wove through her as she strode through the living room toward the stairs. "Tonight? You're not going home?"

"Not until this is settled," he said. "See you soon." The call ended, and Lauren dashed up the steps to the second floor. She had no idea what was going on—Mark had been very light on the details.

To her credit, she wore professional clothes to sit at the table in her bedroom, so she didn't have to change. She threw a couple of extra outfits in a bag, sat at the computer, and looked for a ticket. She had toiletries and everything else at her place in Sweet Water Falls. Truth be told, she had clothes there too. Plenty of clothes.

A flight left Atlanta at ten-forty, and Lauren booked herself a ticket. Then she grabbed her purse, her bag, and her laptop and headed for the door.

Whatever was happening better get resolved quickly, because Lauren would not miss Cass's wedding. Oh, no, she would not.

Chapter Two

Lauren pulled up to the office building where she'd put in the last fifteen years of her life, catching sight of the top row of windows. Lights burned there, and though only one other vehicle sat in the lot—a big F-350 truck—it sure seemed like she'd find more people inside than just Mark.

Her anxiety had been quietly doubling since she'd boarded the plane, almost four hours ago now. It was almost one-thirty in the morning, Texas-time, but that didn't seem to matter. She'd slept a little bit on the plane. How, she wasn't sure.

She pulled into her reserved parking spot, as if that mattered right now, gathered her purse and keys, and headed inside. She normally wore heels to work, but such footwear wasn't practical for airports or driving, and her loafers didn't make quite the same clicking noises as her pumps usually did.

The elevator took her to the twelfth floor, and the *ding!*

of her arrival seemed to screech through the empty building. She stepped onto the floor she'd known so well, almost pushing through the doors because they opened so slowly.

She immediately froze. Nothing currently being digested by her eyes was right.

A long, chest-high counter usually greeted guests who came to the twelfth floor. No one could get into the offices behind them without checking in with either Sheila or Reginald. Lauren didn't expect to see them here tonight, but to have the counter completely gone?

She blinked, wondering if she'd gotten off on the wrong floor.

Cubicles took up the left half of the floor, but the six-foot dividers had been pushed against the walls. Some of them, at least. Some lay in a heap, like a giant had picked them up, broken the hinges, and flung them back to earth.

"What is going on?" she wondered aloud.

She saw no computers. No desk chairs. No papers. No filing cabinets. The right side of the floor held a column of meeting rooms encased in glass. Four conference rooms, usually, that had to be booked through Sheila and Reginald, who of course, couldn't do that anymore. Angry marks on the industrial carpet where their workstation had been glared back at Lauren.

Her throat finally remembered how to swallow, and she did that while her pulse raced through her veins. She gripped her purse tighter, not sure if she should proceed toward Mark's office or leave immediately.

"Lauren." Mark's voice echoed strangely in this now-open space, and she jerked her attention toward him. He wore what she usually saw him in: a white shirt, a tie knotted tightly at the throat, and a pair of black slacks. He didn't look like he'd been working for almost twenty-four hours, or that he was responsible for the complete chaos on the twelfth floor.

"Mark." Lauren moved toward him, somehow wanting to run into his arms and be reassured that she was simply dreaming. She even jogged a couple of steps, and he did catch her against his chest. "This is awful. What's going on?"

She'd had a normal day of work. Meetings with two clients. Her team, both in the morning and the afternoon. She'd gone over marketing specs that had come in from the accounts team, and she'd approved the initial mocks to be shown to a client, for which a meeting was set for next week.

She'd had half of a drink, a chat with her friend, and everything had been so perfectly...normal.

Nothing here was normal. At least not for her memory.

"Are you guys closing this office?" That made no sense, as this was the corporate headquarters. She stepped back and looked up at Mark. He suddenly did wear age and exhaustion on his face.

"We're in trouble," he said. He gestured for her to follow him to his office, which she did. His sat in the back corner, the one with two walls of windows. Hers still stood next to his, but as she walked by the great glass walls, where the blinds had been raised, she could see that they now sat empty, like big fish bowls waiting to be filled with water.

She shivered, the thought of sharks entering her thoughts.

Her office door sat closed, and Lauren had the greatest itch to go inside. She hadn't brought her laptop in from the car either, and she clutched her purse even tighter as if someone might jump out from the wall and take it from her.

The art had been cleared out. The potted plants. Everything. Absolutely everything.

Her stupor deepened as she entered Mark's office. It looked like he'd tossed a bomb inside, then waited in the hall with the door closed until it had gone off. All of the papers, files, and furniture she'd expected to see out on the main floor did live in here. In heaps. In tatters. At odd angles.

Somehow, he sat in a chair that was positioned slightly behind his desk. Lauren only took three steps into the office before she stalled. "Mark," she said, and it sounded like a child's voice. She shook her head. She needed to get a grip on her composure and figure out what was going on.

For it sure didn't look like she had a job anymore. Or, if she did, it had morphed and changed in a single second the moment she'd stepped off the elevator.

"Mark," she barked. The man looked at her now, his dark eyes surrounded by pinched lines and...sadness.

"I messed up," he said feebly.

Lauren's normally dormant maternal side reared up. She wanted to tell him it couldn't be that bad. That she'd help him iron everything out and they'd find a solution to whatever he'd done. He'd always been a highly capable and approachable boss. This couldn't be all that bad.

She indicated the floor beyond his open door without looking in that direction. "Yeah, it looks like it," she said. This was why she hadn't been able to find a nice man to settle down with. She told herself Mark wasn't her boyfriend, or even a friend, really. He was her boss, and if he'd messed up, she'd probably have a price to pay.

"Start at the beginning," she said.

"Yes," another, deeper voice said.

Lauren cried out and jumped to her right—away from the sound of the voice. Two men entered the office, and they looked perfectly refreshed, with their hair combed to the side just-so, and black suit coats buttoned neatly. Honestly, if it wasn't two o'clock in the morning and she'd walked onto a normal twelfth floor, she'd think they'd shown up for a cocktail party.

"Lauren Thelma Keller," one said, and he wasn't asking. "You're under arrest for the embezzlement of corporate funds."

"What?" she demanded. "No, I'm not." She looked over to Mark, who hadn't moved. In fact, the man wept. He *wept*, the tears making slow tracks down his face while he didn't make any sound at all.

"I'm afraid we have to take you in."

Mark finally got to his feet. "I told you she had nothing to do with it." He took a few steps and positioned himself between Lauren and the federal agents. Lauren suspected that was who they were, at least.

"You just want me."

The two men appraised him. Looked at her. Then one another. "We went through her computer?" one asked.

"Yes, sir," the other said.

"Her office?"

"Every inch."

"Where's the laptop?"

"Digital forensics connected to it the moment she touched down in Corpus Christi, sir."

"What in the world is going on here?" Lauren demanded. "I get a call after hours from my boss, telling me I better get on a plane and get here quick. That there's some 'serious stuff' going down. So I do, and I show up to some... some...apocalyptic scene in my office building."

Her chest hurt from the lack of oxygen, and Lauren hated how manic she sounded as she sucked in a breath. She tried to hold it, but it wouldn't stay in her lungs.

"You can't stay here, ma'am," the agent said who'd been reporting to his boss. "If you'll come with us, we'll lay it out for you."

"You'll interrogate me," Lauren said, shying further from them. "I'm exhausted. I've been flying for three hours, terrified of what I'd find here, but it wasn't *this*."

"I'm Agent Toledo," the taller man in charge said. "Come next door with me, please." He indicated the open doorway behind him, and Lauren had no idea what to do. She looked at Mark, plenty of pleading silently thrown in his direction.

"Go," he said. "You'll be okay, Lauren. It's my fault. It's all my fault." The slow weeping started again, and Lauren really didn't know what to make of that. She'd seen Mark angry plenty of times. So angry, he'd throw a tape dispenser or the nearest object he could get his hands on. But weeping?

Never had she seen him do that.

She held her head high and stepped past him. She told herself she could answer any question set to her and do so truthfully. She didn't know why there would be two federal agents at Simple Solutions, and Agent Toledo had sounded like she had an office to go into.

She did that, flanked by both suited men. The lights came on as she entered, the way they usually did. They didn't illuminate total chaos like she'd seen out on the main floor, but there had definitely been a crew of people in her personal space.

On her computer. In her files. Accessing her laptop the moment she landed in Corpus Christie. She started to turn numb, her mind blurring along the edges of her thoughts.

"Ma'am," the agent who hadn't identified himself said. "I'm Agent Bell, and we've been investigating an embezzlement scheme here at Simple Solutions for the past nine months."

She blinked. "What?"

"Please sit down," Agent Toledo said, and Lauren did. Her sleek, shiny black leather couch still sat against the wall, though the framed picture of the ocean she kept above it had been removed. As she stared across her office to her desk, she found the majority of the artwork from the office standing against the far wall. The one she shared with Mark.

"I don't have a job anymore, do I?" she asked.

"We've frozen everything inside Simple Solutions," Agent Toledo said. "Mark Wellington, as well as at least three others, have been siphoning money from corporate funds to the tune of seven-point-three million dollars." He perched on the edge of her desk and picked up a black pen. One of her really nice gel ones, as Lauren wouldn't sign documents with anything else. "And ma'am, you'll forgive me, but as closely as you two worked, I'm finding it hard to believe you didn't know."

He looked up, his eyebrows adding a silent question mark to the statement.

"I didn't." Lauren swallowed and cut a look to Agent Bell. "I only work out of the office about half the time. I'm not over any corporate budgeting. I get told from the accounting team how big the individual account budgets are, but even that I don't touch. I'm in charge of design, communication, and quality assurance for our clients."

Their clients.

She took a long breath in through her nose, trying to calm down. "What about our clients?"

The two agents exchanged a glance. "We can't comment on them at this time," Agent Bell said. He took a seat next to her on the couch and touched her knee. "Miss Keller."

She swung her gaze to him, surprised he was there. Lauren felt outside of herself, and she didn't like it. "I think you should get on home," he said, and these federal agents were definitely Texas-based. She could hear the twang in their accents. Why her brain seized on that, she didn't know, but it did make her feel more comfortable with them.

They knew how things ran in Texas. They understood Texas manners.

"We'll drive you, as we've confiscated your car," Agent Toledo said.

"My car?" Lauren asked.

"Truth be told," Agent Toledo said. "I was hours away from putting your name out to Interpol and launching a nation-wide manhunt for you and your car." He gave her a smile that wasn't meant to be happy.

A *smile.*

Lauren sucked at the air then, full-blown panic descending on her. She'd been holding it back since she stepped into the wasteland that was now the twelfth floor, but there was no stemming it now.

"Jack," Agent Bell chastised, and then Lauren passed out.

ROUGHLY EIGHT HOURS LATER, LAUREN CLUTCHED a piping hot mug in her hands. She wrapped her icy fingers around it, trying to infuse some warmth into herself though the Texas July heat was brutal that day.

Not inside this police station, it wasn't. Her house had been likewise chilled with air conditioning. She'd bundled up in a pair of jeans and a mustard-yellow sweater to come with the agents to give her testimony.

Her *testimony.*

Lauren had never done anything of the sort, and she had

no idea what her life had come to. Agent Bell had taken her phone last night, and Lauren hadn't seen hide nor hair of it since. The only thing they'd allowed her to keep after going through it was her purse.

She felt violated on a level she'd never even considered, and she knew that everything in her home was currently being examined too.

Seven-point-two million dollars. Gone.

Six named thieves.

The company name of Simple Solutions all over the news.

She knew the full story now, and she found it hard to believe. Sheila had always been professional and kind at the same time. She'd calmed irate clients, had a London fog at the precise temperature Lauren liked on her desk each morning, and never missed a memo.

She'd become a grandmother last year, and Lauren pressed her eyes closed so she wouldn't be staring at the cold, white wall. She wasn't sure how long she'd been here. The gray tea she'd been brought was half-gone and cold by the time someone came into the room.

Agent Bell put her phone on the table, and the level of relief shooting through Lauren couldn't be quantified. She wasn't sure why, but she felt connected to the outside world with that phone. She had no idea if anyone had tried to get in touch with her, but she suspected both Joy and Cass had.

At least she hoped so. How pathetic would it be if she had no missed calls? No texts from anyone?

She could literally be arrested, detained, experience a

debilitating panic attack and be anywhere in the world by now, and she didn't have one person who cared.

She didn't reach for her phone immediately, but after several seconds, she couldn't resist the pull of it. "Thank you," she murmured.

"We can't find anything to hold you," Agent Bell said. He smiled at her. "This is good, Lauren. You're cleared. You can go."

Go? she wanted to rage at him. Where was she to go? Back to her house, which had been filled with strangers? Strangers touching all of her belongings?

Lauren had seen crime dramas, and she had no desire to return to her house. Not right now, and not alone.

She could call Bessie and see if she could get off of work and go with her. Then she'd have to tell someone about the past several hours, and she had no desire to do that. She closed her eyes again, this time just in a long blink.

Pure humiliation pulled through her, filling her to the point of choking. There was no way she could tell any of her friends about this.

"Come on," Agent Bell said, standing. "Let's get you processed and out of here."

Processed. Like she was some kind of meat.

Lauren stayed numb and silent through the rest of the process, and when she finally found herself sitting behind the wheel of her car, the doors all closed and locked, and the engine running so she didn't fry in the heat, she leaned her head down and started to sob.

THAT EVENING, LAUREN SAT ALONE ON THE outdoor patio of her favorite restaurant in Corpus Christie. She'd once dated a chef at the resort here, and she loved the deviled eggs with chicharróns, as well as the fried green tomatoes.

She'd only ordered her favorite appetizers, and the three plates sat half-eaten as the sun went down in the west, painting the Gulf of Mexico in pinks, purples, and golds.

The strategy she'd started on after she'd stopped sobbing in her car sat on the table in front of her, anchored in the wind by her coffee mug. She had some savings, and she'd be okay until she found another job.

She'd sell her house here and move to Hilton Head Island permanently. Her thoughts jumbled here, because Bessie, Joy, Sage, and Cherry were so important to her. She'd put stars out to the side of "Sell your house and move to SC" and written, *Can fly in for Supper Club, or video chat like Bea has before.*

She couldn't lose her friends, not when so many other things in her life had crumbled.

At the same time, nowhere on her strategy was the note to tell her friends and family what had happened. Not yet, anyway. Lauren liked to keep things to herself for a while, because it took her a long time to process them in such a way that she could then make sense of them and talk about them.

Every time she closed her eyes for longer than a blink, she

saw Mark weeping. She saw the toppled cubicle dividers. She saw the fish bowl conference rooms.

She had received several texts from people today. At least thirty or forty from former employees of Simple Solutions. They'd all lost their jobs, so Lauren wasn't the only one. Still, that didn't make it sting any less.

Cass, Joy, Bessie, and Bea had texted her, and as she sat at the table and lifted her first and only glass of Prosecco to her lips, another message came in. This one bore Cherry's name, and it said, *How does this dress look for Cass's wedding? I've asked a few other people, but I really trust your opinion.*

Lauren smiled as the picture came in, and Cherry looked stunning in a bright red dress that hugged all of her curves. She was six or seven years older than Lauren, and she and Jed Forrester had no children either. Lauren had seen how blissfully happy they were, and she'd started to see that she didn't need to be a mother to be filled with joy.

She told Cherry, *You look like a million bucks. Wear that for sure.*

Cass won't be outshined?

Not at all.

With this talk, Lauren remembered the wedding. She'd been fine to attend alone before, but now the thought made her shoulders sag and her heart sink to her feet.

Joy said you're in Sweet Water Falls? Cherry asked. *Want to do lunch tomorrow or are you leaving? Too busy at work?*

Lauren didn't answer, because she didn't have a flight booked, nor would she be sleeping in her house. She'd taken out a room at the resort here, on the highest floor they'd give her, so she could witness the Gulf as far as her eyes could see.

She picked up her black gel pen and wrote on her strategy outline. *Get a date to Cass's wedding.*

The words swam in her vision, and she blinked and went to her phone. Now, to find a date.

She scrolled through her contacts, stalling very early in the alphabet.

The B's, in fact.

Blake Williams.

Her heartbeat stalled. Could she ask him to be her date? Would he be there anyway? He was one of Harrison's good friends.

Without planning or strategically outlining her message, her fingers flew across the screen. *Hey, Blake. It's Lauren Keller. Do you have a date to Cass's and Harrison's wedding? If not, I'd love to hang on your arm for the evening. No strings attached.*

Without even reading over it again, she sent the message. She felt wild, impulsive, and oh-so-desperate. But if she could keep the news of her company's failure, her lost job, and her complete and utter humiliation off her friends' radar until after the wedding, she would.

She didn't want Cass worried about her on her honeymoon. She didn't want Bessie texting her every evening. She didn't want Joy to look at her with mournful eyes.

And she absolutely didn't want to attend the wedding alone.

She checked her phone, but Blake hadn't texted back.

An hour passed, and Lauren had her food boxed and she took it up to her room.

He still hadn't answered, and she wondered if she'd shocked him into silence with her invitation. They hadn't exactly been on the best of speaking terms prior to this. The last time they'd truly talked, he'd offered her a job, and she'd laughed and told him no.

"A job," she whispered to herself, wondering if Blake could possibly A) be willing to let her hang on his arm at the wedding and B) still have a job opening.

She wouldn't know until he texted back, and her phone stayed stubbornly silent all the way until she went to bed, and Lauren disliked the unsettled feeling of having something on her list that she'd started but which hadn't been finished.

Chapter Three

Just forget about what I said, Lauren typed out the next morning. Blake still hadn't answered, and her annoyance with his lack of communication reminded her of why she'd not gone out with him in the first place. Or rather, she had agreed to a date, and he'd never shown up.

She sent that text and started typing another. *I was just in a bad place last night, and—*

Her phone rang in the middle of the next word, and she nearly dropped it at the sight of Blake's name on the screen. Her throat narrowed again, and she got transported back to the twelfth floor.

The phone rang again, a shrill tone that made her blink. She flew into motion and swiped on the call. She then lifted her device to her ear in slow motion. "Hello?"

"Lauren Keller," Blake drawled, his Southern voice full of happiness. She wanted to lean into it and borrow it just for a little while. "As I live and breathe, I did not expect to get any sort of texts from you."

Her irritation soared and solidified. "Did you get my latest one?"

"Yes, ma'am, and I can't forget what you said. It's right here in black and blue on my screen."

She wandered over to the window that overlooked the Gulf, trying to come up with something clever to say. Something to flirt back. Something to save her dignity. "I just... I've had a rough couple of days, and I don't want to go to the wedding alone."

She couldn't say the rest of what ran through her mind. Lauren was exceptionally skilled at only saying what needed to be said and holding the rest for later. Or for never. For herself, when she was safe and in the privacy of her own home.

Now, though, she felt adrift, and she really needed something or someone to tow her back to shore. "So I thought maybe me and you...it's not a date. And if you weren't going to go to the wedding, that's fine. I can find someone else."

"Who?" Blake asked, but the word wasn't harsh. "Who else would you ask?"

She didn't know, and her silence said as much.

"I was planning on going," he said. "I don't have a date, and I don't have a girlfriend."

"I'm not interested in either," she said, the words, *Ask him about a job* running through her mind. She kept them contained too. Blake Williams would not be the first person she told about losing her job. Oh, no, he would not be first.

He chuckled, and she could just see the sandy-blond man's face. Those dazzling eyes that had caught her attention the first time they'd met, three summers ago now.

"Will you be at the Fourth of July fireworks this year?" he asked.

"Yes," she murmured. She'd gotten up and showered this morning. Added a few items to her strategy, and one of those was to get back to Hilton Head very soon. Her flight left tomorrow morning, in fact. Today, she'd check out here, drive back to Sweet Water Falls, go to lunch with Cherry, and then start packing up her house. Whatever she could do today would get done, and she'd make a plan to do the rest after the wedding.

"Can we sit together?" Blake asked.

"Yes," Lauren said, when she really wanted to tell him, "I'd like that." But such soft words would reveal too much about how she felt about him. Too much about how much she'd thought about him in the past twelve months.

"Can't wait," he said. "If you want, we could try dinner again."

Lauren smiled to her dim reflection in the glass. "Let's see how the fireworks and then the wedding go, okay?"

"Hey, I'll take that," he said with another light chuckle. "It's not a no."

No, it wasn't a no, and Lauren said, "Good-bye, Blake," and ended the call. She turned back to the small table in the room, which held her strategy. She picked up the pen and bent over the notebook.

At the top she scrawled MY SEASIDE STRATEGY and underlined it three times.

Then, way down at the bottom, leaving lots of room for a dozen more items after "sell house in Sweet Water Falls," she added, "Go to dinner with Blake Williams."

Straightening, she looked at the sparse list. While it wasn't much of a strategy, it was a start, and every project she'd ever began started at zero.

This just happened to be a complete rebuild of her life, instead of a client's portfolio, and the stakes felt so much bigger than ever before.

"No, that one's mine," Lauren said a couple of days later. "Yours is the blue one."

Bea looked at the chair in her hands, which was also blue, but navy. "Are you sure?"

Lauren took the oversized camp chair from one of her very best friends. "Very sure." She nodded to Grant, Bea's husband, as he juggled a myriad of things. "He's already got yours, Bea." How nice for her that she had a handsome man to help her carry her blanket, her cooler, her beach bag stuffed with licorice, nerds ropes, and sweet mint gum.

Lauren had to do all of that herself, and she shouldered the chair by the rough strap and reached for her own tote bag. Hers was light gray and contained her tablet, her eReader, and a paperback book. No notebook of strategies. Not tonight. Tonight, she just wanted to see what happened.

She loved Independence Day as much as anyone could, and while she didn't wear a lot of red, this year, she'd braided her hair back into two Dutch braids, both tied with a patriotic red ribbon. She wore a blue-and-white striped shirt with her denim shorts, and a white pair of strappy sandals. That way, she'd gotten in all the colors without having to wear the flag.

So many people did that, and she didn't mind how it looked on her. She simply liked being a bit more subtle.

"What did you sneak into my bag?" She looked down at it, but the top zipper had been shut.

"Nothing," Bea said innocently.

"It's far heavier than before." Lauren started to unzip it, and someone called, "Bea!" from several paces away.

Bea went to greet Cass, who Lauren would be going home with. She'd spent the afternoon on the beach with Bea, Grant, and his daughter Shelby, so she'd cleaned up and driven to the park for the fireworks with them.

Harrison was supposed to be bringing sandwiches for everyone, so Lauren hadn't eaten. To her knowledge, neither had Grant or Bea or Shelby.

She set her bag on the tailgate of the SUV and opened it. Sure enough, Bea had put in four jarred candles. "My word," Lauren grumbled. Like she needed to be carrying these around tonight, the glasses clinking against each other every time she wanted to switch devices. She removed the candles and closed the back of the vehicle.

As she turned, she realized everyone had gone down the path without her. She'd tread the way alone several times in the past, and she knew right where they'd all be. Laughter echoed on the air, but as she and her friends weren't the only people arriving at the park right now, it could've belonged to anyone.

"Let me carry that for you."

Lauren turned toward the familiar voice, her heartbeat skipping as a sense of rejoicing moved through her. Blake easily took the chair from her shoulder and added it to his. His smile broadcast his happiness, and she had a brief memory of him drinking too much and then coming over to her table to offer her a job.

She suddenly wished she was wearing that red dress from last fall. If she did wear red, she went all out. She would've looked ten times as desperate as she already had, but she couldn't help wondering if she could pull the dress out of retirement...maybe for another date with Blake.

"Thank you," she said. She'd managed not to tell anyone about her company or her job, and as life moved a little slower here on this South Carolina island, she hadn't heard anyone talking about Simple Solutions here.

There wasn't any reason for them to. The nearest office was in Miami, and Lauren had been assigned to that branch while she'd been working remotely from Hilton Head.

"You look simply..." Blake looked down to her red-painted toes and back to her face. "Amazing." He wore desire in his expression, and Lauren would be lying against herself and all of humanity if she said she didn't feel the attraction between them coursing through her.

She did, and she always had. She'd managed to smother it for the past few summers, because she hadn't lived here.

She did now.

He'd had a girlfriend.

He didn't now.

No more barriers existed between them, and Lauren swallowed. "Thank you," she said again. "You look great too." He wore a polo that could've been sewn by Betsy Ross herself. Red and white stripes flowed across his broad chest, with his pocket the navy blue field with white stars stitched in.

He wore a pair of navy blue khaki shorts and white tennis shoes with a blue trim around them. He'd always said *precise* to her, as well as, *I have money*.

She wasn't sure if either were really true; he'd known he'd see her tonight. Maybe he'd simply dressed the part.

"Is everyone else here?" he asked, starting to walk toward the sidewalk that led further into the park.

"Yeah, I think so," she said. "We were running late, because Shelby was flirting with some boys on the beach." She gave Blake a smile, and he chuckled and shook his head.

"Ah, to be fifteen again." He laughed now, and Lauren liked the sound of it. His step slowed, and Lauren automatically adjusted her pace to match his. "Listen," he said. "I just wanted to apologize for how I acted last year, in that restaurant?"

He studied the ground as he came to a stop. Then those glorious blue eyes met hers. "I'd had too much to drink, but

I remember seeing you sitting with another man, wearing this—this—stunning dress, and I was jealous."

"It was Harrison," she murmured. "My best friend's boyfriend. Fiancé. About to be her husband." Harrison hadn't been a threat to any relationship of Lauren's.

"Yeah, I know." Blake nodded. "But you know what? Sometimes jealousy is irrational."

Lauren tilted her head and looked at him. "I think I understand that." She'd often fought with the green-eyed monster. Of course she wanted Bea and Cass to be happy. It sometimes felt wholly unfair that they'd both been married once already and had now found a second chance at love when she was still searching for her One True Love.

Blake smiled, the corners of his eyes crinkling. "What's your schedule like tomorrow?"

Lauren's mind automatically went through her morning routine, which included working out, clearing her inbox, and pulling docs for any meetings she had coming up.

Two of those no longer existed, and she honestly felt like her whole life had come to a stop. She hadn't worked out since she'd flown to Texas and back, and she hated hiding out in her room all day, pretending to work.

Cass is getting married in two days, she told herself. She could wait to say anything. Besides, she could easily say she got some vacation days around the holiday and the wedding, and no one would think that odd.

"Nothing," she said honestly. "My whole day is wide open."

His eyebrows went up, and they started walking again.

"Is that right? No plans with your friends the day before Cass's wedding?"

"We are going to dinner tomorrow night," she said. "Just the six of us. Oh, and her daughters." They'd both arrived on the island for the Fourth, and while Cass had a large house, Lauren almost felt in the way. She'd volunteered to stay at Harrison's, but Cass wouldn't hear of it. "So I guess I'm only free during the day."

"As am I," he said, letting the words hang there. "Although." He drew that word out, and Lauren glanced over to him. He wasn't dark like her ex-boyfriend, and she liked that difference. He was educated and articulate, and she could see why she was so attracted to him.

He smiled at her. "Although?" she prompted.

"I'll have my son." He looked hopeful then. "But we could have breakfast together in the morning without him. I know we're not dating." He whispered the last word and glanced around like someone dangerous might overhear him. "So it's probably far too early to meet my kid."

Lauren's ribs felt too tight for her to take a breath. When she didn't know how to react or what to say, she went quiet. On her video calls, she could cut the video and mute herself, make an excuse in the chat, and compose herself.

Now, standing in front of Blake, she couldn't do any of those things. "I think we should at least be dating before I meet him," she said quietly.

Blake's face broke into a grin. "Are you saying there's a chance we'll start dating?"

Lauren recognized flirting when she saw it. She laced her

hand through Blake's arm and looked down the sidewalk. "Yes," she said simply. "I think there's a chance we'll start dating."

"Hallelujah," he said with a laugh.

Lauren smiled too, this one bright thing in her life making all the darkness and difficult things of the past few days seem dimmer than they'd been previously. "Do you want to really cause a stir tonight?" she asked. One more curve, and the spot where she'd sat with her friends for the Fourth of July fireworks for the past three years would come into view.

All of her friends would be there. They'd see her being escorted by Blake Williams to the picnic.

"I'm always in for causing a stir," Blake said, and his voice carried just the right amount of mischief.

"Yeah, you do seem like the type." She grinned at him, glad her flirting game was still spot-on. "If I hold onto you like this, everyone around that corner will freak out." She took another step, getting closer and closer.

"Will they?"

"Mm hm."

Blake took a moment to respond, and when he did, it was to tighten his elbow against his ribs and say, "I can't wait to see this."

Chapter Four

Blake Williams shouldered the weight of a dozen pairs of eyes, including those of his mother. All conversation had come to a halt, and he and Lauren stood in a gap in the semi-circle of chairs and blankets that had been set up.

"Hey," Lauren said easily. "I think you guys all know Blake Williams." She looked over to him, positively beaming at him, a secret edge in her eyes that told him she liked this kind of attention. Not only that, but she liked *him*.

He honestly wasn't sure what kind of lottery he'd won to get the attention of this gorgeous woman.

"This is Sage Grady," Lauren said. "She still lives in Texas. "Bessie Clifton, also in Texas. Cherry Forrester and her husband, Jed."

"Howdy, brother," Jed said. He rose from his chair and shook Blake's hand.

"Howdy," Blake echoed back to the cowboy. He liked to think of himself as a Southern gentleman, and Jed was the opposite of that. He seemed refined at the same time he was rugged, and Cherry got to her feet and greeted him with a handshake too.

As they settled down, Lauren continued with, "You know Joy, I think. Joy Bartlett."

"Always a *joy* to see you," he said.

Joy rolled her eyes, and Blake didn't blame her. Heat filled his face at such a lame statement. She'd played interference between Blake and Lauren when he'd missed their date last summer.

"Cass, of course," Lauren said. "Harrison, Grant, Shelby, and Bea." She'd just gotten to his mother, and Lauren actually made a little squeak.

"My mother," Blake jumped in. "Linda. Momma, this is Lauren Keller."

"Are you two seeing each other?" Momma asked point-blank.

Lauren looked at him, and he looked at her. She clearly needed to take the lead on this. She faced the group again and said, "We're still deciding. But he's going to take me to breakfast tomorrow, and the wedding on Sunday, and then we'll see."

"You're going to the wedding with him?" Bea asked.

"She replied with a plus-one," Cass said. "It's not a big deal."

"I thought Joy was her plus-one."

"Please stop," Lauren said in a stern tone. She flicked a glance at Blake, who didn't want this to be embarrassing for her. He put her chair down in the empty spot next to Joy and set it up for her. As he did the same for his, Lauren drifted away from him to chit-chat with her friends.

He met Harrison's eye, and the man raised his eyebrows. Blake didn't know what to say to his silent question, so he simply sat down and asked, "How's moving the outdoor kitchen coming?"

Harrison let out a long sigh. "It's not," he said. "I think Cass and I are just going to end up building a new one at her place."

"Your back patio will look like it's lost its teeth if you remove everything," he agreed.

"Yeah," Harrison said. "When I get back from my honeymoon, I want to come see about taking some money out of my life insurance."

"No," Cass said from the other side of him. "I told you we didn't need to do that."

Blake wasn't going to get into the middle of that discussion, and he looked up at Lauren as she moved in front of him. She sat next to him and set her bag down, then busied herself with getting something out of it.

He turned to his phone and tapped out, *I can't wait to go out tomorrow. What's your favorite breakfast food?* and hit send.

Her phone chimed loudly from next to him, and he couldn't help watching her for her reaction as she read the message. Her smile came quickly, and her fingers practically flew across the screen.

She hit one final button, then tucked her phone under her leg.

His phone chimed, and he grinned at her. She reached over and covered his hand with hers. "Guess," she said.

"Your favorite breakfast food?"

Her deep, dark eyes glittered, and Blake could only think about what emotion they'd hold as he leaned closer and closer and closer...and kissed her. She nodded slowly, her perfectly painted red lips curving into a glorious smile.

"Uh, let's see." He could barely think at all right now. "I'm going to go with...quiche."

She shook her head. "I'm from Texas."

"Chicken and waffles?" he guessed.

She giggled, one of her braids falling over her shoulder and providing a hint of red to her otherwise blue outfit. "I do like chicken and waffles, but that's a bit heavy for breakfast, don't you think?"

"I think it's a good time for fried chicken any hour of the day."

"You would." She reached over and took his hand in hers, and Blake sure did like being claimed by her. He settled his fingers between hers, enjoying the buzzing, sparking feeling moving up his arm and into his shoulder.

Like fireworks, he thought, dusk settling around him. Yes, everything about Lauren Keller reminded him of fireworks, and he would only be lucky if she got close enough to burn him.

A COUPLE OF DAYS LATER, HE STOOD ON A WIDE front porch, pillars reaching up to support the roof two stories overhead. The doorbell finished ringing, but no one had called or come to the door yet.

He wore a black tuxedo, complete with a bow tie and tails, every piece of it trimmed in shiny satin. His shoes could reflect his own image back to him, and Blake had taken plenty of time that morning to make sure his hair sat just right, and his cologne wasn't too over-powering.

His mama rode in the backseat of his SUV, and as soon as Lauren came to the door, he'd help her into the front.

The door swung open, and Lauren appeared. She wore blue from head to toe, and *stunning* wasn't a strong enough word for her. Blake lost the ability to do anything but involuntary functions like breathing and blinking.

She cocked a hip and perched one heeled toe. "How do I look?"

"I'm having trouble forming thoughts," he admitted. The dress had practically been painted on her body, as that was the only way it could seriously stay on. There were no straps and no buttons or zippers that he could see. She'd definitely shimmied into that somehow, and Blake wanted to know how.

"Are you ladies ready?" he asked as he remembered his manners. This woman wasn't quite his girlfriend yet. They'd gone to breakfast yesterday, and it had been a fantastic two hours. Best way to start the day for Blake, that was for sure—and he didn't even eat breakfast normally.

Then he'd spent the day on his boat with Tommy, delivered him back to his mother, and retuned home about dark. He and Lauren had texted throughout the day, but she'd made it clear that they were seeing how the date and the wedding went before any definitions or labels were given to their relationship.

He wasn't going to push her to do that. Or to do anything. He counted himself lucky to have this woman in his life at all, and whatever she gave him, he'd be happy with.

"Yes," Lauren said, "Joy's coming down right now."

As if they'd rehearsed it, Joy's heels clicked toward him, and he looked past Lauren and into the foyer. She too wore a blue dress in the exact same shade as Lauren's. Her hair had been swept up onto her head, and Blake grinned at her. She wore more makeup than he'd seen Joy wear—so did Lauren—and he reasoned that their best friend was getting married.

They wore matching black heels that seemed as shiny as his shoes, and when Blake looked back at Lauren, all he could think about was how kissable her neck looked. Her hair normally covered it, but she'd likewise pinned it up, and only a few tendrils curled down below her ears.

"We're ready." Lauren linked her arm through Joy's, beamed at her, and then faced Blake.

He offered her his arm, and she took it. He led them both to his SUV in the circle drive, and first opened Joy's door, then Lauren's. Joy started talking to his mother, and Blake took a moment to bring his arm around Lauren and pull her against him. "You are amazing," he whispered. "I can't wait to dance with you."

One of her hands came up behind his head, lightly

touching the hair along his neck. The other planted itself against his chest, and Blake really liked the way they fit together.

He'd been out with several women since his divorce, and no one had *fit* the way Lauren did. This might be something stupid, but Blake liked how her height complimented his. He liked how she wasn't afraid to look him in the eye and say what she thought. He liked he'd had to *work* to get her to this spot, and he wanted to do the work to have her in his life for a long time.

The moment lengthened while she studied him, and then she finally said, "I do like a good slow dance with a handsome man." Her fingernails sent shivers down his throat as she pulled her hand back, and Blake moved out of the way so Lauren could get in the car.

She liked slow dancing. She liked muffins for breakfast. *It's like an excuse to eat cake for breakfast*, she'd told him yesterday morning. She worked in marketing, had never been married, and had no children.

She was living here on Hilton Head for the foreseeable future, and Blake had laid in bed last night thinking about her for a solid thirty minutes before he'd finally fallen asleep with her face in his head.

He was sweating by the time he rounded the SUV and got behind the wheel. He hadn't cut the engine to go to the door, because this was Carolina in July. Air conditioners ran twenty-four-seven here right now.

After a quick drive down the coast, he pulled into the parking lot at Palmetto Museum, which was one of the most sought-after wedding venues on the island. Of course this was where Cass would choose to get married.

"This place is nice," he said. He glanced over to Lauren. "Have you been here?"

"I toured it with her a few months ago, yes," she said. "It's very nice."

"Isn't she getting married outside?" Joy asked.

"Yes," Lauren said.

"We're going to melt." Blake pulled into a spot and parked.

Lauren gave him a look that made his heartbeat dry up, and he killed the engine. The heat immediately started to infiltrate the vehicle, and he gave her a surprised look. "What? We are."

"It's going to be short," Lauren said. "We'll be on the beach for twenty minutes, tops."

"I'm gonna hold you to that."

"They're doing dinner on the beach," Joy piped up from the back.

"But there will be misters and fans under the tents." Lauren opened her door. "I'm melting in here."

"That's my point," Blake said, and she threw him a tight look before she got out of the SUV. Blake got out and helped his mother out of the backseat. She kept her hand in his arm as they went around the vehicle, and Lauren and Joy had linked arms and started toward the immaculate building.

The kiss of air conditioning met his skin as they entered, and a sharply dressed woman directed them toward the Haslam-Tate wedding. People mingled in a stylishly decorated room, sipping champagne from tall glasses while they waited for the ceremony to start.

Blake plucked a drink from the tray and handed it to Lauren. She took a delicate sip as he took his own glass of bubbly. "Mm," she said. "This is fantastic."

He took his own sip, but he wouldn't take another. Alcohol and him didn't get along, and the last time he'd drunk too much, he'd made a fool of himself in front of a lot of people—Lauren included.

Humiliation filled him, though he'd already apologized. Lauren had texted him, and they were here together. He set his glass down and said, "What's your favorite color?"

She looked mildly surprised, and then she said, "Anything but red."

He hadn't seen her wear a lot of red, that was true. "You wore that killer red dress last year," he said.

"A rare instance," she said.

"What were you hoping to accomplish by wearing it?" He inched closer to her, hoping the distance was appropriate for public but close enough for her to know how very interested he was in her.

Her eyes met his. "I wanted to go out and have a good time," she said.

"Did you?" he asked. "Why were you there alone with Harrison?"

Lauren took another sip of her champagne. "Has anyone ever told you that you ask too many questions?"

Blake grinned at her and nodded. "A few times, actually. Drove my ex-wife nuts."

She gave him a dry look. "I can see why."

"Oh, come on," he said, still laughing a little. "How else am I supposed to get to know people?"

"People?" she asked, lifting her flute to her lips one more time. "Or just me?" She asked the question from behind her glass.

Blake waited for her to lower her glass, and then he made sure she'd locked onto him before he spoke. "Definitely you," he said. "I want to know everything about you."

She gave him a gorgeous smile just as a woman's cool voice said, "Ladies and gentlemen, the bride and groom invite you to join them outside for the wedding ceremony." The wall of windows at the back of the room started to open, and all the guests glided that way.

Lauren set down her glass half-drunk and slipped her arm through his. "You're with me, right, Blake?"

"Yes, ma'am," he said. "I'm right here with you."

She leaned into his shoulder and said, "Thank you for doing this for me."

What she didn't get was that this was a fantasy come true for him, not a favor. He simply nodded as they went outside, flowing with the rest of the crowd. He and Lauren went up front, where she hugged Cass, who already stood at the altar.

Blake clapped Harrison on the back, who also stood up front. They mingled with their closest friends, and after a few minutes, they came together and stood facing the crowd. There was an unspoken note in the air for people to take their seats, and Blake made sure his mother could navigate the sand to her chair before he sat beside her.

"She's lovely," she whispered as Lauren sat on his other side.

"You're going to jinx it," he whispered back.

"Pish," Momma said. "If anyone will jinx anything, it's you, son."

"I'm doing my best this time not to do that," he hissed at her. He turned his attention from her to the couple still standing at the altar. They smiled like today was the happiest day of their lives, and Blake could *feel* their joy filling the tent and seeping up into the glorious blue sky.

He reached over and slipped his hand into Lauren's. She squeezed, and he lifted her hand to his lips and kissed the inside of her wrist. She glanced over to him, a look on her face that said she'd definitely be telling him they could start dating after this wedding.

"Welcome," Harrison said. "I know some of you are hungry, and we can't eat until after the ceremony, so let's get this show on the road." He looked over to Cass, who smiled prettily at him.

Blake was ready to get the show on the road, but not for the meal coming afterward. He just wanted to dance with Lauren.

Chapter Five

Cassandra Haslam wore a simple gown that shimmered in the sunlight the way gasoline did. It had thin, barely-there straps that went over her shoulders, and a neck that draped almost enough to show some cleavage. Since she'd already had her big wedding, she'd wanted this one to be simple and small.

The dress fell all the way to the sand, and she didn't wear shoes right now. Harrison wore a tuxedo, as he claimed he wanted to dress up and look as nice as she did. She'd tried to tell him her dress wasn't anything fancy, but he'd swallowed hard and his eyes had filled with desire when she'd entered his dressing room twenty minutes ago.

I don't want to go out there, he'd murmured in her ear as he'd taken her into his arms. *Maybe we can stay here, and I can examine every inch of this dress to make sure it's appropriate for a wedding.*

She'd giggled into his shoulder, excited to become his

wife, finally sleep in the same bed as him, and merge their lives as they both moved forward into the future.

Out here they had come, of course. She'd kissed him in his dressing room until Bea and Grant had insisted they get in position. She hadn't wanted to be walked down the aisle. She hadn't wanted to invite a lot of people. Her closest family and friends had come from Texas, and Harrison had invited a similar number from around the island. A couple of his best friends at his construction firm. Along with Grant, Blake, and a man named Tyler Parker, who sold a lot of real estate on Hilton Head, Oliver Blackhurst, who owned the smoothie shop where Bea and Grant had first met, and Scott Anderson, who Harrison had sold the landscaping part of his business to a couple of years ago, his party then included his brother, parents, and Beryl. Her golden retriever sure did love Harrison, and Cass was sure it was because of all the hamburgers he fed to the canine.

The pastor walked toward them, and Cass and Harrison turned to face each other instead of the crowd as he took his place behind the altar. He smiled out at them and everyone beyond them, and Cass settled her hands in Harrison's. His were so much bigger than hers, and she felt safe and secure with him in everything they did together.

"Welcome to the union of Cassandra Haslam and Harrison Tate," Pastor Rollins said. "Cass started coming to my services about a year ago, and it has been a pure delight getting to know her."

She gave him a warm smile, glad she'd been able to make a few connections here on the island. She'd worked with several clients too, but she'd only invited one of them to her nuptials. AnnaMae Hank sat on the end of the second row with Sage and Sage's sister, Thelma.

A shot of worry bulleted through Cass. Sage had just finalized her divorce, and yet she sat at Cass's wedding with a smile so wide, Cass would never suspect that she was hurting inside.

She was, and Cass knew it. Bessie beside her wiped her eyes, but Cass knew watching yet another person in their Supper Club get married and leave Sweet Water Falls was difficult for her. Joy, who sat next to Bessie, had struggled the most with the dissolution of their group. She'd invited Cherry Forrester to the group in an effort to keep it thriving, and she sat next to Joy in a ravishing red dress that Cass wanted to try on.

She knew it wouldn't fit her. She stood about six inches taller than Cherry, and the woman had far more curves than Cass did. She was more straight up and down and always had been, even after the birth of her babies.

Her children sat on the first row, along with her parents. She looked past her husband-to-be and smiled at all of them, grateful there hadn't been any drama leading up to this wedding. Of course, Sariah and her husband, Robbie, hadn't arrived on the island until yesterday, and Jane had barely beaten them. Conrad, her only son, lived with her right now, but he worked two jobs on the island in his efforts to save money for college.

He'd go back to Baylor in the fall to start his junior year, and Cass still traveled to Texas plenty to see her kids. Both

Sariah and Conrad lived there, and she wanted to keep her spot in the Supper Club.

This month, they'd do Supper Club here on Hilton Head, because Lauren, Joy, and Bea all lived here. For now. Once fall returned, Joy and Lauren would go back to Sweet Water Falls. Back to their normal lives.

Maybe, Cass thought as the pastor started talking about love and marriage. Lauren sat awfully close to Blake Williams, and she'd shown up to the fireworks picnic with his hand in hers two nights ago. She seemed happy and in control of her emotions, but Cass knew Lauren on a deep level. She could see past the façade that kept most people in the dark about how Lauren really felt.

This wedding was very difficult for her too, and Cass renewed her commitment to make sure her friends knew how very much she loved them. Just because she was getting married again didn't mean she wouldn't be there for them when they needed her.

Bea stood beside and behind her a step, as Grant did for Harrison. That was the extent of the people Cass needed to see and bless this wedding, and she turned to look at the pastor so she wouldn't miss more of the ceremony.

"...seeing people find each other later in life," Pastor Rollins said. "It renews my faith and belief that God's hand is in all of our lives, no matter how old we get or how much experience we have."

He looked up from a small book he held in his hands. "Now, I was told not to carry on too long, so I think we should get right to the part where these two are joined together in marriage." He looked from Cass to Harrison. "Would that be all right with the two of you?"

She nodded, and Harrison said, "Yes, sir," in a somewhat rusty voice. He didn't attend church with her, and she was okay with that. She didn't go every week either. She was a praying woman though, and he supported her in whatever she wanted to do.

"Great," Pastor Rollins said. "Then Cass, I believe you have some vows to read."

She nodded and extracted one hand from Harrison's. Bea handed her a small index card, and Cass glanced at it. She'd gone over the bullet points with her Supper Club last night as they'd gone to dinner together.

"Harrison," she said. "I've appreciated your steady friendship and companionship as I've healed these past couple of years." She drew in a breath, because thinking of West still made her chest pinch. No sadness accompanied the tug on her heartstrings anymore, and Cass knew she was ready to say I-do to another man.

Not just any man.

The one standing in front of her, his features so dark like West's but so different at the same time. He squeezed the hand he still held, and Cass focused.

"You took care of me when I needed it most," she said. "I love you for that. I love you for how you can make me laugh, and how you love my children and my dog, and how I wanted to live in my house even though yours has the outdoor kitchen you've always wanted."

He chuckled and shook his head, his chin dropping

slightly. He was absolutely adorable, and Cass's love for him doubled.

"I love that you're quiet when I'm loud, and you're the complete compliment to all of my flaws, making them smoother and easier for everyone to deal with."

"Not true," he whispered. "You don't have any flaws."

Cass smiled at him, her eyes filling with tears. "I love you, and I want to walk at your side for the rest of my life." She handed the card back to Bea, who tucked it somewhere.

Cass slid her hand back into Harrison's as the pastor prompted him to say his vows. He cleared his throat, his face suddenly filling with a handsome blush. "Cass," he said. "I'm not one for talking too much about how I feel. I wrote these vows at least ten times, but they never seemed quite right."

He hadn't taken out any notes, and he gazed evenly at her as he spoke in a clear, just-loud-enough voice. "My love for you is simple, but it feels complex. I would give up anything to be with you. Sleep, time fishing, and yes, my outdoor kitchen."

A tear leaked out of the corner of her eye. She honestly wasn't sure why she'd been so blessed to have him in her life. West had been so good to her too, and she really wanted this happiness and level of care for all of her friends, especially Lauren.

"Since I'm simple, I didn't prepare anything too long. I love you. I love your children and your dog, because you love them so much. What's important to you is important to me. I know you feel the same about me, and I hope we can work together to make each other happy for a lot of years." He nodded, the end of his speech evident.

They both looked to Pastor Rollins, who said, "Cassandra Aloise Haslam, do you give yourself to Harrison Gaylen Tate, to be his lawfully wedded wife, from now until this mortal life separates you?"

"Yes," she said. "I do."

He nodded and turned slightly to face Harrison. "Harrison Gaylen Tate, do you receive this woman, Cassandra Aloise Haslam, into your heart and life, and give yourself to her, to be her lawfully wedded husband, from now until this mortal life separates you?"

"Yes," he said, no throat-clearing needed. "I do."

"Then by the power of God and the state of South Carolina, I now pronounce you husband and wife. You may kiss your bride."

The crowd started to clap and cheer, whistle and whoop, and Cass stepped into Harrison's arms and kissed him. Their smiles made it hard to do anything too scandalous, and they separated quickly. He lifted their joined hands into the air as they faced the few rows of chairs, and Cass soaked in the happiness streaming her way.

All of the people had gotten to their feet, and their faces were lit with such joy, Cass wanted to take a picture of it. So she reached under the white satin covering the altar and turned her back on the crowd. She lifted her phone high as Harrison yelled at everyone to crowd in close.

She snapped several selfies of her and Harrison in the foreground with all of their loved ones behind them, that joy still prevalent. She needed to be able to see this at any given moment in the future. Soak in this feeling again and remember how amazingly happy she felt too.

After she tucked the phone back under the satin, she stepped into her mother's arms. "You did good, baby," her momma said, and Cass squeezed her eyes shut as she gripped her mother's shoulders.

She had done the best she could, and she figured no one could expect more than that.

Hours later, after the dinner, the toasts, the dancing, and the sparkler send-off, Cass sank into the back seat of a luxurious black stretch limousine. Lauren closed the door, sealing out everyone and everything.

She sighed and looked over to Harrison, who'd gotten in ahead of her. She leaned toward him without saying anything, and he met her halfway for a kiss. She cradled his face in her hand, the touch between them light and electrifying. "Thank you," she murmured against his lips. "That was a beautiful evening."

"I think so too," he said.

She tucked herself into his side, and he lifted his arm around her shoulders. "Did you see the way Blake and Lauren were dancing?" she asked. She let her eyes drift closed as the car started to move.

"Pretty close," he said.

"Cheek-to-cheek," she said. "He had his hands all over her."

"She didn't seem to mind."

"No," Cass said. "She didn't."

"He's a good guy," Harrison said. "Hopefully, he'll figure out how to handle Lauren."

Cass wasn't sure what that meant, so she asked.

"I just mean." Harrison exhaled. "She's a strong woman, Cass. She's not meant for just anyone. She needs someone tailored just for her, that's all. It's not a criticism. I like Lauren a lot."

She nodded, because he was right. Lauren had been in a couple of serious relationships, but her job always came first. She hoped and prayed that Lauren could make an adjustment this time and put Blake first. Maybe if she did that, and Blake could indeed figure out how to handle her, they could find their happily-ever-after.

The drive to the resort on the south end of the island didn't take long, especially at this time of night. The limo came to a stop only a few minutes later, and she emerged from it, Harrison right behind her.

He put his hand on the small of her back and guided her toward the glass doors. He didn't stop for a bag; they had someone to do that for them here. In fact, Cass thought their bags would already be in their room.

A man dressed in a dark suit met them just inside the door, and he said, "Mister and Missus Tate, welcome." He handed her an envelope. "Your room is twenty-one-seventeen, and the elevators are to your left and around the corner."

"Thank you," Harrison said, and Cass gave the man a nod too. They went toward the elevator, and once inside, Harrison took her hand in his. They said nothing, and Cass's stomach swooped with the speed of the elevator. It practically shot them up to the twenty-first floor, and they walked along golden carpets in an arched hallway to the very end suite.

Harrison unlocked the door, and the scent of lavender and apples met Cass's nose. "The chocolates are here," he said.

The door slammed closed behind them, and Cass paused to remove her shoes. She'd changed out of her gown and into a party dress for dinner and dancing, and that had required heels. She'd had enough of them now, and she left them by the door and followed Harrison into the room.

He turned and held a bouquet of roses along with a box of plump, ripe strawberries. He indicated the table to his left. "They left hot fudge for dipping. It's actually warm." He grinned at her, and Cass returned the smile.

She moved into him and took the flowers from him. She set them down on the table next to the hot fudge. Her eyes drifted up to his as she took the fruit and put it back too. She then picked up the jar of hot fudge and started to stir it. "This looks good."

"Yeah?" His voice came out as mostly air.

"Mm." She looked up at him, dipped her fingertip in the hot fudge, and instead of licking it herself, she traced the chocolate along his lower lip. He held as still as a statue, save for his arms which came around her, bringing her flush against him.

She tilted her head back and met him as he crushed his mouth to hers. She licked the chocolate from that lower lip, and wow, she liked the way he tasted in her mouth. The zipper on her dress slid down, and Harrison broke the kiss somewhat violently and said, "I want to lick that from your whole body," in a hoarse, husky, sexy voice.

"Okay," she whispered, and Cass closed her eyes and kissed him again.

Chapter Six

Lauren went into the master bedroom at Harrison's house—her house for now—and put yet another box on her bed. Joy wasn't here right now, and despite it being the middle of the day and hotter than Hades outside, Lauren had decided to haul boxes in and out of the house.

She didn't want Joy to see how much stuff she was moving in anyway. She'd likely find out, and soon, because Lauren had never been a closed-door type of person. Joy would come in and out of her bedroom this summer, and it wouldn't take her long to see that Lauren had a lot more than she'd had at Cass's.

With the bed full, she started to unpack what she'd brought in. A minute or two later, a shrill alarm filled the air, and she spun back to the door. She hurried down the hall and around the corner into the living room. She'd left the front door open, and the security system didn't like it.

She only had two strides left to reach the door when the

alarm wailed. She very nearly went deaf, but she managed to get the door closed. That, however, didn't appease the security system. A large panel sat at eye-level on the wall next to the door, and Lauren poked at it.

Harrison hadn't given her any instructions for this, and the alarm was so loud and so annoying that her brain couldn't form coherent thoughts.

"Hello, this is South Island Security," a voice said over the alarm. "Are you in distress?"

"No!" she yelled. "I just left the front door open on accident!"

"We need your safe phrase," the man said.

"Safe phrase?" The alarm continued to wail, and Lauren reached up and covered her ears.

"Do you know your safe phrase?"

"No!"

"I'm sending the police," the man said.

"No!" Lauren said. The man did not come back onto the speaker, and Lauren couldn't stay in the house while the alarm deafened her. She went out the front door, but the alarm outside there was almost as loud as inside.

She stood as far from the house as she could, wondering if she should walk down the lane to Cass's house or just wait here. Would she get arrested? Could she call Cass and Harrison on their honeymoon?

Cass hadn't given her a day-by-day itinerary, and she didn't know where the two of them would be on their European honeymoon. She couldn't just stand out here on the surface of the sun, wearing a pair of dirty cutoffs and a tank top that barely contained her chest.

Before she could decide what to do, police sirens added to the alarm filling the South Carolina sky. Even if she'd wanted to leave, she'd have to run now, and running indicated guilt. Didn't it?

She stayed on the lawn, even waving as two police cars pulled into Harrison's driveway. Wait. *Her* driveway. She met the first man as he got out of the car. "Ma'am, back up, please."

"I live here," she said. "I'm renting the house from Harrison Tate. I just left the front door open." She didn't get any closer to the police officer, but she didn't back up either.

Before she knew it, she stood in the gravel drive with four male police officers. They all looked at her, and one rested his hand on his hip—on perhaps a weapon? Lauren swallowed and faced them.

"I don't know the safe phrase," she said. "But I am renting this house from Harrison Tate. We got approval from the HOA and everything."

Two of the officers exchanged a glance, and then all eyes moved to the SUV pulling into the driveway.

Lauren's heart leapt to the back of her throat and then sank into her stomach. Blake had just arrived. She hadn't been expecting him, but she would've been happy to see him had she answered the door from the safety of the air-conditioned house.

He came to a stop, and two cops went to greet him. "I'll call Marigold," one of the remaining ones said, and he ducked back into the cop car. The last remaining man stayed with Lauren, and she didn't dare go greet Blake.

She could hear his voice as he talked to the officers, but she couldn't decipher the words. Worry pounded through her, and she glanced back over to the man nearest her.

"Do you have any ID?" the officer asked.

Lauren patted her pockets. "It's in the house." She realized in that moment that her phone was too. She didn't have her car keys. Nothing.

"Let's go get it." The officer started toward the house, and Lauren didn't see an option but to go with him. He made it to the front door, reached for the handle, but didn't go inside. He turned back to her. "It's locked."

Lauren didn't have a key. Her pulse was seriously going up and down on a roller coaster, and she needed this blasted alarm to be silenced. She'd typed the six-digit code for the keyed door into her phone—which she didn't have.

"I have the code on my phone," she yelled.

The officer looked one breath away from arresting her and throwing her into a jail cell without a key. The other officers joined him, and blessedly, the alarm went off.

"Thanks," one guy said.

"The door is locked," the first officer said.

"The door is locked," he repeated into his phone. All eyes came to her again, and Lauren swallowed.

"I have the code on my phone, which is inside. I could call Harrison and get the safe phrase too," she said. Blake came to her side and handed her his phone. Relief poured through her when she saw the texts from Harrison. She said, "It's 'the tide is coming ashore.'"

She looked up, and the officer on the phone repeated the safe phrase. "All right," he said. "Got it. Could you unlock the door for this woman too, please?"

Just like magic, the deadbolt unlatched, the electronic mechanism plain to hear. "Thanks." The officer tried the handle, and the door swung in. All four of them entered before her and proceeded to fan out through the house.

She stayed in the lobby, door closed, absorbing the air conditioning.

"Hey," Blake said, his hand touching hers. She grabbed onto it and held it tightly. "Are you okay?"

She nodded, though she felt similar to the way she had when the federal agents had been in her office. Cold inside, fearful, unsure. She hated feeling like this, but she couldn't just swallow and push it all away. Then, she'd been alone. Now, she wasn't.

"Why did you come by?"

"Thought you might like lunch," he said. "I have food in my car."

She looked over to him and watched his beautiful smile form on his face. "You brought me lunch?"

"Mm, yes." He leaned down and touched his lips to her temple. He then watched the activity in the house as two officers switched sides. Apparently all four of them would search all the rooms. "I took Tommy home, grabbed that roasted beet salad you like, and came here."

"Do you have to go back to work this afternoon?" she asked.

Blake looked back to her, interest in his eyes. "I was going to, yes. I have a client call at three."

Lauren somehow got closer to him, though she stood at his immediate side. "Maybe you could stay here until then."

"You don't have to work today?"

Lauren didn't want to lie to him, but she didn't have to work today. So she said, "No."

Blake's mouth tipped up again. "Where's Joy?"

"Volunteering at the library," Lauren said. The main officer in charge approached, and he carried a bottle of water from the fridge. Lauren frowned at him, but he didn't care one whit.

"We're good here," he said. "Mikey got in touch with Marigold. Your story checks out."

She nodded, ready for them to all leave. She wondered if they'd pawed through any of her things—or any of Joy's upstairs. One by one, they left, and once the front door was again closed and locked, Lauren sighed and faced Blake.

"I'll get the food," he said.

"Wait," she said, so many things flying around inside her brain. "I—I don't have to work today, because I lost my job."

Blake's eyes widened, and he wasted no time in hesitant reactions. He swooped her into his arms and said, "I'm so sorry."

"It wasn't really my fault," she said. She still clung to him like she needed him to hold her up. It sure was nice to be held in a difficult time, and she didn't release him right away. He finally did step back, and she added, "I have savings, so I'm going to take some time before I look for something else."

His blue eyes roamed her face, and he clearly had something he wanted to say. "What would you look for? Something here?"

She ducked her head, pleasure filling her. She reached for him, her fingertips playing with the buttons on his shirt as they moved up toward his collar. "Why? Are you worried I'm going to leave Hilton Head?"

"Yes," he whispered.

She looked up and into his eyes. "I'm not much into long-distance dating," he said. "I can barely keep my head above water with my son on Carter's Cove. I don't want you to leave Hilton Head." He might as well have parted the clouds and opened heaven. Conjured up some angels to sing majestic songs for her.

Lauren wrapped her hands around the back of his neck, and if he'd lower his head, she could kiss him. He didn't, and she figured it was probably too soon for kissing anyway. She hadn't even told him she'd like to see him again. Cass and Harrison had been off on their honeymoon for three days now, and they'd be gone for another ten.

"So you brought lunch today," she said as he settled his hands on her hips. "Do you want to take me to dinner sometime soon?" She looked at him, hoping he could feel the flirty vibe and pure charge between them.

"I'd like that," he said. "I'm taking Tommy to his mother's tonight. Tomorrow?"

"I suppose I can wait until tomorrow." She grinned at him, and Blake returned it.

He released her and stepped over to the door. "I'll grab the food." He opened the door and then turned back to her. "Does this mean you want to start dating? Strings attached and all that?"

"Yeah," Lauren said. She reached up and brushed her hair out of her face. "That's what I'm saying. Strings attached."

His face burst into a shining star. "Great," he said. "I'll be right back." He jogged outside, the door drifting open as he left. She went to close it, because the last thing she needed was a repeat of the alarm and then more cops showing up.

"Listen," Blake said as he opened the door and came inside with one of the fanciest brown bags Lauren had ever seen. "I know I messed up last time, but I really do have a job for you at my firm."

He met her eyes with trepidation in his. "I'd love to tell you about it if you'd like."

Lauren cocked her head and appraised him. "Depends on what's in that bag." She nodded to it and laughed lightly. It felt good to have told someone about her job, though she hadn't gone into specifics. Blake would surely ask, but Lauren wouldn't mind telling him.

She'd harbored the news to herself for long enough, and she'd tell Joy tonight too. Then, she'd spill the beans at Supper Club once Cass returned from her honeymoon.

"Oh, you're gonna like what's in this bag." Blake's smile rivaled the sun in brightness. "Come see." He went past her and toward the kitchen, and Lauren turned and went with him.

With him.

It felt really nice to be...with him.

Chapter Seven

Blake felt like he'd just blown on some dice and tossed them down the craps table. Lauren hailed from Texas, so it wasn't a huge stretch to assume she liked meat. Red meat. Beef.

He set the brown paper bag on the counter and looked at her, really playing up what was in this bag. She responded, her smile sexy and playful at the same time. Not only that, but she barely wore anything today, the line of her tank top dipping low enough for him to see plenty of cleavage.

She hadn't been happy when he'd arrived, and in fact, he'd thought for a split second there she might run. She wouldn't have made it far in shorts that short, though she did wear a pair of trendy tennis shoes.

"There's this great roadside stand coming out of Carter's Cove," he said. "Tommy and I stop there all the time after I pick him up and we're back in the car." He opened the bag and reached inside. "I just found out they opened a brick and mortar store here in Hilton Head, so I stopped by." He wrapped his fingers around the sandwich and pulled it out.

To the casual observer, it simply looked like a foil-wrapped log. Blake could already taste the Swiss cheese, the grilled onions and peppers, and that perfectly seasoned steak.

"It's a cheesesteak," she said. She laughed, and Blake sure did like the sound of that. "I love cheesesteak." She narrowed her eyes at him. "Did I tell you that?"

"No, ma'am," he said. "You did not. I took a wild stab that a fine Texas woman like yourself would like steak."

"And *you* like steak," she pointed out.

"Guilty," he said. He rounded the island and started opening drawers. "Knife, knife."

"Far left drawer," Lauren said. "Harrison keeps the knives in there."

Blake opened the drawer she'd suggested, and sure enough an array of knives sat in slots, waiting to be used. "For a second there, I thought I might have to go outside and rummage through his outdoor kitchen."

"Surprisingly, he keeps a lot of stuff in here," she said. "I don't know why, but I've never used an outdoor kitchen."

"I've grilled outside," Blake said. "Does that count?"

"In my book, yes," Lauren said. "I don't cook much at all, so grilling is like the fancy kind of cooking." She gave him another light laugh, and it was such a nice gift.

He took out a serrated knife and cut the monster-sized Philly cheesesteak in half on the bias, the way a real chef would do. He didn't put it on a plate, however, because one simply fisted a cheesesteak to eat it.

Using the tip of the knife, he nudged her half closer to her. "Go on," he said. "Try it." Blake didn't know Lauren super well, and he thought she might be the type of woman to take a dainty bite, deem it delicious and leave the rest. She hadn't eaten much at the wedding, he remembered that.

Today, though, she picked up the cheesesteak, pushed the foil wrapper back, and bit into the sandwich like she meant business. Blake didn't want to have heat shooting from the soles of his feet to the back of his brain—it just happened.

"Wow," he said, chuckling. "You *went all-in*."

Not only that, but her shoulders, which she always kept so boxed and rigid, fell. She sighed and then moaned, her eyes rolling back in her head as her eyelids fluttered closed. He could only stare then, which he could do without shame, because her eyes were shut.

She was the picture of "stunning." If he flipped through the dictionary, he'd only find Lauren under that word. Her eyes opened as she finished chewing, and her smile filled her face after she swallowed.

"That is amazing." She took another bite, and Blake told himself to wake up. Get out of this trance he'd fallen into. She grinned at him, and he took a bite of his half of the sandwich. Pure flavor filled his mouth, from the perfect caramelization on the onions to the seasoned beef. He groaned too, and Lauren hid her mouth behind a napkin and giggled.

"So," he said between bites. "What are you doing today?"

"Moving in," she said. "Always."

He nodded. "Moving takes too long."

She agreed and looked out the window. "Then, I don't know. I think I'll go lay on the beach. Feels like that's something an unemployed person would do." She looked at him, and Blake wasn't entirely sure, but she almost held a challenge in her eyes.

"The job," he said. He hastened to put down his sandwich. "It's not exactly marketing. I work with a national firm, in a private office."

"I know how financial investors work," she said. "You have the backing of a big company, but you have to fund your own office. You have to find your own clients. All of that."

"Yes," he said.

"We did marketing for the big companies," she said. "Signage, logos, commercial campaigns. All of it."

She was extremely overqualified for what he needed. *Don't tell her*, he told himself. The last thing he needed to do —again—was embarrass himself. He reached for the cola he'd brought. "I got you a Diet Coke," he said, indicating the cup.

"Thanks." She smiled at him. "Yours isn't diet."

"No." He took a long drink of his sugary soda. "I like the hard stuff." They'd talked about this at the wedding. He'd been texting her a lot too, and Blake had just been told she wanted to attach strings. He could do that, and he wondered if she knew she already held quite a few of his heartstrings in the palm of her hand.

Probably. Women like Lauren knew.

Her dark eyes drank him up, her smile wide and revealing those straight, white teeth. She didn't wear any makeup, but she was still flawless, and Blake wanted to cancel his whole afternoon and stay here with her. He wasn't even sure what his afternoon held, which was why he needed Lauren.

"It's an assistant position," he said. He cleared his throat. "I can pay decently well, but nothing like I'm sure you were making at your marketing firm." Or even close. "I don't know what Harry's rent is, or what you need. There's some medical and vision benefits. It's a full-time position."

Lauren kept eating, nodding as he talked. He told himself not to say more. She could ask questions if she wanted additional information.

"Your assistant?" she asked.

"Yes," he said. "My personal assistant."

"How big is your office?"

He studied her for a moment. "Like, square footage? Or personnel?"

She grinned at him, and he had no idea why. "Let's go with both."

"The office is half of a building. It's got four or five offices in it. A couple of bathrooms. The front reception area. You'd work out there. Greet people when they come. Come get me and bring them back. Offer drinks." He cut off. "This sounds like a terrible job. I'm sorry, Lauren. You're not a waitress."

"I wouldn't have to waitress," she said slowly.

He shook his head. "No, I don't want you to do it. It's way below your skill set."

"I'm not sure there's something with my skill set here." Her eyes widened, and she clapped one hand over her mouth. "Oh, biscuits and gravy. I sounded so arrogant right there. I'm sorry." She shook her head, her already somewhat olive skin turning a glorious shade of red. "I'm not all that. Really. I mean." She exhaled. "I lost my job. The whole company shut down in a few hours, and I had no idea anything was wrong. Nothing."

She hadn't said much about what had happened at her job, just that she didn't have one anymore. Blake watched her for a moment, and the carefully composed, classy, and educated Lauren reached up and wiped the corner of her eye.

He loved seeing her be real with him. He loved the softness she suddenly possessed. He wiped his hands and moved closer to her. He took her hand in his and said, "Hey, things happen. So many things that are out of our control."

She looked up at him, and he nodded at her, his smile slow and stretching just right across his face. "You wanna go lay with me in the hammock?"

She nodded, wiped the one eye again, and sniffed. "Yeah. I'm exhausted."

Blake led her outside, making sure the French doors he moved through weren't locked—they didn't need a repeat of the alarm that had been blaring when he'd arrived—and settled in the hammock first. She then deftly curled into his side, resting her arm across his torso as he put his around her shoulders and down her forearm.

She smelled like feminine sweat, soft cotton, and sunshine. She smelled like a new beginning for him, something that made his blood buzz and the possibilities for his future open all the way up.

"I like you," he whispered. "I think working together might ruin things between us, as new as they are."

"I don't want to work for you," she said back, her voice as equally as quiet. "But I am considering coming to your office to kiss you."

He smiled up into the sky and said nothing. At least he wasn't the only one thinking about kissing. His eyes drifted closed, and they drifted together in the hammock, and it was really, really peaceful. Quiet. Perfect.

He did need an assistant, but it wouldn't be Lauren. No, she was going to be his girlfriend—just as soon as he could figure out how to kiss her without giving away how hard he'd already fallen for her.

"Tommy," he called as he entered his house sometime later. "I'm here. Let's go." He hadn't gone back to the office, and he'd ended up doing a conference call with some clients out of Raleigh from the patio table while Lauren scrolled on her phone nearby.

He'd stayed as long as he dared with Tommy here alone, and he found his boy lounging on the couch, his shoes having been clearly kicked off. They'd landed at odd angles several feet away, and Tommy clearly didn't care. He also wouldn't be able to find them later.

He'd just turned thirteen at the end of last year, and Blake swore his brain had fallen out of his head. He'd been klutzy for a couple of years now, as his limbs and feet had grown so fast. Too fast for him to know how to use them. He was getting better now, but he still lumbered sometimes, and he dragged his feet all the time, and Blake counted himself blessed that they hadn't been to the ER yet this year.

"We're goin' to your mother's," he said, surveying the damage in the living room. An empty ice cream pint container, with melted pale green liquid in it. A bowl with a couple of swallows of milk Blake assumed would be room temperature. Two empty bottles of Diet Mountain Dew tossed casually onto the nearby cushions.

"Oh!" Tommy yelled and jumped to his feet, the video game controller still in his hand. "Did you see that?"

Blake had not seen it, but he said, "Yeah, that was a good shot." He smiled at his son. "You're going to Mama's for the rest of the week, remember?"

"Yeah, I'm ready," he said. He wasn't, and Blake repressed a sigh as he bent to pick up the dishes and trash. Tommy finished his game while Blake debated telling him about Lauren. He normally didn't alert Tommy to his dating adventures—and they had been adventures lately—until the relationship was pretty serious. He didn't need to be introducing Tommy to every woman he went out with, as he wanted to protect his son.

He also felt a great duty to show his son how to date a woman properly. How to treat her with respect and kindness, as a human being who should be treasured and loved. He never spoke ill of Jacinda in front of Tommy, and they co-parented the best that they could.

"We're gonna be in the island traffic now," he told Tommy. They'd have to wait forever for a ferry to Carter's Cove, and then Blake would likely stay there for a while until the traffic coming back to the mainland thinned too. He could grab a drink at the Heartwood Inn and sit on their outdoor patio or beach for a while.

He knew Gage Sanders and his wife—one of the Heartwood sisters—and they'd let him do whatever he wanted even though he didn't have a room at the inn.

"Get your shoes and your bag," he said to his son. It took Tommy another half-hour to get everything he wanted to tow back to his mother's. When he'd been packing up his game machine and taking it back and forth, Blake had nearly lost his mind. He'd finally bought Tommy one to have here, and he had a permanent bedroom with a desktop computer in the kitchen that only he used too.

At least Blake got a few more emails answered while he waited, and since it was the height of summer, the sun would be shining for a while yet.

"Dad," Tommy said once they'd settled in the SUV and were making the drive off Hilton Head and around to the ferry port that would take them to Carter's Cove.

"Yep." He glanced over to his son, who wore a nervous

expression. He wasn't very good at hiding how he felt, and Blake actually liked that. "What's wrong?"

"I got some weird texts today," Tommy mumbled.

Blake leaned closer, trying to hear better. "Weird texts?"

"From a girl." Tommy sighed and shoved his phone under his leg. "They made me feel weird."

Blake didn't like the sound of this. "Read them to me."

"No." Tommy shook his head. "They're too embarrassing. I'm not reading them out loud."

"I'm reading them when we get to the ferry," Blake said.

Tommy said nothing, and the fact that he couldn't read his son's phone right now sent anxiety through him. He drove faster, but there was traffic, and the highway system couldn't handle his impatience.

They finally made it, and Blake took his son's phone the moment the car wasn't moving anymore. He scanned the texts, and he could instantly see why Tommy was uncomfortable. "Who is this?" Blake asked.

The girl wasn't labeled in Tommy's phone, and she hadn't identified herself.

"Sally-Ruth," Tommy said. "She lives a couple of blocks over from Mama."

"She wants to send you pictures." Blake didn't want to see those. "How old is she?"

"Fifteen," Tommy said. He got out of the SUV and opened the back door. He collected his backpack and turned toward the ferry station. Blake scrambled after him.

"Where did she get your number?"

"She said Gwen gave it to her."

Blake knew Gwen. She was Tommy's best girl-friend, and they'd been friends since the first grade. She lived only a few doors down from Tommy and Jacinda, and she still came over all the time. At least according to Blake's knowledge.

He had no idea what to tell his son. They joined the line for the ferry, as they had permanent passes they only renewed once a year. "You did the right thing by telling me," he said. "And not deleting the texts."

He took screenshots of the texts and sent them to himself. Then he'd be able to show Jacinda without needing his son's phone, and he couldn't believe it, but he kind of wanted to talk to Lauren about the messages too.

He'd never been a great single parent, because he needed to bounce his thoughts off someone else. He loved talking things out and over, just to make sure his mind wasn't making too big of a deal out of something or making too little of it.

He didn't like silence either, though this afternoon in the hammock with Lauren had been soothing.

They made it to Carter's Cove, and then they waited in line for the shuttle that took people around to various places. In the summertime, they ran all the time, so they didn't have to wait long. People also zipped around in golf carts, and Jacinda owned one of those, which she drove over to her shop every day.

She made candles, bath bombs, and other scented bath and body items out of her house. Then, she sold them to tourists and locals in the afternoons and evenings, when the streets and the beaches were filled with people.

They got off the shuttle only a half-block from the house, and Blake swore he could smell oranges in the air already. *At least she uses something that smells good*, he thought.

Blake walked in silence to the house, still lost in his thoughts about what to tell Tommy and what to say to Jacinda. "Tommy," he said when they started crossing the lawn. "I don't want you to respond to that girl."

"Okay." His son kept going, and Blake reached out and tugged on his arm to get him to stop.

"She's too old for you, and she's clearly doing and saying things you're not interested in."

"Yeah." Tommy met his eyes, and Blake pulled his son into a hug.

"You're a good boy," he said. "Don't let her take that from you."

"I won't."

"And tell Gwen that you don't want her texting you anymore."

Tommy pulled away, his face full of worry now. "Do you think she'll be mad?"

"No," Blake said. "Even if she is, Tommy, she shouldn't have given your number out without asking you."

Tommy nodded, and he pulled out his phone and started typing. Blake led the way into the house, calling, "Just us," as he did.

"On the back patio," Jacinda called. The scent of

cooking meat filled the air here, and Blake walked through the house—which was a complete wreck, as usual—and outside to the back deck. All of the houses on Carter's Cove were there for the outdoor living space, not necessarily the indoor accommodations. Jacinda's house was no exception.

"Hey." He bent and kissed his ex-wife's cheek, then swept his gaze over to her boyfriend. "Hey, Cason."

"Howdy, Blake." They didn't shake hands or anything.

"Jacinda, can I talk to you for a sec?" Blake hooked his thumb over his shoulder and back toward the house. Tommy came outside too, without his backpack but with his phone.

"Is there a steak for me?" he asked.

"Sure thing, bud," Cason said, and he got up and opened the grill. "You like medium-well, right?"

"Yes," Tommy said as Blake followed his ex inside.

"What's going on?" Jacinda asked. She had long, dark hair that curled of its own accord. Her pale skin didn't match her dark eyes and hair, and her lips had always been nearly as thin as sheets of paper.

"Tommy got a bunch of sort of sexual texts from a girl today," Blake said. He spoke quickly, almost under his breath. He took out his phone and gave it to her. "I told him not to respond. I told him to tell Gwen not to give out his number and that he doesn't want this girl texting him. They made him uncomfortable."

Jacinda looked up, her eyes wide. "They make me uncomfortable." She handed him his phone. "He told you about them?"

"Yes, on the way here."

She nodded, wrapped her arms around herself, and looked outside to Tommy. "I'll talk to him too, just so he knows we both know about it and are here to help him."

Blake nodded and swallowed. "It's really early still, but I started seeing someone new."

Jacinda's gaze came back to his. "Have you told Tommy?"

"Not yet," he said. "Just telling you, in case when I do… if he has any questions he won't ask me."

She nodded again. "Okay." She patted Blake's bicep as she went past him. "Good to see you, Blake." She went back outside, and Blake watched her rejoin Cason and Tommy. He and Jacinda had been so young when they'd gotten married. Tommy had come along almost immediately, and Blake honestly wasn't sure he even knew what love was.

Romantic love, that was.

The love for his son, he knew. He understood that, and he touched his fist over his heart when Tommy looked his way. His son smiled, got up, and came inside. "Bye, Dad. Love you."

"Love you too, bud. You tell your mom if that girl texts again, ya'hear?"

Tommy nodded, and Blake turned to leave. *On the way to the Heartwood Inn*, he texted Lauren. *Gonna hang at the Heartwood Inn for a little bit until the ferry lines die down. Wish you were here.*

She didn't respond right away, and he wondered what

she was doing right now. Probably something with Joy. Or looking for a job. Or texting all of her Supper Club ladies.

No matter what she was doing, the simple thought of her made him smile, and Blake wore that all the way to the beach, already planning the perfect date for the next evening.

Chapter Eight

Lauren laughed as she texted Blake. He could flirt, and Lauren did like that about him. The thing with him was she knew he'd say out loud the things he typed too, and she enjoyed their back and forth conversations about the people he was watching on the beach.

Part of her wanted to figure out the fastest way to get to Carter's Cove. The biggest, nicest inn on the island was the Heartwood Inn, and Blake had bragged about knowing the owners. They let him come hang out there and order food and drinks to his beach-side lounger even though he didn't have a room.

Stop bragging, she typed out now. *It's not a good look for a man.*

I'm not bragging, he said. *I'm celebrating my accomplishments. There's a difference.*

Sure, she said. He'd been talking about his friendships, his relationship with his mom, how he handled some tough texts his son had gotten that day, and no, he wasn't really bragging.

Lauren liked that he was somewhat of an open book. She felt closed off all the time. At the very least, she didn't rush to tell others everything going on in her life. Sometimes she never did, and she simply dealt with everything internally.

She wasn't sure which was better. Getting it all out and making other people worry over her, or holding it inside herself and dealing with the constant anxiety.

"Hey," Joy said, and Lauren looked up from her phone. Joy wore a bright blue polo with the Hilton Head Library insignia embroidered over her heart. She looked bright and happy, and she carried a blue pastry box that made Lauren love her more. "Look what I brought."

"That better have a chocolate croissant in it." Lauren cocked one eyebrow.

"They were out." Joy put the box on the table and sank into the chair Blake had used for his conference call earlier in the day. Since he'd left, Lauren hadn't done much of anything. That wasn't entirely true. She'd carried in a few more boxes, but they all just sat in her room, still full and taped closed. She'd made tea and sipped it to the tune of the ocean waves down the sand. She'd been texting Blake.

"But I got a raspberry fritter," she said. "They looked incredible, and it was the last one." She opened the box and pulled out the humongous doughnut. "How was your day?"

"I set off the alarm here," Lauren said. "The cops came."

Joy froze with the mammoth fritter in her hand. "What?"

Lauren smiled and shook her head. "It's a long story. I'll tell it after we get food. What do you want?" She swiped on her phone to order delivery. She raised both eyebrows at Joy, who shifted in her seat. Something was going on.

"I, uh, ate after work," she said. She did work part-time at the library four days a week. She went in one or two others as a volunteer, and that had been today's shift.

"You did?" Lauren normally didn't care. She wouldn't tonight, if Joy's face hadn't turned a pale shade of pink that made her freckles pop out. "With whom?" She really enunciated the M on the last word, because Joy had some news to spill.

You do too, Lauren thought, and she told herself to tread carefully. In all honesty, she was surprised Joy hadn't already sniffed out the fact that Lauren didn't have a job. They'd been busy with the holiday, the wedding, and lastly, the moving in.

"There's this man who delivers packages to the library every day," Joy said. "He asked me what time I was done today."

"Classic," Lauren said, grinning.

"His name is Chester. He's nice."

"Nice." She nodded. "A good quality."

Joy grinned and shook her head. "Stop it. This is...terrifying and new. I didn't really like the date."

"You didn't? Why not?"

"It wasn't him." Joy sighed and looked toward the house

at something only she could see. "It was just…weird. I'm forty-seven years old. I shouldn't be going out on awkward first dates." She blinked, her gaze moving back to Lauren's. She only held it for a moment before dropping it to the doughnut in her hand. She tore it in half and wouldn't look at Lauren again. That was a quintessential Joy move. She didn't like looking people straight in the face when she felt vulnerable, exposed.

Lauren understood, and she looked past Joy too. A dog barked somewhere down on the beach, and Lauren thought it might be Beryl. He was still at the house three down, staying with Conrad while Cass and Harrison were on their honeymoon.

"I told Blake we could start dating," she said.

"That's great," Joy said, and she sounded like she meant it.

Lauren nodded. "He came by with lunch while the cops were here. He stayed almost all afternoon." She smiled then, because she couldn't hold the gesture back.

"All afternoon?" Joy asked, faking her shock. "And what, pray tell, did the two of you do here—alone—all afternoon?"

Lauren looked at her and they laughed together. "Nothing," Lauren said truthfully. The words she needed to say clogged her throat. "Joy, I have to—we talked about a job he has at his financial firm."

"Not the job again." Joy rolled her eyes. "You have a job, Lauren. A really good job. Why does he…?" She trailed off, as

Lauren had started shaking her head a couple of sentences ago.

Tears filled her eyes, but they weren't because of the job. Her lost job. The job she'd once had. They came, because she still felt so stupid about how things had happened at Simple Solutions. "I lost my job," she said, the words finally bursting free from her throat. "Before the Fourth. When I went to Texas for those few days."

"You what?" Joy's eyes had grown as wide as dinner plates. "You can't lose your job. You're the VP of the whole company."

"Simple Solutions doesn't exist anymore." Lauren reached up and wiped her leaky right eye. It couldn't contain the tears as easily as her left for some reason. The skin in the corner and underneath her eye was tender and raw, as she came to near-tears several times a day. Still.

"There were several people there doing some embezzling," she said. "Something like that. When I got to Texas, the whole building had been torn apart. There were these federal agents there in the middle of the night, and they kept me for questioning." Her voice caught on itself, and she shook her head.

Joy's hand covered hers. "You're okay, though, right?"

Lauren sniffled and sucked in a breath, hoping it would help her compose herself. It only sort of worked. "They didn't find any evidence they could use against me, so they had to let me go."

"Why didn't you tell me?" Lauren gave her a sharp look,

and Joy held up her free hand. "Okay. You're you. I get it. I mean, I don't, but it's you, so it makes sense."

Lauren wanted to ask her what that meant, but she didn't trust her voice.

"You didn't want Cass to worry," Joy said. "And you're so headstrong, you think you can take on the world by yourself."

"No," Lauren said. "That's not true. I don't think I can take on the world by myself. I *have* to take on the world by myself. There's a difference." She glared at Joy, who simply studied her in return.

She finally dropped her eyes and said, "Okay, Lauren."

"I'm not like you, Joy. Besides, you told me about Wendell leaving a few years ago—when you could. That's what I do too."

"What are you going to do?"

"Get another job," she said with a shrug. "People do it all the time."

"Did you call Jess?"

Lauren gave her another sharp look at the mention of her brother. "No," she said slowly. "Why would I do that?"

"Because he's your brother, and because he probably employs entire marketing teams."

"In LA," Lauren said. "I'm not interested in living in California."

Joy covered her hand again, and this time Lauren turned hers over and braided their fingers together. "Did you like Chester? Did you hold his hand like this?"

"No," Joy said. "I mean, yes, I like him. No, he didn't

hold my hand." She gave another wistful sigh. "Like I said, it was awkward. I'll be shocked if he calls me for another date." She took a bite of the doughnut and chewed thoughtfully.

"I'm going to get pizza," Lauren said. She swiped around to do that, ordering on the app, but things didn't chill between her and Joy. "What else is going on with you?"

"Nothing." Joy gave her a smile that strained along the edges. "Just worried about Lexie. She's got another interview with HP."

"That's her third or fourth," Lauren said. "Right?"

"Her fourth," Joy said. "They've hired several people after only two interviews, and she's not sure what she's doing wrong."

"Maybe she's not doing anything wrong," Lauren said. She often felt like she'd been doing things wrong in her life. She thought back to when her daddy had died. Her mama had gotten remarried about five years later, and the very moment Lauren had graduated from high school, her step-dad had announced they were moving back to Minnesota. They'd taken their baby girl and gone, and Lauren had barely seen her mother since.

Jess was older than her and already in California. He'd gotten married a few years later, and then his kids had started to come. Lauren had been alone for a long, long time, and she'd wondered for years if she could've done things differently. If she'd done "something wrong" to be so isolated from her family.

Then she'd found Bea and Cass and the Supper Club.

She excelled at her job—and yet, she'd still lost it. Had she done something wrong to cause that to happen?

She'd never been married. Not only that, but she'd never even been close to getting married. Never engaged. Never even talked with a man about getting married. Had she been "doing things wrong" all this time?

Since last summer, she'd really been pondering these things. "Maybe she's not doing anything wrong," she said again, her voice quieter this time. "Maybe she's just not meant to work at HP."

Joy nodded, but she still wore a troubled expression. Lauren squeezed her hand to let her know she was there, and Joy squeezed back. Lauren said, "I'm glad you're here with me, Joy."

Their eyes met then, and Joy realized the weight of what Lauren had said. "I love you, Lauren. You're my favorite person in the world."

Lauren grinned at her and said, "Same. But are you sure about me? What about Chester?"

They both laughed, and that helped to lighten the mood. Then Joy said, "So you told Blake about some strings. What's next for you two?"

THE NEXT NIGHT, LAUREN BENT HER HEAD TO PUT in her earring, carefully threading the wire through the hole in her earlobe. The doorbell rang, and her phone lit up and started playing the National Anthem. She and Joy had set the chime to that after Harrison had given them access to his security system app. The Fourth had been a few days ago, but apparently the patriotic songs would be available for the whole month of July.

The security app brought up the doorbell cam, and she saw Blake standing there. He wore a pair of black slacks and a light blue shirt, open at the throat. Her pulse sped at the sight of him holding a huge bouquet of white roses. She smiled and looked at herself in the mirror. She'd told him last night that she didn't like red roses.

"Tacky" she'd called them.

The door opened, and Joy's voice came through the app. "Come on in," she said. "She's almost ready."

Now that Lauren had told her she'd lost her job, she'd also admitted she was going to sell her house in Sweet Water Falls and move here. Joy had cried a little, and Lauren understood. She'd sworn Joy to secrecy until they could have their Supper Club once Cass returned from her honeymoon, and she trusted Joy explicitly.

She didn't want to think about how Bessie would react to the news, and Lauren had to once again coach herself that life changed. She needed to leave Texas, and she knew it deep down in her core.

After lightly brushing her fingers through her hair, she deemed herself ready, and she left her bedroom. To Joy's surprise, Chester had called her, and they were going out tonight too. Lauren was glad she wouldn't have to be home alone tonight, and she looked stunning in a white dress with big bell sleeves and a full skirt that looked like the perfect thing to wear for a stroll along the beach with a handsome man.

Blake had given Lauren only a few details about tonight, but he'd said they might be walking a lot. Because of that, she'd skipped the heels and opted for a pair of comfortable leather sandals. They went well with her eggplant shorts and the retro, short-sleeved sweater in beige, purple, and yellow she'd paired with it.

She picked up a pale yellow sun hat as she passed the couch. "Hey, you."

Blake whistled, his eyes roaming to her feet and back to her eyes. "You are gorgeous."

"I'm going to tell Chester to greet me like that when he gets here." Joy grinned at her from the kitchen.

Lauren giggled and positioned her hat on her head. "Ready." She slipped her hand into Blake's and squeezed.

"Good to see you, Joy," he said somewhat absently, and they left the house. Outside, Blake stepped in front of her. "Seriously, Lauren, I don't know what I did to catch your eye, because you're..." He swallowed. "Honestly." He chuckled. "Out of my league."

Lauren had heard that before, usually during a break-up. She shook her head. "Don't say that. It's not true."

"Oh, it's true."

Frustration filled her. "Blake." She exhaled, not sure what to say. She hated not knowing how to express her feelings, but she often didn't. "Look, just promise me something."

"Okay," he said.

"Don't break up with me because I'm 'out of your league.' I've been through that before, and I'm standing right here, saying out loud, *I* don't feel like that. *I* don't feel like you're beneath me. There are no leagues. We're just people, and we're on even ground." Her chest stormed, and she searched Blake's face, desperate for him to understand. "Okay?"

His expression changed instantly, and he dropped his head. "Okay."

"I'm not sure I believe you." Lauren tried to slip her hand out of his, but he gripped her fingers before she could get them away.

"Okay," he said in a stronger voice. "We're just people, and we're on even ground."

"Yes." She re-settled her fingers between his. "Now, I believe you promised me an amazing date." She took the first step toward the edge of the steps. As they moved down them, she asked, "Where are we going?"

"I was thinking of this place down in Sea Pines," he said. "Where the historical lighthouse is?"

"I've been down there," she said. "There's a big shopping center."

"Yes," he said. "Have you been on the harbor cruise?"

Lauren's eyebrows went up. "There's a harbor cruise?"

"I got a couple of tickets. They serve dinner, and we'll watch the sunset, and then they have live music on the beach. We can stay and dance or leave. Go for a walk along the shore." He shrugged. "I'm open to suggestions after the cruise."

"That sounds great." She smiled as he reached to open her door, hoping Lauren could curb her slight fear of boats long enough to get on the ship. She turned into him and reached up to smooth her fingers along his collar. Their eyes met, and Lauren enjoyed the crackling energy between them. "I think you might be out of my league, Mister Williams."

She wanted to kiss him, but the date had just started, and she didn't want to set that precedent. Instead, she brushed her lips across his cheek and moved to get in his car.

Her heartbeat quivered in her chest as he closed the door and rounded the vehicle to get behind the wheel. She wasn't sure if that buzzing came because she was too desperate for this relationship to work, or if Blake was so special and so perfect for her.

Please don't let me make a fool of myself this time, she prayed as he started the vehicle, all the same crackles and snaps and pops blitzing between them.

Chapter Nine

Blake's cheek burned where Lauren had kissed him. He hadn't been on a first date in over a year, as he hadn't dated since he'd broken up with his previous girlfriend so he could go out with Lauren. *On a date that never was*, he told himself.

He glanced over to her, riding with her legs crossed in his passenger seat. They'd finally made it on a date, and Blake kneaded the wheel, his fingers aching with how tightly he squeezed.

He swallowed and told himself he'd spoken to her before. They'd been texting for days. He knew things about her. "What did you and Joy do today?"

"Got arrested," she said.

"What?" Blake turned his head and stared openly at her. She grinned at him, and he shook his head. His adrenaline still coursed through his body, and he said, "That's not nice."

She laughed, and Blake relaxed. The sound of her happiness filled the car, and he wanted to collect a sample of it so he could listen to it later.

"Yeah, but it's better than what we did."

"Which was?" he prompted. "I mean, it can't be worse than staring at numbers, clicking from one spreadsheet to another, and answering email." That was what his day had been. Boring. Lifeless. The only thing keeping him going had been this date. This moment with Lauren Keller.

"We sat on the beach for a while. Beryl came out and joined us. I looked for jobs and read them to Joy. She said none of them sounded good." Lauren uncrossed her legs, and Blake dang near drove them into the car in front of them. His safety systems on his car actually vibrated his seat and a red flashing light shone on the window.

He jammed his foot on the brake and said, "Wow," the walls of his throat sticking together slightly. She wore classy clothes, paired perfectly from the sun hat to the stripes in her sweater, and Blake definitely felt out of her league. He pushed the thoughts away, because she wouldn't like them.

Lauren swept her hand along her thigh, brushing something invisible away. "Yeah. Then Chloe got in a vocal argument with Oscar—they haven't settled in well here—and I had to put her in her carrier for a time out. That was honestly the most exciting part of the day." She looked over to him. "Talk about boring."

"I'd come be bored with you," he said.

"Yeah?" She turned slightly toward him. "What would we do?"

Blake's face heated, because he could think of a few things he'd like to do with Lauren. "Talk," he said. "I'd show you pictures of Tommy, and tell you about him when he was a little boy." He glanced over to her, and her smile encouraged him to keep talking.

"You'd tell me how you take your coffee, and if you're a morning person or a night owl, and then, I'd ask about your family." He raised his eyebrows, but his next glance away from the road showed Lauren completely closed off.

"What did I say?" he asked.

"Nothing." She looked out the window.

"Oh, don't be like that." He started to laugh, but the mood in the car had changed. "I said something."

Lauren took her sweet Southern time answering. Enough time that Blake had to think through what he'd said. Tommy. Coffee. Morning person. Family.

She'd said absolutely nothing about her family. Not her parents. Siblings. No distant cousin somewhere. No one.

He swallowed again and reached for the bottle of water in the middle console. "Is it Tommy? You don't want to hear about him?"

"I'd love to hear about Tommy," she said quietly. "I don't talk about my family."

"Why is that?"

She speared him with a withering look, and Blake kept his eyes on the road so he wouldn't turn to dust completely. "I just said I don't talk about them."

"Do you not have any family?"

"You're not going to let this die, are you?"

"I mean, I don't want to. I think this is what people do when they're dating. They talk about their lives. The good, the bad, the ugly. All of it." He did look over to her then. He kept driving, and when he eased the SUV to a stop at a light, she sighed.

"It's not good or bad or ugly. It's...nothing. I don't have a relationship with my mom. My dad died with I was young. I was ten. My mom got remarried and she has a new family now." The slightly bitter tone of her voice indicated it was definitely more than nothing. She had feelings about this, but Blake felt like he'd be pulling every one of her teeth to get more than she'd already said.

"I'm sorry," he said. He got the SUV moving again when the light turned green, glad he'd lived here long enough to navigate easily. She sounded like she wanted a relationship, but simply didn't have it. "My momma would love to talk your ear off any day of the week. I can give you her number if you'd like."

Lauren gave him a subdued smile and shook her head. "My brother lives in California. He's a big-wig movie producer something-or-other. He has three kids and a wife, and he doesn't need his needy little sister bugging him."

Blake wanted to say he was sure her brother didn't feel like that, but he held his tongue. No need to poke the bear. She'd already said she didn't want to talk about them, and then she had. He could be satisfied with that.

"I'm sorry," he said again.

"I have my friends," she said. "I had co-workers. I was getting along."

He glanced over to her and found her once again shrinking into herself. He made a right turn, the highway to Sea Pines opening before them.

"What about you?" she asked. "Brothers and sisters? Only been married the one time?"

"Yes to all of it," he said. "Married the one time. My ex is Jacinda, and she lives in Carter's Cove. She makes a variety of bath and body products and sells them to hotels and bed and breakfasts there on the island. Some on Hilton Head too, actually. Sells them in a stand on the beach to tourists. That kind of thing."

"Sounds fun," Lauren said. "The total opposite of you."

He chuckled. "We were pretty opposite. She's more of a free spirit. I'm buttoned to the collar."

Lauren reached over and brushed her fingertips along his collar. "Not tonight. You've got a couple of buttons undone."

"Just for you, sweetheart." He gave her a smile, and when she returned it, he finally relaxed into himself. "I've got an older brother and an older sister. Both married. Both with kids. Tommy's not quite the youngest grandchild. Lindsey has a daughter who's ten, and she's the youngest."

"They must not be too close," Lauren said. "You've never brought them to the fireworks."

"Charleston," he said. "Peter's in Charleston. Lindsey is a bit north of there, in a smaller town. It's close enough for big holidays like anniversaries or birthdays, but not quite pop-in status."

She tucked her hair and adjusted her hat. "Something tells me you like that."

"Them not popping in? One hundred percent," he said. "I hate the pop-in."

"You popped in with lunch yesterday."

He looked at her to see if she was teasing, and she clearly was. Her eyes shone like diamonds, and he rolled his eyes. "Fine," he said. "I won't do that anymore."

"I was teasing," she said.

"Yeah, because you want me to pop in with lunch every day."

"I wouldn't say no to it." She took his hand from the steering wheel and laced her fingers through his. "And I'd love to learn about Tommy and meet him when you think the time is right. I might even call your momma."

Blake made the final turn into the parking lot, which wasn't super easy with only one hand. "Oh, boy," he said. "Sounds like I've opened a can of worms I shouldn't have."

"You're the one who said you'd like to be bored with me."

He eased down a row of parking spots, looking for one. "I would, Lauren. Slow, carefree days with you on the beach? Sounds like heaven."

"Not every day can be carefree on the beach," she said.

"Why not?" He spotted an empty space up ahead and swung into it. He parked and looked at her. "Why not?" he asked again when she didn't answer.

She shook her head. "That's not real life. Real life is work and deadlines. Dealing with people and projects and trying to make a living." Her dark eyes sank into his, and Blake really wanted to kiss her.

Don't, he told himself. *Do not. You'll make a fool of yourself.*

"Yeah, it is like that sometimes," he said.

"That's what makes the slow, carefree days so special," she said. She took a deep breath. "All right, Mister Williams, I feel like I should confess something."

"Ooh, a confessional. I like where this is going."

She laughed as Blake got out of the SUV and went to get her door for her. She waited for him, and he took her hand in his as she stood from the vehicle. He gave her no room to move away from the car or him, and she stepped right into his personal bubble.

"I'm just the teensiest bit afraid of boats."

Blake's eyebrows shot up. "You are?"

"Mm hm." She fiddled with his collar again, the length of her body nearly pressing into his. From toe to chest, all Blake could feel was her, her, her.

"Well, maybe we shouldn't go on the cruise," he said.

"Once I get on, I'm usually okay," she said. "It's bridging that gap between land and sea I don't like."

"Do you get sick?"

"Not usually." She looked up at him, and Blake forgot about everything else. He forgot he wasn't going to kiss her. He forgot they had a ticket and needed to be somewhere on time. He forgot all of the promises he'd made to himself about not falling in love too fast.

With her gazing up at him, the scent of her hair or skin

or whatever that rosy, feminine smell was, her hands on his chest, all Blake could do was bend his head and kiss her.

He did, and Lauren certainly didn't complain. Her hands slid along his shoulders and into his hair, and wow-oh-wow, he had not experienced fireworks like this with a woman in a decade. Longer.

Ever.

She seemed made for him to hold, her lips slick and glossed and tasting like cherries. He wanted more, and he deepened the kiss. She went with him, seemingly gladly, and Blake couldn't believe he stood in a parking lot kissing the amazing, sexy, outstanding, totally out of his league Lauren Keller.

He finally remembered they had zero privacy and ducked his head enough to break the kiss. He had to pull in a long breath to satisfy the needs of his lungs, and with Lauren's fingernails sliding along the back of his ear, pure electricity arced down his back.

Clearing his throat, he finally backed up to give her some breathing room too. He couldn't go far, because of the car parked beside him, and she came with him anyway. He closed the door and took her hand in his again.

There was no awkwardness between them. No regrets. He lifted her hand to his mouth and kissed it too. "You ready for this?"

She looked at him, and he liked that she wasn't shy or giggling or acting like kissing him had been something silly or weird. "Yeah," she said. "I think I am."

He grinned at her and took her toward the small

boathouse where they checked in. The sun had started to dip in the sky, and Blake's stomach grumbled for food. The scent of steak rode on the air, and they checked in and joined the line of people getting on the boat.

It moved slowly, and Blake said, "When Tommy was born, he was balder than a billiard ball."

Lauren grinned, and Blake sure liked that. Some women he'd dated hadn't been thrilled that he had a son. "Do you like kids, Lauren?"

"Sure," she said. "I don't have any of my own, of course. And very little experience with them, so maybe? Maybe I like them?" She looked at him with sudden confusion in her expression. "I don't really know."

"Do you want kids?"

"Blake." She glanced to the couple in front of them and edged closer to him. Her other hand came around his, and he liked how claimed he felt by her. "I think I'm too old to have kids. So if you want more...I'm not the woman for you."

He ducked his chin to see her better, but he couldn't. Not with how close she stood. "I'm fine not having more kids," he said in an equally quiet voice. "But just out of curiosity. And you can break-up with me and stomp back to the car if you want. But...how old are you?"

"How old are you?" she asked.

"Forty," he said easily.

"I've got you beat by four years," she said.

Blake nodded and said, "That's not too old, Lauren."

"I guess you never know," she said. With a deep breath,

the murky cloud over her disappeared and she smiled. "It's almost our turn. You'll help me, right? Because that walkway thingy just wobbled, and I'm about to bolt because of that, not you asking me how old I am."

Blake hadn't even seen the walkway move. People walked up it to the ship, and it seemed to be swaying a normal amount. "I'm right here, baby," he said. He pressed a kiss to her temple. You can close your eyes if you want, and I'll guide you right to our table."

"There is no way I'm closing my eyes," she said. "You're insane."

He looked at her, the couple in front of them handing over their tickets. "Do you trust me or not?"

She searched his face, swallowed, and came up with, "Yes," in a froggy voice.

"Then close your eyes." He waited for her to do it, and then he handed his tickets to the man standing at the entrance to the gangplank.

He ripped them and handed them back, said, "Table twelve, sir," and gave Lauren a strange look.

"All right," Blake said, taking the first step. "We're walking. Just move with me, baby. I won't go fast." He didn't either. He had several feet between him and the couple in front of him, and they had to go up a couple of stories on the ramp to get to the boat.

"Slight incline," he murmured, and he was glad she hadn't worn heels. He checked to make sure she wasn't peeking, and she sure wasn't. He loved the lines of her face and the way she'd painted her lips pink tonight. He hadn't smeared it at all with that kiss either, and he'd have to do a better job of that next time.

Just thinking about kissing her again set his blood to boiling, but he managed to ease her around the corner and back up the next ramp. "Going up again."

"I can't believe we're going up," she said. "Now when I fall in the space between this very shaky sidewalk and the boat, I'm going to plummet to my death."

"Nope." He squeezed her hand and kept her close to him. "I won't let you fall." He moved slow enough that he didn't have to stop them to wait for the couple ahead of them to get on the ship.

He moved around the next corner with, "To your left, Lauren." She moved with him in sync, and he felt like they were completing a dance neither of them had done before with anyone else. But together, it made perfect sense. Together, they could do anything. Together, all of the moves were fluid and easy.

"Another left," he said, and it was the last turn. But he didn't want her to know that. He didn't want her to know she'd moved from "shaky sidewalk" to ship at all.

They stepped over the threshold together, and Blake gazed at all the tea lights and people enjoying champagne on the ship. He'd been on these harbor cruises before, and they never stuffed them too full.

He tugged Lauren to the right so they'd be out of the way, and said, "Open your eyes, Lauren." She did, first gazing around at the upper deck of the ship. "Oh," fell from her lips, and Blake thought he could end the date right then and be the victor. She drank in the luxurious atmosphere on the boat, and a waiter approached with champagne.

"Thank you," she said, but he waved it away. Not only was he driving, but he'd committed to not drinking for the foreseeable future. She sipped hers, the magic of the harbor cruise sinking fully into her eyes.

"You're on the boat," he pointed out.

Lauren looked over to the people still embarking. "Yes." She smiled at him. "Thanks, Blake. That was so much easier than if I'd been looking." She stretched up and kissed him, and he was drunk instantly. Not from the tiniest taste of champagne on her tongue, but from the woman herself.

He'd been thinking about her for a solid year—longer than that, if he were really being honest with himself—and actually being with her was far superior to any fantasy he'd had.

She rescued him from his boredom, and he thought he could endure any spreadsheet if he could kiss Lauren at the end of the day.

Chapter Ten

Joy Bartlett bustled around the outdoor kitchen, realizing why Harrison liked it so much. There was so much room, with counter space galore, and hooks for all the utensils she used on the grill. She was bursting with news, and she couldn't wait for their monthly Supper Club to start.

Cherry Forrester wouldn't be here physically, but everyone else had stayed through Cass's honeymoon. She and Harrison had returned yesterday, and Joy couldn't wait to hear all about Europe, the castles, the river cruise, the landmarks, everything.

"They're going to die," she said gleefully. "When you tell them about Chester." She grinned at the watermelon on the grill and then started removing it. She just wanted the smoky, charred flavor, and then she'd chill it again. Behind her, a cat meowed, and it would be Chloe. Oscar rarely came outside unless forced, and Joy hardly saw him in the house either.

Lauren said he liked to lurk under couches and beds, while Chloe liked to sit in the sunshine and imagine herself to be a great bird-catcher. Joy had caught the gray and white cat in the window, pawing at the glass, a time or two.

She turned now and found Chloe on the patio table. "Hey," she said. The cat barely looked at her. "Get down, you. Go on." She waved the long, grilling tongs at Chloe, who gave her a doleful look and hopped to the stones. "Thank you."

Chloe stalked to the edge of the patio and jumped up on the wall there. She looked over the beach, and Joy wondered if she thought she was some sort of Lion King. Surveying the lands she owned. The grasses would bow to her.

She giggled at the thoughts and turned the grill off. She and Lauren were hosting the Supper Club that evening, but Lauren had gone into town for a job interview at a real estate agency. Joy wasn't sure if Lauren wanted the job or simply needed it. It wasn't exactly in her field of expertise, but Lauren was smart and could do anything.

The listing had said they were looking for someone with "an eye for marketing," and that had been why Lauren had applied. She was probably terribly overqualified for the position, and Joy worried she'd be bored in a matter of days. A bored Lauren was never a good thing, and Joy was actually surprised she'd made it this long without a job.

It was mid-July now, and that meant Lauren had been

unemployed for almost three weeks. She had been busy moving in here and dealing with her house in Sweet Water Falls from a distance. She'd been out with Blake every night since she'd deemed them "strings-attached," and listening to her talk about him made Joy feel like a college freshman with her first serious boyfriend.

He did treat her well, despite their rocky start, and as Joy slid the grilled watermelon into the fridge, she glanced at the clock. Still a few hours until Supper Club. She still wore her swimming suit from her lunchtime picnic on the beach with Lauren, and she snatched her sunhat from the dining room table and went back outside.

Harrison didn't have a pool like some of the houses in this community, but his access to the beach was spectacular. He did have a hot tub, but it was far too hot to use it right now. Joy thought it would be amazing in the cooler months of the year, and a pang of sadness hit her that she wouldn't be here then to try it.

She played with the strap on her suit, her cover-up falling off her shoulder, as she moved to the steps that led down to the beach. Was she really going to go back to Texas when autumn arrived?

"Why wouldn't you?" she asked herself. She had a house there. She'd lived there for over twenty-five years. She had a job at an elementary school, working with students and teachers whom she loved.

The very idea of returning home to her house, alone, made her head ache. Her fingers went round and round the strap on her shoulder, and then with one loud *snap!* it came apart in her hands.

Stinging shot down her arm, and Joy looked at her wrist as if the injury emanated from there. Her strap hung down her bicep, the clasp holding the front part of it to the back part separated. She finally realized what had happened, and she picked up the end of the strap. It didn't look broken.

She couldn't quite reach the back strap, as it had fallen down her ribcage on the left. Her arms weren't long enough to reach it, and she twisted and turned in a full circle, trying to get it. Anyone who saw her would think her an inept fool, and she sighed in exasperation. Not only that, but Joy was well-endowed enough to require two straps on her swimming suit. This one was particularly low cut, and she was practically hanging out on the left side.

Deciding she'd attempt to get the strap one more time before she headed inside to switch suits, she stretched and reached, groaning as she did. She could not reach it, and to her great horror, a man said, "Let me help you."

His warm hand slid along her back to the strap she was so desperately trying to reach, and he caught it and lifted it over her shoulder to hand it to her.

She'd frozen upon the introduction of his voice to her life, and she could only stare at him.

Taller than her, but that wasn't hard to do. Tall for a man, probably at or just over six feet. His light brown hair shone with a slight red sheen, and Joy's mouth dropped open. Was God trying to torment her or send her a gift?

She was a real sucker for a ginger, she knew that. The Lord knew it too. "Mercy," she whispered as the man smiled.

"Sorry," he said. "I was spraying the weeds when I saw you in real trouble." His eyes slid down to her chest, and pure humiliation filled Joy from top to bottom. She spun away from him, but that only made her girls bounce a little too hard. She pressed her eyes closed and drew in a deep breath.

She got the clasp back together and pulled the straps up and tight before she faced him again. His blue eyes twinkled with mischief, and dare she think it? Desire? Attraction?

Don't be stupid, she told herself. This man wasn't attracted to her. She knew, because she'd met him before.

"I'm Scott Anderson," he said, clearly not remembering meeting her. Why would he? Joy had been invisible to men for years now. "I own—"

"Anderson Landscaping," they said together. "I know," Joy added. "We've met before."

His eyebrows went up. He shook his head as his smile grew. "I don't think so. I'd remember you."

"You came to a barbecue at this very house. I was here too." There were a lot of people, but not so many that she hadn't met them all. "Oliver Blackhurst was here. Bea and Grant. Cass and Harrison. Lauren was here. Bessie. Sage." She held up her fingers as she counted. "Blake Williams tried to come in, but Lauren didn't want him to. You were here. I think I even sat beside you while Grant told us about that one renter who'd wadded up wet toilet paper and thrown it against all the walls and the ceiling."

She cocked her head at him and folded her arms, practically challenging him to contradict her.

His expression shifted, but his smile remained in place. "I was there for that party," he said. He glanced around as if trying to see her out on this very patio. "I don't remember you though."

Joy exhaled and rolled her eyes. She'd lived with her invisibility her whole life, and she was tired of it. Tired of fading into the wallpaper and wishing the men around her would see her.

Today, she took a step closer to him and looked right into those pure blue eyes. Even the ocean wasn't this blue, and Joy would have a hard time getting them out of her head tonight.

"Here's a hint, Scott." She reached up and patted his chest in a semi-condescending way. "When you don't remember meeting a woman, you don't tell her that." She stepped past him and started for the house. Suddenly, she didn't want to spend any more time in the sun today.

"What's your name?" he called after her.

Joy kept going, only pausing when she got to the French doors that led inside. "Ask your friends," she said over her shoulder. "They all know my name." With that, she went inside, and she did not look back at the gorgeous Scott Anderson standing on the back patio.

She didn't want to think about what he'd seen as she'd struggled with her strap and then spun around. She held her head high as she grabbed her phone from the counter and headed for the steps. Lauren lived in the master bedroom here on the main level, as she'd be staying here for longer than the summer. Joy only had about five weeks left in paradise, so she'd taken the largest bedroom upstairs. It had an attached bath and essentially functioned as a second master bedroom.

She shed her suit and got in the shower, and when she got out, her phone flashed with texts and messages. As she stood in the bathroom, a towel wrapped around herself, she could only stare at the several she had from the same person.

From Harrison: *What did you say to my friend Scott?*

He wants your number.

Cass says I can give it to him...

Can I give it to him?

Okay, you're not answering, so I'm going to trust my wife and give it to him. I'm sorry in advance if this is not what you want.

She swallowed, because Scott had asked his friends for her name. And her number.

After backing out of that string without answering, she saw an unknown number which had sent three messages.

Joy almost didn't dare tap on them. She did, however, and her eyes bugged out of her head.

This is Scott Anderson. I asked Harrison for your number, and he gave it to me.

Joy.

What a lovely name. I'm sorry I didn't remember you, and thanks for the tip about not telling a gorgeous woman that. I'll keep that in my back pocket for next time. Hope you get your suit fixed.

She looked up and into her own eyes. "What is happening right now?" She honestly had no idea. Scott hadn't asked her out. He had apologized. He'd...she had no idea what to think now.

Chapter Eleven

Scott Anderson finished the yard work at Harrison Tate's house, his gaze wandering to the nearest window every other moment. That made the job take twice as long, and he seriously needed to pull himself together.

He honestly couldn't remember meeting the lovely Joy Bartlett—a name he now knew, thanks to Harrison.

He'd practically had to grovel to get the woman's number. He'd asked four times, finally telling Harrison that he'd said something rude to her and needed to apologize. She wasn't happy, and he had to have happy customers.

The business angle was a bit devious, but he'd gotten the woman's number. He'd texted her a half-hour ago. He had no idea if she'd read them or not. "You didn't exactly ask her anything," he said as he tossed the weed eater into the trailer attached to his truck. He loved owning his own business, setting his own hours, and working and building toward his own success.

Harrison had owned a large part of the landscape company at one point, but as his construction career had taken off, he hadn't been able to maintain both. He'd sold all of the landscaping equipment and clients to Scott, and he'd been working like a dog ever since.

His brother worked with him, and they'd just hired two more full-time people to mow, weed, and trim for the summer. He also had a full-time secretary in the office, and Carly was a lifesaver for him and Jeff.

He looked back to the house one more time, and Joy leaned one of those curvy, beautiful hips into the pillar at the top of the steps. Scott immediately moved toward her, his pulse skipping ahead several beats. His imagination went wild, and he barely had time to censor himself and his thoughts before he said, "Hey, did you get my texts?"

"Yes," she said. Those arms folded, and wow, she had the sexy librarian getting mad at the patron who was too loud down pat. Perfectly. Everything about her called to him, and he simply could not believe he hadn't remembered meeting her.

This afternoon, it had felt like he'd been struck with lightning the moment she'd turned and looked into his eyes. She had eyes the color of slate, and he had to look and look to decide if they were blue or gray.

Blue, he told himself.

No, gray.

Her blonde hair had been piled on top of her head earlier, but now, it was damp and curled around her ears. She wore it short, but with her long neck and heart-shaped face, she was still very feminine.

Scott imagined himself fisting her hair as he pulled her head back to kiss her, and he practically burst into flames.

"I'm really sorry," he said. "Maybe I was blind last year."

"Do you remember the party?"

"Vaguely."

"You must go to a lot of parties."

"I talk to a lot of people," he admitted. "I was probably in overload." He held up both hands at the displeasure in her blue-gray eyes. "I'm not making excuses. I'm apologizing. And I'm wondering if you'd like to go to dinner with me, so I can make it up to you." He smiled at her, because no one had ever turned him down when he turned on the full Anderson charm, complete with this smile.

Joy softened right in front of him, but Scott refused to be smug about it. Jeff, his brother, did that, and it wasn't a good look on a man. Women didn't like it, at least. He tucked his hands in his pockets and rocked back onto his heels. "I can wait until you decide," he said.

She tucked her short hair behind her ear. "I'm seeing someone already."

No! Scott cried in his head. The word very nearly came out of his mouth. He had somewhat poor impulse control, which was why he'd walked right up to this woman and helped her with that errant swimming suit strap. That thing would haunt him forever, he was sure of it.

"Who?" he managed to ask.

Joy backed up a step. "I don't think that's your business, Scott." She started to turn, and he really didn't want his time with her to end.

He couldn't reach out and grab her, so he simply watched as she crossed the wide porch and opened the front door. She turned back to him and said, "I accept your apology. I hope you have a good evening."

"You too," he said. "And hey, if it doesn't work out with you and...whoever, you can text me. I'd love to go out with you." He very nearly bit his tongue, because he hadn't meant to say that.

Joy smiled, though, so maybe she liked his bluntness and his inability to control his mouth. *She won't for long*, he told himself. Most women didn't, and Scott had learned how to manage his business fairly well without too much of a filter.

Relationships, on the other hand... He was quite hopeless at those.

For Joy, he thought he could try harder than he had in the past, when she said, "I'll keep that in mind, Mister Anderson. Good night." She stepped into the house and closed the door, and all the air rushed out of his lungs.

He turned away from the door, his smile covering his face and extending for a while beyond it. "Well, that wasn't so bad." It wasn't good, but Scott had stopped aiming for good. "Not so bad," was his goal now, and seeing as how he had the woman's number now, perhaps he could slide into her text messages and woo her away from this other boyfriend.

Scott opened the door to The Mad Mango, the annoying bell Oliver kept on it singing with the movement. There hadn't been many cars in the parking lot, and the number of people inside matched.

Oliver Blackhurst looked up from behind the counter, his face breaking into a smile when he saw Scott. "Hey, buddy," he said. He tossed the rag and came out from behind the counter. "You want your check."

"That," Scott said. "And I need the Bridge Over Troubled Water. It's *hot* out there."

Oliver twisted back to the woman still behind the counter. "Bridge," he called. "I've got to run into the office." He gestured for Scott to go with him.

"You've got enough help this summer at least," Scott said.

"Yeah," Oliver said. "Took a learning curve, but I learned to hire in April. Let the high school kids work afternoons, because then they all want as many hours as they can get." He grinned at Scott. "You?"

"Always short-staffed," he said. His mood darkened. "I just lost Ralph too. His wife got a job in Miami, and they moved last week."

Oliver stopped just inside the office and plucked something from a magnet board there. "Here you go. Thanks for making this place look like someone takes care of it."

"Someone does take care of it." Scott tucked the check into his back pocket. "Is your cousin still looking for a job?"

"You don't want Leo." Oliver shook his head. "I tried, trust me. He's *my* cousin, and *I* fired him." He grinned at Scott. "Have you checked the community board?"

"Yes." Scott sighed. "It's fine. I'll figure something out." They went back out into the shop. Only one couple remained at a table, and Scott moved over to the counter. His smoothie wasn't quite ready yet, and he leaned against the counter where the cash register waited.

He pulled out his wallet as Oliver rung him up. "Harry's back from his honeymoon. Are you going to his barbecue tonight?" He acted like he didn't care, but if Oliver wasn't there, Scott probably wouldn't go.

He liked hanging out with Grant, Harrison, Oliver, Blake, and whoever else Harrison would invite. Sometimes his brother came. Sometimes Grant or Blake would have their kids with them. But Grant and Harrison had wives now, and while Scott wasn't upset about that, he certainly didn't want to listen to them talk about how he needed a girlfriend.

He got enough of that from his mother, and his sister. Sometimes his secretary even tried to set him up with her sister, her friend down the street, or someone she chatted with at the grocery store for five minutes.

Scott really didn't want to deal with that tonight, even if Harrison could grill a mean hamburger.

"I should be going, yeah," Oliver said. "You?" He took the twenty Scott gave him and started to make change.

"Maybe," Scott said. He suddenly didn't want to commit.

"You just don't want to listen to Grant talk about Bea." Oliver grinned at him.

"Do you?" Scott took his change just as Carolina set his smoothie on the counter. "Thanks," he said to her and picked up the drink.

"It's not so bad," Oliver said with a shrug. "I mean, I'm seeing Rosalinn now, so it's...not so bad."

"Rosalinn?" Scott took the first, thick sip of his smoothie, the orange and pineapple tart and cold on his tongue. "Who's Rosalinn?" He tried not to sound disgusted, but Scott was afraid he didn't quite pull that off.

"I met her a couple of weeks ago."

"She came in to interview," Carolina said in a voice drier than the desert.

Scott looked from her to Oliver. His throat burned from the chill in the drink. "What?"

Oliver's face turned a ruddy shade of red and he shrugged. Scott burst out laughing, really setting his throat full of hurt. He couldn't stop himself though, because Oliver had seriously asked out a potential employee instead of hiring her.

He thought of Joy Bartlett, who he'd texted a few days ago, after the swimming suit incident, but she hadn't returned his message. He'd spoken to her outside, but he hadn't liked what she'd said.

She was seeing someone.

Seemed like everyone but him was seeing someone.

"Maybe I should put out an ad for a new secretary," he joked. "Then I can ask out the women who come in to interview." He grinned at Oliver, who rolled his eyes. What Oliver didn't know was that Scott was seriously considering doing it. Otherwise, he'd forever be screening what events he went to and always be defending himself to his mother.

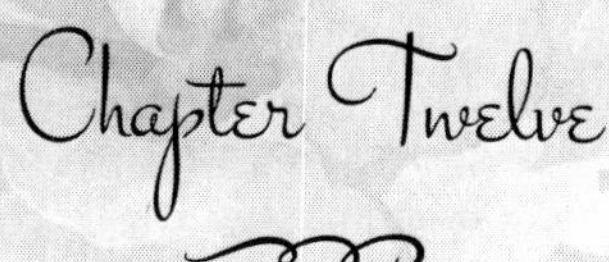

Chapter Twelve

Lauren walked down the sidewalk with Joy, both of them carrying something they'd spent the day making. Lauren wasn't the best in the kitchen, but she could put together a killer batch of cowboy cookies.

When it was her turn to host Supper Club, she catered while Bessie took a day off of work to prep all the food for their dinner that night.

"Harrison seemed surprised we hadn't torn his house to the ground," Joy said. "Did you notice that?"

"I noticed." Lauren smiled at her. "I think he thought we were going to party our brains out or something."

Joy laughed, and while Lauren hadn't found a new job yet, she also hadn't entered panic mode about it.

"What was he saying about...what was his name? Steven?" Joy tensed up, and Lauren knew there was something there. "You're holding out on me."

"No," Joy said.

"You are." Lauren peered at her, and Joy wouldn't look at her. "Look at me, then."

Joy's eyes flitted over to her, not truly locking onto Lauren's. She sighed, which made her shoulders slump. "So there was this guy. His name is Scott, not Steven."

"Sure, Scott," Lauren said. "The landscaping guy."

"Yeah," Joy said. "The landscaping guy. He, uh, asked me out."

Lauren stumbled. "What?"

"I basically flashed my chest at him, because my swimming suit was malfunctioning, and well, he asked me out, but that was after he told me he didn't remember me." She looked at Lauren then, a burning fire in her eyes. "I've met him before. We had dinner together with everyone, right there in Harrison's house, and he *didn't remember meeting me.*" Joy spoke with such vitriol, and Lauren's heart bled for her.

She linked her arm through Joy's which wasn't super easy because of the big bowl of cowboy caviar Joy carried. "I'm so sorry, honey. I see you."

"I know," she whispered. "You always have. What I don't understand is why no one else does."

"They do," Lauren said. "We all do, Joy. Scott obviously did whenever he asked you out. Chester did." She grinned at her friend. "You have two men who want to go out with you, Joy. *Two.*"

Joy shook her head. "Scott was blinded by my stunning white flesh." She giggled and shook her head. "He doesn't really want to go out with me."

"How did Harrison know about him?"

"Scott texted him for my number."

"Okay," Lauren said. "So the guy asks you out. You say no, right?"

"I'm seeing Chester," Joy said. "Of course I said no."

"And he texts to get your number?"

"It didn't exactly happen in that order," Joy said as they turned down Cass's driveway. "I don't want to talk about it anymore. It's nothing."

"Are you going to tell everyone tonight?"

"Not about Scott," she said. "Only about Chester." She speared Lauren with a. look. "Okay? Only Chester."

"Yes, ma'am," Lauren drawled. "Only Chester." Her own stomach rolled as she thought about telling everyone about her employment situation. She somehow made it into the house without turning and fleeing, and she expected to hear laughter and chatter.

It was far too silent. Lauren let Joy go ahead of her, and then she closed the front door. "Where are they?"

"There's no one here," Joy said.

Lauren followed her into the kitchen and set the cookies on the bar. The evidence of food preparation existed on the counter, mostly in the form of several loaves of banana bread. "That isn't dinner," Lauren said. The scent of something savory hung in the air, but Lauren couldn't place it.

"I'm calling Cass," Joy said. She already held her phone to her ear, and she turned away as she said, "Cass, where are you?"

The garage door opened and in spilled Bessie and Sage.

"There you are," Lauren said. "What's going on?"

"Cass messed up the meat," Bessie said with a smile. She'd been in town for a couple of days, but she still moved right into Lauren and hugged her. "It's so good to see you."

Lauren held her tightly, somehow not wanting to let go. "It's good to see you too." When they did step apart, Lauren took Sage into her arms. "And you."

"We ran to get more drinks," Sage said. "Cass is picking up tacos. She'll be back soon." Sage moved back and wiped her hair out of her eyes. She grinned at Lauren. "You look good, Lauren. Very relaxed."

"Thank you," Lauren said.

Cass bustled into the house in the next moment, saying, "I need help carrying things in." She wasn't the picture of relaxation, but Lauren wouldn't be either had she been cooking only to have to then go buy something.

Lauren went outside with everyone else, and with all of them, they got in the foil trays of chips, beans, rice, meat, and tortillas in one trip. The chatter and laughter she'd been expecting started up, and she listened to Cass detail how she'd been browning the ground beef for her own homemade tacos, but when she'd salted the meat, the lid had come off. She didn't think she could salvage it, so she'd tossed it in the trash, called Bernardo's, and gone to pick up the tacos.

"I've got sour cream, guacamole, and other toppings in the fridge," she called. "Ranch dressing. Lettuce. I really did cook."

"No one cares, Cass," Lauren said. "Where's Bea?"

"Is she not here?" Cass surveyed the kitchen now that she'd put down the tray of tortillas. "I don't know." She gathered her hair into a ponytail and sighed. "I need to calm down. This is Supper Club; I'm not feeding the President of the United States."

Lauren grinned to herself and at Cass, but she was still stressed and didn't look at Lauren. She helped by peeling back the lids on the trays to see what they had, and Cass lined it all up the way she wanted.

Bea came rushing into the house through the front door. "I'm so sorry I'm late." She stopped when she saw they were all just hanging out in the kitchen. "You haven't started yet."

"I messed up the tacos," Cass said. She smiled at Bea. "Look at you." She scanned Bea down to her flip-flopped feet. "Did you come straight from the beach?"

"Yes," Bea said, lifting her chin. "I was with Shelby, and she didn't want to leave."

"Where's Grant?" Bessie asked.

"They're all at Harrison's," Lauren said. "Or our place. Whatever. The house down the road."

"Grant's not there yet," Bea said. "He's running home to shower first, but I didn't want to miss the announcements."

"Who says there are announcements?" Cass asked.

"Aren't there?" Bessie asked. "I actually have an announcement."

Cass glowered at them. "Not until we have food in front of us." She went over to the fridge and opened it. "And wine." She pulled out a couple of bottles of rosé. "I had these out earlier, so they should be okay."

She then smiled around at everyone. “Let’s get food and go out onto the patio. Then we can do announcements.”

Lauren liked the sound of that, and she opened the rosé closest to her. The scent of it lifted from the bottle, and Lauren smiled. She didn’t drink a lot, but she sure did enjoy a good glass of wine from time to time. She poured one for Joy and handed it to her.

The next one went to Cass, who stood out of the way as Sage filled her plate with beans, rice, lettuce, and shrimp, then doused the whole thing in Ranch dressing. “It’s a shrimp taco salad,” she said.

Lauren thought she was doing pretty well for how new her divorce was. She and her husband had been together for so long too, that even Lauren had been shocked by the split. Sage didn’t seem to be, and Lauren supposed she never really knew what went on behind closed doors.

“Get some food, Lauren,” Cass said.

“You look good,” she said back. “Happy.”

Cass’s lower lip trembled for just a moment. “I am happy.”

“I’m so glad.” Lauren hugged her, and she definitely felt a change inside Cass. Inside herself too, and she hoped it was for the better.

She made two tacos—one shrimp with pineapple-mango salsa, and one beef with all the traditional toppings—and took her laden plate outside with her glass of wine. The lights on Cass’s back patio cast everything in a romantic light, and Lauren set her plate down next to Bessie.

Joy took the spot on her other side, and Cass came outside last and sat down with all of them.

"I want all the news from Europe," Bea said.

"That's not an announcement." Cass looked at Bessie. "We'll do those first, okay? Then I can talk about Europe if you really want to hear it."

"I do," Lauren said, and all the others agreed.

"Announcements first," Cass insisted. "Bessie?"

She wiped her mouth, her dark green eyes shining with what Lauren could only describe as mischief. "First, I don't want anyone to freak out." She looked over to Joy as she said that, and Lauren did too.

"I'm not going to freak out tonight," Joy promised.

"The Bread Boy is thinking about opening up for franchising," Bessie said. "I'm thinking about opening a franchise of it." She sparkled she was so excited, and Lauren couldn't contain her own smile.

"Wow," Bea said. "That's amazing, Bessie." She looked around the group, and Lauren heard the unspoken words. Bea wouldn't say them. No one would but her.

"That's not something you'll do in Sweet Water Falls," she said.

"No," Bessie said. "I don't know where yet. Wynona is in Peachtree, so maybe up there. Maybe somewhere else."

Again, a somewhat strained silence covered the table. Lauren really wished someone else could say the hard things. She determined not to do it this time, and she looked over to Cass.

"Maybe here on Hilton Head," Cass said oh-so-casually.

Bessie didn't confirm or deny anything. "Maybe," was all she said.

"My announcement is that I got a job," Bea said. She puffed out her chest like she'd just said she'd climbed Mount Everest. "I'm working mornings at The Mad Mango with Oliver, and I don't hate it."

"You're what?" Joy asked. "Why would you do that?"

"Because Grant is gone all the time anyway, and Shelby sleeps late. This way, I can work a little in the morning and still go to the beach in the afternoon." Bea gave Joy a sharp look. "Why do you work?"

"Because I need the money," Joy shot back, indicating that Bea didn't. Everyone knew she didn't.

"I'm bored," Bea said. "It's a valid reason too."

"I can't believe you're bored here," Sage said. "It's such an amazing place."

Lauren agreed with that. She'd spent a lot of the past two weeks looking at job boards, roaming the island and visiting the historical pieces of it, and chatting with Joy while she cooked or baked.

"It is," Bea said. "But I don't want to explore it by myself."

"She needs her hot tour guide husband to go with her," Cass teased.

Bea didn't deny that, and Lauren laughed along with the others.

"My announcement is that I'm really happy to be married to Harrison," Cass said, beaming out at everyone.

"And I'm really happy you're all here for Supper Club, in Hilton Head."

"Cherry's not here," Joy said.

"No," Cass said. "You're right."

Cherry Forrester wasn't an original member of their club, and while Lauren really liked her, she also didn't miss her as much as she would've one of the other ladies.

All eyes moved to her side of the table, and Lauren realized only she and Joy hadn't given their announcements yet. Joy looked at her, and she looked at Joy. She lifted her eyebrows, but Joy remained silent.

"Your news is bigger," Joy said. She then took a big bite of her taco, a clear indication that she expected Lauren to go first.

"Fine," Lauren said. She drew in a deep breath. She'd been thinking about this moment for a long time. Weeks. She could've planned; she *had* planned. She'd imagined how she'd tell her friends and how they'd react, but now that the moment was here, it was much harder than she'd anticipated.

"Just say it," Cass said. "You're making me nervous."

Lauren looked at her. She looked at Bessie, then Sage, then Bea. These were her people. They'd rally around her and support her, not judge her. "I lost my job," she said, the words flowing evenly from her mouth. "I lost my job at the beginning of July actually, when I went back to Texas for those few days?"

Stunned silence draped the table, and Lauren felt like she was trying to outrun a herd of wild mustangs. "I'm surprised none of you heard about it. Simple Solutions closed down due to some embezzlement allegations. They arrested several people, including Mark."

She took a breath, and her chest expanded so much easier than it had been since she'd gone to Texas last. "I'm planning to sell my house in Sweet Water Falls and move here permanently. I'm looking for a place, but I won't move until Joy goes back to Texas in the fall."

She smiled at Joy, who nodded, a silent encouragement that Lauren had done a good job succinctly delivering her news.

"Embezzlement?" Sage asked.

"I interviewed with the FBI," Lauren said. She popped a chip laden with guacamole into her mouth. "I was terrified, but ultimately exonerated."

"Of course you were," Bea said as if anything but Lauren's complete innocence would be ludicrous.

"And she's dating Blake," Joy said. "She left that out."

"I didn't leave it out." Lauren frowned at her. "I just hadn't gotten to it yet." She shook her head. "Why don't you tell them about your *two* suitors?"

"What?" Bessie practically screeched.

"Two suitors?" Cass asked. "Oh, this is the juiciest Supper Club we've had in a while." She looked absolutely gleeful, and Lauren enjoyed the commotion around Joy's boyfriends. Plural.

"You're dating Blake?" Sage asked. "Like, you've been out with him already?"

"A few times," Lauren said. "He kissed me before the

harbor cruise last week." She grinned around at all of her friends. "I might just pull a Bea and fall in love in a single summer."

"I'm never going to live that down," Bea said.

"You don't need to," Cass said. "What you and Grant have is wonderful. You didn't need more time. Don't listen to her."

"Seeing as how Lauren kissed Blake *before* the cruise, at the beginning of their first real date, mind you," Joy said. "I don't think she's saying you did anything wrong, Bea."

"Nope," Lauren said. "When there's chemistry, there's chemistry." She and Blake had it in spades, and she was too old to apologize for it.

"I have got to move here and find me a boyfriend," Bessie said. "Lauren's kissing on the first date. Joy has *two* boyfriends." She shook her head. "I can franchise here, I'm pretty sure."

"I do *not* have two boyfriends," Joy said. "I can't even believe I'm going out with one. I don't live here." She shook her head, some of the life she usually held leaving her face. "It's all a disaster."

"Start at the beginning," Cass said. "I had no idea I'd miss so much while I was on my honeymoon."

"Oh, you didn't miss that much," Lauren said.

Cass gave her a withering look. "You're not done talking either, Missy. So get your story ready. You're going right after Joy tells us about her dual-beaus."

"If one more person says I have two boyfriends, I'm leaving!" Joy practically yelled. That caused everyone at the table to erupt into laughter, and though Joy was the last one to join in, she did eventually smile and laugh while she shook her head.

Lauren basked in the energy and friendship at the table, and she never wanted to leave it. Sometimes these women drove her crazy. Sometimes she got a little jealous of them and what they had that she didn't. But no matter what, she always loved them, and they loved her, and she was so happy to have this place to belong among them.

Now, if she could figure out what to do with her life next, that would be great.

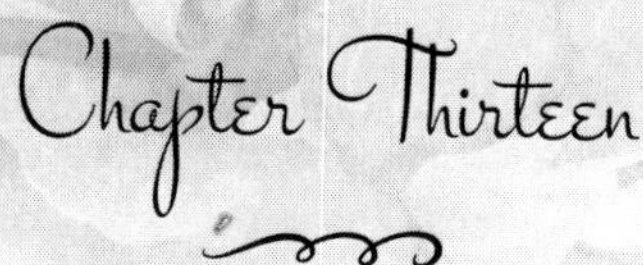

Chapter Thirteen

Blake pulled into the parking lot at The Mad Mango, and not two seconds later, Lauren emerged from the shop. He still got out of his SUV to meet her, grinning all the while. "Are we this connected?" he asked. "I hadn't even put the car in park."

"Bea saw you through the office window." Lauren smiled at him and extended the pale pink smoothie toward him.

"Dang." He took the drink. "Here I was thinking we had this incredible connection."

Lauren gave him a heated look that made him laugh.

"You can admit it," he teased.

"Admit what?" She set her smoothie on top of his vehicle and pulled her high ponytail tighter.

"We have an incredible connection." In his opinion, at least, and he wasn't usually far off when it came to women.

He'd known his previous girlfriend wouldn't last. They'd broken up through texting, for crying out loud.

His relationship with Lauren, though less than a month old, already felt wildly different than the one he'd had with Camille last year.

"Fine," Lauren said. "We have an incredible connection. Happy now?"

"Not when you say it like that," he shot back, clearly teasing her. She finally cracked and put the straw on her drink in her mouth. Blake watched her lips close around it, everything inside him now at last five hundred degrees.

They got in the car, and Lauren set her smoothie in the cup holder. "Thanks for driving me."

"Anytime," he said. She didn't have a car here on the island, but when she went home with Joy in another month, she'd be driving back from Texas. "I almost hate to ask." He looked at his back-up camera as he spoke. "But you've said precious little about your residency here in the great state of South Carolina." He added quite the Southern twang to his words, hoping they wouldn't rile her up.

He hadn't asked again since the day he'd brought her lunch and found her outside with cops. Three weeks ago now. Almost four, actually.

Lauren glanced over to him, and their eyes met for the briefest of moments. "I have a strategy," she said.

"Oh?" He lifted his eyebrows. "I'm quite familiar with the word."

"I'm sure you are," she said dryly. "I'm just...I'm going to see if I can afford anything here first. If I can, then I'll call my realtor in Sweet Water Falls. We'll list my house, and I'll make a plan for when I'll go back to Texas to pack."

"You're flying home with Joy at the end of August still, right?"

"Yes," she said. "We've already got that all strategized."

"How many places do you need to look at to know if you can afford something here?"

"Well." She blew out her breath. "We have three showings this afternoon, and then I guess we'll see after that." She gave him a smile, but Blake wanted something more concrete.

He did spend a lot of his day entrenched in "strategy." Meetings, phone calls, portfolios. He knew how to take a new client with no savings and no retirement fund and strategize with them for what they should invest in first. Where to put their money, depending on their age, their occupation, the risk factors involved.

Blake knew all about financial strategy and risk strategy, but his knowledge of Lauren Keller's strategy still eluded him. He knew he didn't want her to leave Hilton Head for any length of time, and he'd communicated that much to her previously.

He would not have looked at real estate here first. It would've been something he'd have done almost near the end of the strategy, and it sounded like Lauren hadn't even decided on tactics *until* she saw the housing market here.

"You know Ty, right?" Lauren asked.

"Yes," Blake said absently. "He comes to barbecues and

beach bashes with Harry and Grant sometimes. He's a great agent."

"He just texted to say the first house we were going to look at is now pending." She tapped on her phone, her eyebrows drawn down. "Someone else put in an offer." She sighed and looked out the window, tucking her phone under her leg as she did.

"So I'm not going to Penchance Lane?" he asked.

"No," she murmured, but she didn't give him another address.

Blake felt her melancholy rising through the car, and he wished he could take it and bottle it for her so she didn't have to feel that way. "Hey," he said gently. He reached over and took her hand in his, and she looked at him like she was just now realizing that he was a human being and not a robot.

"I need to know where we're going next."

She retrieved her phone and said, "Uh, let's see. O'Hare Road."

Blake eased off the accelerator. "Really?"

"Yes," she said. "Why?"

Blake tried not to make a face, but he obviously had. "What's that look for?" she asked.

"It's just...I can't believe Ty is showing you something on O'Hare Road." He turned off the main road and came to a stop on the side street.

"Is it trashy?"

"It's...not nice," he said. "It's on the east side of the island, where the big bridge is. Lots of traffic, on and off the island, all the time. It's nothing like where you live now."

"I can't afford to live where I live now," she pointed out.

"You sure? Harrison got an amazing deal on his house, I heard."

Lauren cocked her head, and Blake spoke enough Female to know she didn't enjoy being challenged. "Where do you live, Mister Williams?"

"Do we have time to drive by?" he asked.

"Ty said we can go by O'Hare Road anytime," she said. "The house is vacant."

"Probably for good reason," Blake muttered, and Lauren gave him a withering look. "I'll show you where I live. It's not beachfront like Cass and Harry, but it's nice."

"I don't need beachfront," she said.

"That's not part of your strategy?" he asked.

"Affordable is part of my strategy," she said.

Blake got the car moving again. "Do you always have a strategy, Lauren?"

"Usually," she said.

"For everything? Like, when you're getting ready for church, is there a strategy to that?"

She blinked at him, and he had his answer. Yes. She still said, "I mean, I choose the clothes first—sometimes. Sometimes a piece of jewelry I want to wear dictates what clothes I can wear, obviously."

"Obviously," he teased, though he had no idea how a ring or a bracelet couldn't be worn with anything and everything. He knew Lauren always looked completely put together, and it probably was because she strategized from a single piece to a bigger whole.

"I'm not going to tell you about it if you're going to make fun of me."

"I'm not," he said, quickly backpedaling. "I was kidding."

Lauren folded her arms, and Blake kept driving. After a few more turns, they entered Whispering Waves, and he said, "I live in here. There are some cookie cutter houses that went up after a developer bought the surrounding land, but my house is one of the original ones."

He wove around the curved road to the pale blue house. It had a darker blue door, and a black roof, and Blake did love the two-story design of it in this community of mostly single-story homes.

"Wow," Lauren said, her previous ire with him suddenly gone. "It's gorgeous. How old is it?" She got right out of the SUV, and Blake hastened to follow her.

"Oh, okay," he said as he tried to catch up. "It was built in nineteen-thirteen," he said. "We have a lot of retired people here on the island, and they don't want anything with two levels."

"Hm." Lauren stood on the front sidewalk and admired the house. He joined her and slid his hand into hers. She didn't immediately squeeze, and he wondered if he was still in the doghouse for his strategizing comments. Most likely. Women like Lauren could put on a brave face and a fancy façade when they had to.

"I love old things," she said. "Houses, papers, books,

photos. They possess...charm, don't you think?"

"I do," he said quietly. "I got her for a great price, too. Maybe you'll find something like this you can afford."

She leaned into him, and Blake figured he might not be as sidelined as he'd thought. "I'm on a deadline, though."

"You are? Why?" As far as he knew, Harrison wasn't going to be moving back into his house. If Lauren moved out, he'd have to take care of it. Sell it. Something. In his ritzy gated community, they wouldn't put up with anything less.

"My strategy hinges on the house," she said.

Blake smiled at his front door. "All right, well, let's go look at O'Hare Road then. I hope I'm wrong." Ty didn't usually show junk to clients, and Blake was pretty sure he'd met Lauren before.

Lauren turned back to the SUV. "It's a beautiful house, Blake."

"Thanks," he said. "You know, you could look at Carter's Cove. It's island-y too. Very small-town vibe." He looked at her across the hood of the car.

"I'll think about it." She got in and re-buckled, and Blake did the same.

"Do you want to come back here for dinner tonight?" Blake cast her a look out of the corner of his eye. Tommy was away at camp, and that meant Blake could have Lauren over if he chose.

"Do you cook?" she asked.

"I'm actually decent," he said with a smile. "Not as good as Harrison or anything, but I can put together a meal."

"I'd like to see that," she said, smiling.

Blake let her put the address into his GPS, and the car navigated them to O'Hare Road. It was precisely what Blake had been expecting, but the house he pulled up to had obviously been remodeled. The lawn sat in patches of sod, and the whole house practically shone in the sunlight.

"It's really bright," Lauren said. "Have you ever seen a house that white?"

"Oh, I'm sure I have," Blake said, because he didn't want to ruffle her feathers further. Ty pulled up behind them, and he looked in the rearview mirror. "He's here. Do you want to go in?"

"We're here," she said, and they got out of the vehicle. There weren't any towering trees here as there were in Blake's and other neighborhoods, and that made it feel twice as hot.

"Blake," Ty said with a laugh. They shook hands, and then Ty pulled him into a one-armed hug. "What are you doing here?"

"Escorting the lovely Lauren around the island." Blake tucked his hands into his pockets. "She doesn't have a car, and I've been deemed the driver."

"That is not true," Lauren said. She wore a professional smile now, and Blake marveled at how quickly she could turn that on. In her line of work, she probably had a lot of experience hiding headaches, the hardships of real life, and anything else she didn't want clients to see. "Blake and I are together."

"Together?" Ty's eyebrows went clear up into the

stratosphere. "You do always have a pretty woman at your side." He guffawed like that was just so funny, but one look at Lauren told Blake it wasn't.

"I do not," he said, mostly to Ty, but he maintained eye contact with her. "I haven't dated anyone in a year."

"I guess that's true," Ty said. "Now, Lauren, don't let this street deter you from this home. It is fantastic inside." He prattled off the features, which included quartz, and land out back, and hardwood.

Blake knew the moment he opened the door that Lauren would not be buying this house. She didn't care about land or hardwood. She had all of that already.

No, Lauren wanted charm, and Blake realized as she shot him a wide-eyed look in the kitchen—which he could admit was nice—as Ty went on and on about the animal zoning this property had that she was looking for extraordinary.

And not just in a house.

In her life.

He immediately thought he wouldn't fit the bill, that she was completely out of his league, and he should get out of the game before he lost limbs, internal organs, and more.

She'd asked him not to do that, but as they got back in the car and she buckled up again, he couldn't quite do it.

She looked at him and sighed. "I will listen to you from now on," she said.

He only smiled. "Plug in the next address," he said. "It may be the one." He hoped he could be "the one" for her, but he now knew that outward appearances couldn't make up for bad bones.

As they drove across the island to the southwest side, he gave her a few details about the plantations down here, and she did seem impressed with the history of the area. She liked the neighborhood too.

"All right," Ty boomed from the street. "Don't let this one fool you either. She may look one wind away from falling down, but she has a solid foundation." He started for the front door, but Blake and Lauren stayed on the sidewalk.

"If I sneeze, that house is falling over," Lauren said. Ivy climbed the front of it, and Blake actually liked that. He didn't like the dirt and rust it left behind, nor the weed-infested lawn. He looked next door, and whoever lived in that pristine house probably hated this property with their whole soul.

"Are we going in?" he asked as Ty bounded—yes, literally bounded like an antelope—up the steps. He turned back to them, and Lauren heaved a sigh.

"I guess," she said.

"Come on, guys!" he called.

"I don't know how he has the energy," Blake said. "He's at least a decade older than me."

Lauren giggled then, and Blake couldn't help the smile that filled his soul. She didn't want a fixer-upper. She didn't want a place that had been fixed up to hide flaws. No, Lauren Keller wanted—and demanded—perfection, and Blake couldn't help feeling like he'd never achieve that.

Still, she kept her hand cemented in his, and he wasn't going to deny her that.

Chapter Fourteen

"Yes, that's right," Lauren said, her phone chiming as she spoke into it. A notification from the security system came up that said someone had triggered the camera on the porch. "I was the senior marketing manager for an enormous firm. I worked with clients as big as Nike, and as small as the mom-and-pop diner down the street."

She tapped on the notification and saw it was just Joy getting home from the library. Chester had not dropped her off tonight as he had in the past, and she carried a couple of brown bags of groceries in her arms. With any luck, Lauren would emerge from this bedroom with a job—and dinner waiting on the table.

"Your résumé says you led teams of up to sixteen people."

"Yes, sir," she said. "I was the team lead over design, and that required meetings with clients, and then interpreting their ideas into designer speak and communicating that with my team in-house."

"You worked in the office?"

"Regularly," she said. "Though we have—had—corporate offices all over the country, and I'm able to work remotely too." She swallowed at her slip, but surely Jameson Langley knew what had happened to Simple Solutions. It had been national news. Everyone knew about it. "I was based out of the South Texas office for years," she said. "More recently, my files were transferred to the Miami office, as I've been working on Hilton Head."

She held her breath, waiting for him to dismiss her. She wasn't sure why she couldn't see the potential in herself. Joy had sat her down that morning and told her in no uncertain terms that KM Marketing Group would be lucky to have her.

"Lucky, I say!" Joy had ranted. "What are they? Some local Carolina marketing firm? You eat firms like that for breakfast."

They'd both dissolved into giggles then, and Lauren smiled just thinking about the conversation now.

Not only that, but KM was based out of Charleston, which was only an hour from here. Lauren had put up with far longer commutes in her life, that was for sure.

"We do two work-from-office days here," he said. "Two from home. Four days, from nine to one, without a lunch break. You get one, thirty-minute break, almost always at eleven-thirty. This isn't a full-time position."

She'd known that going in. In fact, it was part of

Lauren's strategy to only work part-time. She wanted time to rest, to relax, to recline on the beach for hours if she so chose.

"That's wonderful," she said, her professional marketer voice clipped in place. "I'm assuming I can get in touch with anyone on the team during regular business hours, home or office?"

"Yes," he said. "I think I'm going to put you on the..." Papers shuffled or a keyboard clicked or something on his end of the line. He didn't speak, and horror filled Lauren as she thought they might have been disconnected. "Creative Licensing team," he finally said. "They make sure we can use fonts, photos, images, that kind of thing, in our work."

She knew what the Creative Licensing team did, and it was a far cry from her previous job. "Great," she said brightly. "That sounds great."

She still had some money in savings, but she'd been out of work for a month. The pay wasn't great either, but it was enough to keep Lauren in her current lifestyle, if she leaned on her savings for major purchases.

"Wonderful," Kenneth said, the K part of the KM Marketing firm. "Can you come in...Thursday to do some paperwork?"

"Yes," she said, though she didn't have her calendar open in front of her. They agreed on a time, and Lauren ended the call. She sagged back into her office chair, her mind whirring and her heart sprinting and every muscle relaxing.

Then she sprang right back out of her chair and burst out of her bedroom. "Joy!" she yelled. She jogged down the hall to find her best friend standing in the kitchen, eating the reddest, ripest tomato Lauren had ever seen.

Joy looked up as juices dripped down her face. At least she was leaning over the sink. Her eyes widened, and she looked as caught as a child sneaking cookies before dinner.

"What are you doing?" Lauren asked as she continued into the kitchen. She grinned the closer she got, because she knew about Joy's nightshade obsession.

"This is the most incredible tomato I've ever had." Joy sprinkled a little salt and a little pepper on the flesh and went in for another big bite. She groaned like it was the best thing she'd ever put in her mouth, and Lauren laughed.

"Well, I'm glad." She sat on a barstool and cradled her face in her hands. "You're looking at an employed woman."

Joy made a yelping sound and lifted the half-eaten tomato into the air. "I knew it! Congratulations, Lauren."

Lauren bowed her head as if accepting a royal award from the queen. "Thank you, thank you."

"Which department?" She took another squelching bite, and Lauren didn't like the wet sound of it.

She winced and made a face. "Admittedly, the Licensing."

"Oh, the one you didn't want."

"It's okay," Lauren said. "It's a job, and I only have to drive to Charleston twice a week. I work here two days, and I have three days off every week." It almost sounded too good to be true.

Part of her strategy here on Hilton Head was to find more joy in the simple things. Sleep in at least twice a week—

yes, she'd actually put that on her Seaside Strategy. Sleep was important, especially as she aged.

She jogged on the beach a few times each week, but if she didn't feel like it, she skipped a day. Her Seaside Strategy was to find joy and purpose in her life, not punish herself and exist on four hours of sleep.

Lauren had lived that life, and she didn't want to go back to it. She wouldn't. Already, she was happier than she'd been in Sweet Water Falls, and so much had changed that she couldn't pinpoint the exact thing that had increased her mood.

"Have you told Blake?" Joy asked.

"I just got the job," Lauren said. "Two minutes ago."

"So I was first to know." Joy grinned at her, and the doorbell rang in the next moment. "Oh, shoot. That's Chester." She shoved the last of the tomato into her mouth. "I wemd fah mimts," she said around the fruit.

Lauren laughed. "I'm sorry. I didn't get that at all."

Joy's eyes turned fierce, and she held up five fingers. "Fahv. Miuhtes."

"Five minutes." Lauren slid from the stool. "You got it."

Joy dashed up the steps, still chewing her tomato, while Lauren went to get the door. She'd been out with Blake a lot in the past few weeks since Joy had started dating Chester, and she hadn't met him yet. When she opened the door, she could only stare.

The man standing there had to be a professional basketball player. Maybe volleyball. Both. He was so tall, he'd have to duck to get through the door. Lauren gaped at him, taking in the neat, trim beard and the bright brown eyes.

Yes, he'd tucked in his polo, and he carried a bit of a paunch, but not all men could be body-builders. He was handsome in a Joy-kind of way, but not Lauren's type at all. "You must be Chester," she said.

"Guilty," he said with a laugh. "It's great to finally meet you. Joy talks about you all the time." He extended his hand for her to shake, and Lauren had to reach up to get to it. She wasn't as short as Joy, and he had to be a good foot—or more—taller than her. Which meant he was fifteen or sixteen inches taller than Joy.

"Same," she said. "Joy says you deliver packages?"

"That I do." He wore a friendly smile, and Lauren had no reason to disbelieve him.

She loved the intricacies of people, and she liked talking to them. It had made her extraordinarily good at her job, and Mark, her former boss, had always said her mother must've taken her to Ireland and had her kiss the blarney stone for how talented she was at talking to people.

"Have you always done that?" Lauren shifted her weight and looked up at him. "You're so tall. You didn't play sports or anything?"

Chester's smile dimmed some. "I..." His gazed shifted beyond Lauren, and he said, "Joy." He ducked under the top of the doorway and into the house without being invited.

"Sorry," Joy said somewhat breathlessly. "I spent longer at the farmer's market than I intended." She gave Chester a smile, and Lauren found the pair of them comical.

Do not laugh in front of Joy, she told herself. Besides, it wasn't like she and Blake had anything on them. Since he'd driven her to look at two properties last week, they hadn't been out again.

He'd asked for the one evening he didn't have his son, and Lauren had allowed herself to put up a low wall between them. Yes, she had a strategy in mind for her move to Hilton Head Island. It wasn't a crime, and she didn't have to explain herself to him—or anyone else.

"We're going to the theater in the city," Joy said, tugging on the left sleeve of the dress she'd put on lightning-quick. "So I'll be back late."

"I'll be here," Lauren said. She quickly smoothed Joy's hair as Chester moved past her, and she hissed, "You've only got one earring in."

"Shoot. I had two." Joy's hands went to her ears, and she searched the floor.

"I'll find it," Lauren said. "Go without. It's fine."

Joy pulled out her single earring and dropped it into Lauren's hand. Then she flashed her a somewhat pained smile and hurried after Chester. Lauren went to close the door, thankful it hadn't been open long enough to trigger the alarm again. She had the safe phrase memorized now, so she supposed it wouldn't be a big deal if it had.

She found Joy's other earring on the second step leading up, and she put the pair of them on the kitchen counter. Looking around the silent house, she wondered, "Well. What now?"

Lauren looked at the hooks beside the garage door

entrance. A single set of keys hung there. She didn't have a car, but Joy had gotten a long-term rental so she could get to the library and back every day. She plucked her phone from her pocket, a strategy forming in her mind.

Can I borrow your car tonight? she sent to Joy.

It needs gas, she said.

I'll fill it up.

Where are you going?

Lauren didn't want to answer her, but she didn't want to leave Joy in the dark either. *I just have something to do. I'll tell you about it tomorrow.*

Okay, but I'm holding you to that.

Lauren didn't answer that one, because if she didn't take the keys and go now, she might not go at all. She grabbed her purse and swiped the keys on her way out to the garage. She didn't know the island as well as Cass, Bea, or even Joy, but she was exceptionally good with directions, and if she'd been somewhere before, she could almost always get back to it.

And she'd been to Blake's century-old house.

She connected her phone to the Bluetooth system in the car, and she said, "Call Bea," as she pulled out of the garage.

"Calling Bea," the car repeated to her, and her friend answered on the second ring.

"Lauren," she said, a smile in her tone. "What's up, girl?"

Lauren blinked, not sure how to answer. Bea pealed out a stream of laughter, and Lauren could see and hear and feel how happy she was. Since she'd come here for vacation, met Grant and fallen in love, her life had changed dramatically.

"Sorry," Bea said through her laughter. "Shelby dared me to say that."

Lauren finally smiled. She waited for the gate to trundle open, and she said, "What are you doing right now? Can you talk for a second?"

"Yep. What's up?"

"I..." She exhaled. She just had to admit it. "I put a little distance between me and Blake, and I'm currently driving to his house." She gripped the steering wheel. "Tell me it's not a bad idea."

"It's not a bad idea," Bea said dutifully. "You like this man, Lauren. Why would you put distance between the two of you?"

"Because I'm self-sabotaging?" Lauren guessed. "Because he teased me about having a strategy for everything?"

Bea remained silent for a few moments. "Honey, you do have a strategy for everything."

"I know." Lauren exhaled.

"It's like me and my lists," Bea said. "Y'all tease me about them, and yeah, sometimes it makes me feel stupid. Or like I should do something different, but you know what? I make lists. That's what I do. You strategize before you do anything. You think four or five moves ahead, and you won't make one until you can see that path. It's fine. It's who you are."

"What if he doesn't like who I am?" Lauren whispered.

"He does," Bea said. "I've seen the two of you together, and he does. He was teasing, probably because he's nervous."

"He has nothing to be nervous about."

"Men get nervous," Grant yelled. "Trust me on this."

"Did you hear that?" Bea asked.

"I heard." Lauren smiled, because she did like Grant Turner a lot. He had a sunny personality, and he complimented Bea perfectly. She drew in a big breath and kept driving. "Okay," she said. "Wish me luck."

"You don't need it," Bea said. "But good luck. Call me back after you talk to him."

"I'm not going to do that," Lauren said.

"Why not?"

"Because, if things go well, I won't have time, and if they don't, I won't want to talk about it."

"Fine," Bea said with a sigh. "I'll call you tomorrow."

"Now, that's a good plan." They laughed together, and Lauren's fingers released their death-grip on the steering wheel. She finished the drive, relief flooding her when she saw Blake's SUV in the driveway.

She didn't know if he'd have Tommy or not. He hadn't asked her out for tonight. "Probably because you've turned him down the past two times," she murmured to herself. She pulled up to the curb and parked, but she didn't get out.

She had no strategy here. She couldn't predict what Blake would say or how he'd react to her pop-in. A groan started in her stomach. "He hates the pop-in."

But she'd driven all this way—fifteen minutes, tops—and she wanted to make things right between them. Lauren reminded herself that she'd been questioned by FBI agents not that long ago. She'd done presentations for Fortune 500 companies, to men with nine zeros in their bank accounts.

"You can talk to your boyfriend." She got out of the car and made her way across his lawn. The doorbell rang inside and out in the quiet neighborhood. Lauren almost fled when he didn't answer in the first three seconds.

She waited what felt like a long time, and finally, the door swung open. Blake stood there wearing a pair of gym shorts and nothing else. Lauren's mind went on the fritz. Even if she'd had a strategy, with a well-crafted speech prepared, it would've fled at the sight of those abs.

All the muscles in his pecs. His shoulders went on for days, and there was no farmer's tan in sight. Just golden, glorious skin forever.

"Hey," he said, leaning into the open door. A smile touched his face. "What are you doing here?"

"Is your son here?"

"Down the street." He nodded to her left, but she couldn't look away from him. "He won't be home for a while. A friend of his invited him to play video games."

Lauren's eyes drifted down his body again. She swallowed and said, "I don't like the distance between us, so I decided to come erase it."

Blake's smile faded. "Where did it come from?"

"I put it there," she said. "Because that's what I do, Blake."

He stepped out of the house and took her wringing hands in his. "Come inside, Lauren."

She let him tug her into the house, and she instantly felt at-home here. The floors bore a light gray wood, and the house opened right into the living room. The TV flickered with something on it, and Blake owned comfortable looking couches in dark brown leather.

He let go of her hands and grabbed a shirt that had been draped over the back of the loveseat. He pulled it over his head and faced her again. "Why do you put distance between yourself and others?"

"Self-preservation," she said. She'd been to therapy before. She knew why she did things, but sometimes she couldn't stop herself. "If I keep other people out, then when they leave, it's not that hurtful."

Blake tilted his head and studied her.

Now that she'd come inside, she wasn't too nervous. "You teased me about my strategizing, and I don't know. I started building a wall. It's pretty low right now, and I decided I didn't want it there at all."

"I apologize for teasing you about strategizing," he said. He was completely serious, not an ounce of sarcasm in his voice.

"Thank you," she murmured. "I know I do it. It was literally my job for decades, and I'm very good at it."

"It works for you," he said. "Don't stop doing it."

She moved closer to him. "Why'd you put on the shirt?" She slid her hands up his chest, feeling those glorious muscles she'd seen only a few minutes ago.

"I felt a little too exposed," he whispered. He held his ground with her, and Lauren sure did like that. He put one hand on her hip and brought her flush against him. "I missed you this week."

"I'm sorry."

"Tell me," he said, dipping his head closer. He touched his lips to her neck, and fire shot straight to her core. "If you go quiet on me again, if you start turning me down for dates, should I assume you're building another wall?"

"Most likely," she said, her words more of a gasp.

"And do you want me to break it down?"

Lauren had never had a man ask her these kinds of questions before. She didn't know how to answer them, but she knew the electricity flowing through her, and she knew the scent of his cologne that made her lightheaded, and she knew she didn't want anything between them.

"Yes."

He slid his lips up the column of her neck to her mouth, and Lauren kissed him slowly, truly savoring every touch, every spark, every sound of his breath in her ears. He pulled away first, leaving her wanting and far too warm.

"Okay," he said quietly. "Do you want to stay for a bit? I was just watching TV."

"What if your son comes home?"

Blake reached out and tucked her hair out of her face. "Hon, I just kissed you like I'm falling in love. I think I can introduce you to him anytime now."

Lauren made a squeak, and Blake gave her a smile. "Too soon. Got it. I won't say it again."

"It's..."

Blake turned and led her over to the couch. "I've been painting my office, and I can't stand," he said. "We have to sit." He practically collapsed onto the couch, and Lauren curled into his side.

"It's not too soon," she said. "I've just..." She let her words trail off.

Blake wasn't one to let her disappear and give him incomplete sentences. "You've just what?"

"I've never had anyone fall in love with me before," she said, glad she could watch the moving images on the TV instead of having to look him in the eye. "My mom left me behind. My brother forged his own path and never looked back. I've had a string of boyfriends over the years, but I've only had one tell me he loved me, and it turned out he didn't actually...so."

"Mm." Blake stroked his hand through her hair, almost mindlessly, and it made Lauren feel cherished. "His loss, Lauren. Seriously."

She closed her eyes and snuggled deeper into his chest. This reality—this slow, easy evening, with a beautiful, handsome man—this was what Lauren wanted. This was the ultimate goal of her Seaside Strategy.

"Oh," she said. "I got a job this afternoon."

"You did? That marketing firm in Charleston?"

"Yep, that's right."

"That's amazing," he said.

Lauren pushed up and looked at him, because he genuinely sounded like it was amazing. "Thanks. Part-time, which I wanted. Four days a week." She leaned down and touched her lips to his. "I think I'm ready to look at a few new places. Would you come with me again?"

"Sure," he said easily. "Whatever you want."

She searched his face, and it sure did seem like he'd do whatever she wanted.

"Can I ask you something?" he asked.

"Sure."

"Do you strategize your love life?"

Lauren smiled at him. "No, Blake. This is all me flying by the seat of my pants, which is why my love life has been so pathetic for forty-four years."

He chuckled and said, "Oh, it can't be that bad."

"It has been, but I don't want to talk about it." She leaned closer, but Blake pulled back.

"You just came to kiss me," he accused.

"But it wasn't part of any strategy."

He laughed and then he obliged in kissing her. Lauren wasn't sure how long they sat on his couch kissing. She couldn't hear anything but the beating of her own heart and the way Blake exhaled like he really was falling for her—until someone said, "Dad, what in the world is going on here?"

Chapter Fifteen

Blake pulled away from Lauren and stood, all in the same motion. He extended his hand to Lauren, who got to her feet in a much slower fashion. He liked how close she stood to him, and he liked that he found her downright sinful in a simple pair of shorts and a tank top. She usually dolled herself up for their dates, which he also liked, but what he needed was someone real.

Lauren felt very real to him, especially as she'd told him about how she kept people out. Now that he knew that, he'd have to work to keep the walls from building up.

He cleared his throat and focused on his son. Another boy stood with him, and Blake glanced to Ryan. "I told you I was seeing someone new," he said. "This is her." He indicated Lauren, who lifted her hand in a wave. "Her name is Lauren Keller, and she...popped in for a minute."

Tommy's eyebrows pulled down, and then he straightened them out. "I guess I forgot."

"I've been out with her while you've been here," he said.

"You have?"

"Remember when I took you to your grandmother's?" Blake asked. He shook his head. "Like, two weekends ago?"

Tommy obviously didn't remember, or if he did, he hadn't realized it was so he could be babysat. "That was so I could take Lauren to the grand opening of Fisher's."

"Excellent fish there," she murmured.

"Lauren, this is my forgetful thirteen-year-old, Thomas." He indicated the boy. "He's the tall one, obviously. His friend is Ryan Shaffer from down the street."

"We just came because Tommy said you had soda pop." Ryan looked between Lauren and Blake, almost like they'd jump into action and serve it to him.

"Sure do," Blake said. "Help yourself."

Ryan went to do just that in the kitchen behind Blake, but Tommy approached him slowly.

"It's great to meet you, Thomas," Lauren said. "Your dad calls you Tommy. Can I call you that?"

He blinked and said, "Sure."

"Great." Lauren stuck out her hand when he got within arm's length, but he just stared at it.

"You shake her hand, son," Blake said. He worked very hard not to roll his eyes.

"Oh, right." Tommy shook Lauren's hand, and that seemed to break him out of his trance. "Can we take some popcorn too? Ryan's mom is at work, and they have like, zero snacks."

Concern spiked in Blake. "Does he have food?" He kept

his voice low. "Like, real food? Should I order pizza or something?"

"She left pizza," Tommy said. "But their fridge is pretty bare." He'd leaned forward, but he straightened as Ryan re-entered the living room. "We'll just take two each." He handed two cans of soda pop to Tommy.

Blake nodded and smiled. "Sure," he said. "Take some popcorn or chips or something."

"Can we?" Tommy asked, and Blake released Lauren's hand to go help his son pull down some snacks.

"Can I sleep over there, Dad?" Tommy asked. "He has a bunk bed in his room. I don't even need a sleeping bag."

Blake had met Ryan's mom and dad, and he looked to Ryan. "Is your dad okay with it?"

"He said yes," Ryan said. "My mom will be home in an hour too. She said it was okay." He wasn't the type of boy to lie, so Blake nodded.

"Fine," he said. Tomorrow was Saturday, and Blake didn't have to work. He and Tommy would likely end up somewhere for breakfast, and then they'd go to the beach. "Get some pajamas and stuff them in your snack bag."

Tommy's face split into a grin. "Thanks, Dad." He hustled down the hall to his bedroom to get his pajamas, and Blake handed Ryan another box of cheese crackers. Ryan took everything he was given, and several minutes later, Blake sent his son back out the front door, each of them carrying a plastic grocery sack full of snacks.

He sighed as he closed the door, and he turned on the spot and leaned into it. Lauren had taken a seat in the living room, and she looked up from her phone. Her smile only increased her beauty, and she got to her feet.

"Well," she said. "I think that's my cue to leave."

"Aw, come on," he said. "You don't have to do that."

She approached him, her smile slipping in measures until it was gone. The sparkle remained in her eyes though. She ran her fingertips lightly down the side of his face. "I sure do like you, Blake Williams."

A glow started within him, and he smiled. "I sure do like you too, Lauren Keller." He wanted to ask her to sleep over with him, but he wasn't sure they were to that spot yet. She certainly didn't need to leave now, not when Tommy had already come home and left again for the whole evening.

"Is he going to be mad at you later?" She nodded to the right, as if toward Ryan's house.

"Probably not," Blake said. "I did tell him about us. He knows I don't introduce my girlfriends to him until later in the relationship."

"He didn't seem thrilled."

"He's thirteen, and he thinks I'm an idiot." Blake smiled at her. "He's a good boy. I love him dearly, but I don't think he cares who I date."

"No?" Lauren's eyebrows went up. "What if you marry someone he loathes? What if you then die, and he's left with this evil step-mother who forces him to live in the basement, tending to the fireplace?" She revealed her straight, white teeth as she smiled.

Blake burst out laughing. "That's not going to happen."

"It could," she said.

He gazed at her as she dropped her hand. "First of all, this house doesn't have a basement."

She backed up a step and said, "I want to do things with him, Blake. I don't want to be the unknown step-mother."

He pulled in a breath. "You're talking like we'll get married."

She didn't nod or shake her head. She didn't shrug. She just looked at him. "Were you thinking we'd date forever?" she asked. "Or break-up?"

"I don't—I wasn't thinking about it at all."

"Mm." Lauren pushed her ponytail over her shoulder. "I suppose women do think of these types of things sooner."

"Are you sure you don't want to...stay?" He looked down at the ground and then up at her through his eyelashes. "I might not be thinking about marriage, but I'm thinking about other things."

Lauren did shake her head this time. "I don't stay overnight unless there is a wedding first."

Blake cocked his head at her. "Really?"

"Really," she said. Her throat worked as she swallowed, and Blake recognized that as her tell. She had something to say to him that would be hard for her, and he waited. "I have before," she said. "But it ruined me. I was completely broken when he left only a few weeks later, and I vowed—no sex until after marriage. I want it to be this amazing, beautiful act of love. Not just a sleep over."

"It can be both," he said.

She smiled and tipped up to kiss him again. He wrapped her in his arms, wanting her to stay very much. He didn't expect her to, and when she sweetly broke the kiss and rested her forehead against his, she whispered, "I'm sure it can be both," she said. "We won't know until after we're married —*if* we get married."

He nodded, his eyes still closed. He could wait for this woman, because he was falling in love with her.

THE FOLLOWING DAY, HE AND TOMMY FINALLY made it to the beach about noon. He'd texted Lauren long after she'd left last night, and he'd told her he'd let her know where they ended up and when.

He set up their chairs and pounded the umbrella into the sand. The wind always seemed to blow here on Hilton Head, and he'd lost many umbrellas to a big gust. Once he had that done, he sprayed Tommy with sunscreen and his son bent to pick up his boogie board.

"I'm going to text Lauren and invite her," he said. "Is that okay?"

Tommy shrugged. "Fine by me." He started to leave.

"Tommy."

His son turned back to him, and Blake gestured him back into the shade. He sighed as he came, and he rolled his neck from side to side. "What?"

"What? What do you mean *what?* Can't you feel this attitude you're throwing at me?"

Tommy growled, his frown growing deeper. "I just—don't care about Lauren."

"I haven't dated anyone in a long time," Blake said. "I haven't introduced you to anyone in at least three years. Your mom has a man living with her. They go on trips to the Bahamas and stuff. Why am I being villainized for having a girlfriend? I don't get it."

"It's just—it was gross watching you kiss her." He scuffed his feet in the sand.

"It was? Why? You don't want to kiss a girl?" He'd talked to Tommy about sex. He'd taken him to his fifth-grade maturation program. He'd bought the boy his first stick of deodorant, and Tommy had always been open with him.

"It looked like you were eating her face," Tommy muttered. "I don't know. I've seen it on movies and stuff, but it was just...different, I guess. I mean, you're *my dad.*"

Blake's heart softened toward his son. "Yeah," he said. "And I like her. She likes me. So we've been kissing for a few weeks. I'm sorry you walked in on us. I didn't know she was coming over or anything."

"Did she stay overnight?"

Blake was suddenly glad she hadn't. He didn't want to admit to his thirteen-year-old that he'd slept with a woman when he didn't want his son to be doing that. "No," he said. "She didn't. She left right after you did."

Tommy looked at him, and Blake smiled at him. "She wants to get to know you. We're pretty serious, bud. If things stay serious, I might could marry her, and then she'd be living in the house with us. She'd be your step-mom."

Tommy nodded. "Do you think Mom will ever marry Cason?"

"I don't know." Blake drew in a breath and blew it out. He watched the waves roll ashore. "Your mom...she's a free spirit, buddy. She didn't like being married, and I'm not sure she'd ever do it again."

"Why didn't she like it?"

Blake had an answer for his son, but he didn't feel like it was his to give. He looked across the beach and back to his son. "You'll have to ask her that."

"You guys are still friends," Tommy said. "Ryan says it's kind of weird. His aunt and uncle got divorced, and he says they have huge screaming matches at family parties."

Blake blinked and then laughed. "I don't think that's normal either, bud." Nothing could really be counted as "normal," could it? "People have different relationships. Me and your mom are friends, because I really want you in my life. She wants you to be happy. We both do, so we work together to make sure that happens."

He nodded and grabbed onto Blake. "Thanks, Dad."

"Yeah, of course." He had no idea where this emotion had come from. Tommy sometimes seemed so much like a child, and then other times, he surprised Blake with his maturity. "If you don't want Lauren to come, that's fine. There will be other times she can join us."

Tommy pulled away and picked up his boogie board again. "She can come. It's fine, Dad. See if she'll stop and get us sodas from On the Rocks." He ran off then, his long stride almost athletic. If Blake hadn't been in the hospital with him twice last year, he might even mistake Tommy for someone who ran the beaches every morning.

Then he stumbled, and there was the kid Blake knew. He grinned, sank into his chair, and started texting Lauren. *We're on the east side, near Library Downs Plantation. Beach four, straight to your left.*

None of those directions make sense to me, she answered. *You can't just put in beach four and have it take you there, can you?*

Blake chuckled, this new feeling of being alive—truly alive—vibrating in his chest. *I'm sending you my pin right now. Just tap on that, and you'll come right to me.*

Half an hour later, Lauren dropped a folding beach chair. "This is all Harrison has. It works for his beach."

Blake jumped to his feet. "Why didn't you call me like you said you would?" He took the two white paper bags from her, the scent of something savory and creamy mixing with something sugary sweet.

"I saw you right here," she said. She put down her beach bag and bent to unfold her chair. She'd be sitting almost on the ground, and Blake would be above her. He grabbed the blanket they always brought to the beach and nudged his chair out of the way so he could spread it on the sand.

He sat on that while she sat in her chair and started pulling food out of the bag. She wore a white, blue, and green tropical print dress, and it hiked up her leg almost all the way to her hip, where he caught a peek of a dark blue swimming suit.

His face heated, and he pulled his eyes away from the length of her leg as she handed him a foil-wrapped sandwich with the words, "Ham and cheese melt." She eyed it and then him. "That actually smells really good."

"I told you it was. You switched out the Swiss for muenster?"

"Sure did." She looked out toward the water. "Is he going to come in and eat?"

"When he's ready," Blake said. "We have no schedule at the beach, sweetheart. He plays and comes in, goes out, finds someone to throw a Frisbee with, whatever."

She shaded her eyes. "Where is he?"

Blake had just seen him right before Lauren arrived, and he quickly scanned the area to his left where Tommy had been. Sure enough, he spotted him several yards out. "He's over to the left," he said, pointing. "See the kid with half his torso out? That's him."

"He's so tall." She looked at him as she unwrapped her sandwich. It wasn't grilled, which meant she hadn't gotten the hot ham and cheese the way he'd suggested. "Where'd he get that height from?"

"I'm almost six feet tall," he said.

"Are you?"

"Yes." He shook his head. "Tommy's over that now. I don't know. Jacinda's barely five-four."

"And that's your ex-wife."

"Yes, ma'am."

"Why did you two get divorced?" She took a bite of her sandwich, a moan coming from her mouth. "Oh my word." She reached for a napkin and wiped her lips. "I asked the guy at Heaven's Hoagie what to get, and he recommended this. It's incredible. Try it."

She handed him her sandwich, and he looked at the variety of ingredients between the two pieces of wheat bread. He must've made a face, because she started to laugh. "Never mind." She tried to take her sandwich back, but Blake jerked it away from her. "You can't have any. Not with that look on your face."

He met her eye, his smile spreading. "What look?"

"You look like that tomato is going to stab you as it goes down your throat."

"I don't really like tomatoes," he said.

"Then give me my sandwich back."

"I've never seen anything like this at Heaven's Hoagies."

"The guy said it's their California Beach Club, and I thought that sounded fitting."

"Are these—?" Blake poked at the flimsy sprout things. "Sprouts?"

"Yes." Lauren managed to grab her sandwich from him, and he grinned at her as she settled back into her chair. "They're good. It won't kill you to eat vegetables, you know." She took another bite of her sandwich and made a big deal out of moaning over its greatness.

Blake laughed while she did, and then he took a bite of his sandwich. Ah, yes. No one made sandwiches like Heaven's Hoagies, what with the bread all toasty on the outside like that, but so soft under that initial crunch? He loved it, and he loved the simplicity of the mayo-mustard mix, warmed slightly on the inside of the sandwich, with that salty ham, and the melty cheese.

With this sandwich and with Lauren on the beach with him now, Blake could honestly say this was about as close to perfection as life got.

Tommy came jogging up to their little umbrella as Blake finished his sandwich. “You got lunch?”

“Heaven’s Hoagies,” Blake said. “Lauren got your favorite.”

She bent to get it out of the bag, and she handed him the sandwich. He looked at her and took it. “Thanks, Lauren.”

“Anytime.” She smiled at him, and Tommy sat on the blanket with Blake.

“The water’s choppy today,” he said. “It looks smooth, but it’s not.” Just then, the siren sounded, and Lauren yelped.

Neither Blake nor Tommy got too bothered, because they’d been through this before. “It’s a warning siren,” he said—yelled—over the noise. “It means you have to come out of the water. See how everyone is coming in?”

“Why do they have to come in?” Lauren yelled back.

“They’ve spotted something out there they don’t like.”

Lauren seemed alarmed, but she really didn’t need to be. The siren continued for another minute or so, and then it silenced. “That is so loud,” she said.

“No sirens on the private beach, I’m assuming,” Blake said.

“I never get in the water,” she said. “But no, I’ve never heard a siren.”

"You wore your swimming suit," he said. "You weren't planning to get in the water?"

"No." She looked at him, but she'd put on a pair of sunglasses, and he couldn't really see her eyes. "Are you?"

"Yep," he said. "It's hot, and the water cools you down."

"The shade keeps me cool," she said. She actually reached into her bag and pulled out a sun hat. She settled it on her head and took another bite of her sandwich. "So, Tommy," she said. "You like to boogie board?"

"Yes, ma'am," he said. He didn't add anything else to the conversation, and Blake felt the tension under the umbrella tick up a notch.

"What do you do when you can't come to the beach?" she asked.

He looked at her, the ends of his hair curled and still dripping salt water. "We can always come to the beach."

"Well, you can't go in the water right now. So you'd..."

He looked at Blake, who didn't want to bail him out.

"Wait for them to blow the all-clear horn?" Tommy guessed.

Lauren's shoulders went down, and she smiled. "I see."

"She means what do you do when you're not at the beach at all, bud."

"Oh, like go to the skate park or play video games."

"Yes," Lauren said. "That's what I meant. What's your favorite video game?"

Blake wanted to warn her away from this path, because once Tommy got talking about SquareSpaces, he wouldn't stop. Actually *couldn't* be stopped.

"SquareSpaces," he said.

"Tell me about it," she said, and Blake wanted to start waving his arms at her.

Tommy started telling her about it, and fifteen minutes later, he knelt next to her in the sand, showing her the live tournaments that got live-streamed all around the world.

Lauren looked like she'd been learning Japanese and would then be expected to speak it fluently, and when the video ended, he said, "So it's fun."

"Yes," she said. "I can see that. You play alone, or you play with a group like those people?"

"Sometimes I coordinate with my friends," he said. "And we all join the campaign together. But sometimes I just join whoever's playing online."

"Sound on," Blake said, finally joining the conversation. "No headphones when he plays with strangers. I want to hear what everyone's saying."

"I have the minor tag, Dad. Everyone knows they have to keep it clean when they play with a minor."

"Still." Blake exchanged a glance with Lauren. "You can never be too careful with kids these days." He thought of the texts Tommy had gotten a few weeks ago. "Did you ever get any more texts from that girl?"

"No," Tommy said. "And Gwen apologized for giving out my number."

"That's good," Blake said.

Tommy had finished eating while he chatted about SquareSpaces, and Lauren took his trash from him. "I brought chips too," she said. "And those sour gummy worms."

Tommy blinked at her. "You like those? Sick."

She smiled at him and reached into her beach bag. She pulled out the bag of them, ripped it open, and then removed a red and orange gummy worm. It had lots of sour sugar on the outside of it, and she put the whole thing in her mouth.

"Mm," she said. "Just more for me to have."

Tommy shook his head, but Blake saw the smile on his son's face. Lauren had said she didn't interact with many kids, but she was calm and cool with Tommy. Blake barely knew how to act around teenagers, and he'd known Tommy for every day of his life.

She offered the bag to Blake, and he took it. He too didn't particularly enjoy this kind of candy. He didn't really like candy at all, preferring junk food to it ten to one.

"Are these your favorite candy?" He took out a blue and pink one, but the thought of putting it in his mouth had his throat closing.

"No," she said. "My weakness is that of many other women around the world: chocolate."

"You should go to Ryan's uncle's candy shop," Tommy said. "He makes the best chocolate truffles in the world."

Blake nodded and casually dropped the sour gummy worm back in the bag. He was not eating that.

"Do they?" Lauren asked.

"They do tours and stuff," Tommy said. "They'll show you how to make the truffles. My grandma tried once, and they were good, but they weren't as smooth as you get at the shop."

Lauren looked over to Blake, and while he couldn't see her eyes, he felt the locking, clicking connection between them. "They do tours?"

He grinned, picked up his phone, and started looking how to book a private tour at—"What's the name of it again, Tommy?"

His son didn't answer, and Blake stopped trying to remember and looked up. Tommy wasn't sitting five feet from him anymore, and Blake hadn't heard him get up or leave. "Where'd he go?"

Lauren giggled and pointed to the right, and it only took Blake half a breath to find Tommy standing with a group of teenagers a couple dozen yards away. He couldn't determine their ages from this distance, but he didn't recognize any of them either. Why would he? He didn't work with teens.

Tommy clearly knew them, as he razzed the boy next to him and then inched closer to the girl on his right.

"Oh, boy," Lauren said almost under her breath. "That boy is in troub-ble."

"What do you mean?" Blake leaned forward, as if the six inches he'd gained would help him see better. He squinted, and that didn't help either.

Just then, the girl on his right, brushed her fingers along Tommy's. The boy across from him laughed, but Tommy didn't. The next thing Blake knew, his son was holding hands with that girl, and his blood burned like lava in his veins.

He sucked in a breath and got to his feet. Then Lauren stood in front of him, one palm against his very bare chest, her touch burning into him. "Don't go over there," she said. "Blake. Blake!"

He blinked and looked at her. She shook her head, and he came to his senses. His pulse throbbed through his whole body, but he managed to sit back down. When he looked over to the group again, they'd broken up. Someone had a spikeball set, and Tommy currently stood on the sidelines while four other people played, including the girl he'd been holding hands with.

She wore a pair of cutoffs that showed the pockets hanging out of the front of them they were so short. On top, she had on a yellow sports bra, and her long, blonde hair had been tied on top of her head.

"She's really cute," Lauren said. "Who is she?"

"I have no clue," Blake said darkly. "Tommy hasn't mentioned a girl at all." At least not one he liked, one he might hold hands with, and one he'd very obviously thought about kissing. And to think, he'd been "grossed out" by Blake kissing Lauren last night.

He shook his head, some of his laid-back attitude returning, especially when Lauren stroked her fingers through his hair. "It's cute," she murmured. "It's like puppy love."

"Except he's not a puppy," Blake said. "He's a hormonal thirteen-year-old boy who told me that he thought we were 'gross' by kissing on the couch."

Lauren giggled, and Blake liked the sound of that. He looked back at her, and she leaned further forward over her legs, clearly wanting to kiss him right now. He wouldn't say no to that, but because they were on a public beach and not a private one, he kept it chaste and quick.

After all, he now had to keep a very close eye on Tommy —and not only because of the cute blonde. Once his son's turn came to play spikeball...Blake could be looking at a trip to the hospital.

Chapter Sixteen

"This is the one," Lauren said, her voice pitching up in excitement. She looked over to Cass and Bea, both of whom had come with her today to look at "the perfect house."

She'd found it less than forty-eight hours ago, and she'd immediately texted Ty to set up a showing and then Blake to ask him about the neighborhood.

"Look at it." She almost got out of the SUV while Cass was still driving it, but the handle flipped back as the door was locked.

"You're like a tween getting her first makeup," Cass complained. "At least let me put it in park first. Jeez."

"It's so stinking cute," Bea said, and that only fueled Lauren's excitement. Cass finally put the vehicle in park, and the door locks disengaged. Lauren flew from the SUV and stood in front of the house, the sidewalk outside pristine. Two huge trees sheltered the home, one on either side of the sidewalk, and flowers, bushes, and shrubs had been planted all along the front of it.

The porch came from the eighteen hundreds, when steps were wide so men and women could pass one another without touching.

Lauren loved everything about Southern architecture. The traditions. Why they'd built things the way they had. The colors and lines and shapes she saw in each design.

This house exuded charm, and Lauren closed her eyes and breathed it in. It was not on the beach, like Bea's and Cass's houses, nor like the one she had now. It was probably one-third the size of Cass's house, but Lauren didn't have three children who could drop in to stay with her at any time.

This house had soul, and it spoke to Lauren's. "I want it," she said.

Ty pulled up then, and when he got out, he said, "Well? What do you think? First impressions?"

"I want to put an offer on it," she said.

He laughed and handed her a sheet of paper. "Let's at least go inside first, should we?" He led the way, and Lauren practically skipped after him, Cass and Bea at her side. Lauren had seen the specs already, so she simply brought the paper along for the ride.

"Two bedrooms," Ty said as he unlocked the door with his special realtor code. "Two bathrooms, one of which is in the master suite, as requested." He gave her a winning smile as he pushed into the house.

The door squealed like Satan himself was trying to enter,

and Ty frowned at it. "I can fix that for you," he said. "Easy." He spread his arms wide. "This house has such great charm to it. Good bones too, and the owners have recently renovated it in anticipating of renting it. But." He hit the T really hard. "They decided not to. They're leaving the island, and they didn't want to hire someone like Blake to manage it for them."

He drew a breath as Lauren squeezed in beside him. She paused, the sight before her glorious and bathed in light from heaven above. She could see down the entryway, which was much wider than she'd expected it to be. Newer homes had front offices or formal living rooms. This house didn't have that, but the flooring was a deep, dark rich wood, met by white baseboards that gave way to light blue walls.

At least they looked blue. The palest of blues, like the sky in the early morning before the sun truly said hello. She wasn't sure, because of the floor-to-ceiling windows at the back of the house. They gave light to the house, and the sun shone through them with vigor. That light lit Lauren's soul, and she now really wanted this house.

The garage fit two cars, but was detached, and the home had exactly two entrances—the one she'd just come through, and a set of sliding glass doors off the master bedroom in the back corner. So this sight would greet her each and every day when she got home.

She needed this in her life, as she'd started the job in Charleston, and coming home to glorious windows with rays of sunshine would do so much for her.

Ty stepped down the hall, chattering about the drapes,

the furniture, the appliances. "They want it all to stay," he said. "If that's a problem, let me know."

Lauren didn't know if it would be a problem or not. She hadn't sold her house in Texas, and she wasn't sure what she wanted to bring with her and what she could leave behind.

You left it all behind, she told herself. She had packed up a lot and brought it with her weeks ago.

"I'll let you know," she said, her voice almost a vague rendition of itself. She went through the kitchen, her fingers trailing along the quartz countertops, and she went down the hall with Ty. A small, narrow office sat right off the living room, and Lauren had worked in much tighter spaces.

A guest bathroom and bedroom took up the front quadrant of the home, with the master suite behind it.

"Walk-in closet," Ty said, pulling open the door. "It's actually a walk-through closet. It connects to the linen closet in the hall." He beamed like this was a great feature for a home to have, and Lauren smiled back. It was unique, at least.

She stopped dead in her tracks at the master bathroom. Blues, grays, and whites reflected like diamonds in her eyes. "Wow," she said.

"Marble counter tops." Ty glanced at his tiny clipboard. "The tiles in the shower and powder room are glass, frosted and clear. We've got ceramic tiles on the floor and the sinks are cement."

Lauren adored them, how they sloped from left to right, where the drain ran the width of them.

"Standing shower," he said. "With a rainfall head, and of course, your tub."

"It's copper," Bea said. "I love it."

"I want to take a bath here," Cass said.

Lauren moved over to the coppery tub, surprised everything in the house had been cool, made of grays, whites, and blues—until this tub.

She looked at Ty. "Can I afford this?"

He grinned at her. "You sent me the listing."

She bit her thumbnail and turned in a full three-hundred-sixty-degree circle. She looked at Cass, who nodded with the widest grin on her face. Bea was already bouncing on the balls of her feet, her hands clasped together near her throat.

"Lauren, you have to live here." Bea clapped then and launched herself into Lauren's arms. They laughed together, but Lauren knew that just because she liked something didn't mean she'd get it.

"This house was built for you," Cass said. "A hundred years ago, and you're both just now realizing it."

Lauren pulled away from Bea and took a deep breath. "Okay." She straightened her blouse and turned to Ty. "I want to put in an offer. Full asking price, and I won't require an inspection. I want them to come back to me if they have other offers so I can consider increasing mine."

Ty cocked his eyebrows. "I'll keep that to myself for now," he said. He tugged his phone out of his front jacket pocket. How he wore a jacket in the dog days of summer, Lauren didn't know. Her lightweight, nearly sheer blouse was suffocating her. "I'll go call the listing agent right now and get a feel for how many people have seen the house, if he has other offers, all of that."

"Sounds good."

Ty left the bathroom and Lauren reached for the hands of her friends. "I'm not crazy, am I?"

"Yes," Cass said. "You absolutely are." She giggled, the sound growing into a full laugh. "But it's good, Lauren. You need a change, and this will be a huge change for you."

"I hate my job," she said next, sudden worry diving through her. She hadn't always overthought things in her life, but lately, she felt like she could go round and round in circles and never come to a decision.

"Then get a new one," Bea said. "Do you really need to work that much? You've worked for almost twenty years already."

And she'd never been married. It had always been just her, paying her mortgage and her car payments. No one came asking for money, and Lauren had had a good, healthy six-figure annual salary job.

"I'll see," Lauren said, because she hadn't discussed her finances with anyone. Of her friends, she probably seemed to be doing the best from the outside. She traveled a lot, and her clothes came from designer department stores. Her job had paid for all of that, and Lauren had been extremely grateful.

"I need to list my house in Sweet Water Falls," she said.

"I'll give you my realtor's number," Cass said, already on the job with her fingers flying across her phone screen.

Lauren turned to Bea while Cass did that. Together, they left the master suite, which Lauren did love. She could see herself relaxing here. She wanted to be here. "This isn't too insane, is it?"

"I don't think so," Bea said. "But I fell in love with Grant and got married in a few months." She lifted one shoulder and glanced at Lauren. She'd always been able to read her very well, and she paused and turned back to her in the hallway. "You can't worry about Joy. Or Bessie, or Sage. They're grown women."

"Yeah," Lauren said. "That's easy for you to say. You're already here, locked in with the amazing beach and the gorgeous husband." She smiled so it wouldn't sound like she was criticizing Bea. She wasn't. It was simply easier for her to tell Lauren to do what she wanted and not to worry about anyone else.

Lauren didn't want to be that person. She loved Joy and Bessie and Sage, and she didn't want them to be upset that now their group was completely split. Half in Sweet Water Falls, and half here in Hilton Head.

Bea blinked a couple of times, and then her surprise melted away. "I know. But Sage told me she's thinking of moving here now that her divorce is almost final. She can do hair from anywhere, and Bessie's already looking into a franchise with The Bread Boy."

"And Joy?" Lauren asked. "I worry about Joy the most."

Her time in Hilton Head was almost up, and Lauren felt it moving through her keenly. She tried to grip it with all ten fingers, but it just wisped away like smoke. "She's already packing, and I hear her sniffling through it."

"We have Beach Day," Bea said. "And one more Supper Club. She'll be okay."

Lauren wanted to ask, *And then what, Bea?* but she didn't. Because memories of Beach Day and Supper Club didn't actually mean she and Joy could meet for lunch at the Thai place they liked. Not if they didn't live in the same city.

Cass joined them, and she and Bea started chit-chatting about the groceries they needed for Beach Day that weekend, and Lauren followed in their wake. She couldn't help wondering if that was what she was doing again—simply following them from Texas to South Carolina.

Outside, she walked down the length of the sidewalk and turned back to the house while the others got in the car. She loved it, and her heart swelled at the blue eaves that blended up into the dark gray roof and shingles. It looked straight out of a magazine, and when Ty got out of his car, saying, "No, I'm faxing over the offer within the hour. They'll have it by five p.m. to consider with the other one," Lauren's concern grew.

She met his eye, but he waved his hand. "It's a fantastic offer, Ben. Just let your clients know it's coming." He grinned. "Yes, from a very enthusiastic young woman who would love to live in their masterpiece... Uh huh. Buh-bye."

Lauren didn't judge him for the professional talk and mannerisms. Lord knew she'd gone through the motions many times too. Anything for the client. The customer was always right. That type of thing.

"Well." He sighed.

"They have another offer," he and Lauren said together.

"They just got it this morning," Ty said. "They've only had three showings, but they do have two more tomorrow."

"So what does that mean?"

"Most likely, they'll pick one of you tonight," he said. "List it as pending, and the showings tomorrow won't happen."

"When will I know?" she asked.

"They technically have twenty-four hours to accept, deny, or counter with another offer," he said. "My secretary is putting it together now. It'll be off within the hour."

Lauren nodded and tried to tamp down the anxiety rising through her. "Okay, well, that's all I can do, right?"

"Yep," he said. "Leave the rest to me, Lauren. I'm going to get you this house." He smiled like that gesture alone could seal the deal, and she decided she had to trust him. He knew Blake, Grant, and Harrison, and he'd come with a great track record and plenty of praise.

She joined her friends in the car, and Bea asked, "Where should we go to dinner?"

"We're going to dinner?" Cass asked. "I'm pretty sure Harrison put meat on the grill. He got his new one on the back patio this morning."

"I was going to go to Blake's," Lauren said. "Sorry, I didn't know we had dinner plans too."

Bea looked at Cass and then back to Lauren in the back seat. "I guess I assumed. It's okay. I can grab something and eat it on the deck while I watch the ocean."

"That sounds amazing," Cass said. "Do you want to do it from my deck? I'm sure Harrison will have enough for you."

"And crash your newlywed beach dinner? No thanks."

"I've been married for almost two months," Cass said with a laugh.

"Aren't you a newlywed for a year?" Bea asked.

"Maybe when you're twenty," Cass joked. She let out a peal of laughter. "Which I so am not."

Lauren had never been married, and she let her mind wander as Cass drove her over to Blake's house. The trip only took a few minutes, and she said, "Thanks for coming with me, guys. Thanks for lunch too, Cass."

"It was so fun," her friend said, and Lauren got out of the car. She walked toward Blake's front door, taking in the perfectness of his house too. His SUV sat in the driveway, so she wasn't surprised to find him opening the door as she put her foot on the top step.

"Hey, pretty girl," he said.

"I put in an offer on the house." She held up her phone. "Do you want to see the pictures?"

"I looked at the listing, but absolutely I want to see them again." He grinned and motioned for her to follow him into the house. "I also texted you about five minutes ago, asking if you'd be stopping by here or going back to the house, but you didn't answer."

"Sorry," she said. "I didn't get it." Her phone chimed just then, and she glanced at it to see his name flash up at the top. "There it is."

"I was hoping," he said, and he hadn't stopped moving yet, so he'd gone all the way into his kitchen. He opened the oven and pulled out a tray with a couple of round, aluminum containers. "I got those Mediterranean bowls you were talking about."

"You're kidding." Her stomach growled as if on cue, and he grinned at her.

"Cold toppings in the fridge. They've been here for five minutes, so super fresh."

She moved into his side as he took off the oven mitts. She leaned into him, took a big lungful of his cologne, the masculine scent of his skin, and his pure goodness. "I want to eat with you."

"Mm, good." He leaned down and kissed her, and Lauren wanted to do a lot more than just eat with him. He didn't linger long, as the timer on the oven went off, and he broke their kiss to silence it. Then he busied himself with getting out the cold toppings, and he put together their Mediterranean rice bowls and served her at the kitchen table.

"Blake," she said. "There's another offer on the house. Either way, I'm going to call a realtor in Texas and list my house tomorrow. I'm going to move here." She stirred in her pickled vegetables and took more green goddess dressing. A smile formed on her face. "And I'm really excited about that."

"Me too," he said. "Absolutely me too."

Lauren could just see her picture-perfect life in that cottage, but as their conversation continued with talk about his day, and her job, and the upcoming Beach Day expectations, she couldn't help wondering what she was doing.

He lived here. He had three bedrooms and a son. If they ended up being serious—really serious—and getting married, they surely wouldn't live in the house she'd just fallen in love with.

But maybe falling in love with a beautiful man is more important, she thought. She had no idea how to rationalize with it or argue with it, so she simply let it sit there in her brain and circle.

For now.

The following day, Lauren paced in the enormous kitchen at Cass's house. Harrison hadn't gotten home from work yet, but Cass had been entertaining her and Joy that afternoon. Evening was almost upon them, and Lauren threw a nervous look to the clock on the double oven.

"Why haven't I heard yet?" she asked. "Ty said twenty-four hours, and it's been twenty-three and a half."

Joy had a date with Chester in an hour, and once Harrison came home, Cass would need to be ready to go too. They had a dinner appointment at a fancy place in Charleston that Cass just loved, which left Lauren alone tonight.

Blake had gone to Carter's Cove to get his son, and they had plans to get hot dogs there before catching the last ferry back to the mainland. Then they had to drive around to Hilton Head again, and Lauren had planned an evening with pizza, popcorn, and pineapple sherbet in the big house three doors down.

Put on her favorite movie, surround herself with her favorite things, and celebrate—if only she had something to celebrate.

"He'll call," Joy said. "Give him a minute. Maybe he's working that magic."

That only made Lauren worry more, and she threw Cass a nervous look. Her friend wasn't even watching her, and Lauren's frustration skyrocketed.

It took another fifteen minutes of pacing—and two more questions of when she'd hear—before her phone rang and Ty's name sat there.

Lauren swallowed and brushed her loose hair back. She hadn't worked that day and having nothing to do certainly didn't help her anxiety. "Hey," she said as casually as she could.

"Lauren," Ty said, his usual jovial self. A pause came through the line, and she held her breath, not daring to even breathe into it. "You got it!" he yelled.

Lauren sighed, her smile huge and the relief rushing through her with the strength of a stiff beach wind. "Oh, praise the stars," she said.

Ty laughed and went over the paperwork and details he'd have his secretary send. Lauren said she'd watch her email, and then she hung up.

"You got it." Joy rushed at her and wrapped her up into

a tight hug. "I'm so happy for you." Her voice broke on the last word, though, and Lauren pressed her eyes closed to keep her tears in.

"You'll come stay in the guest bedroom every weekend," she whispered.

"Heck yes, I will," Joy whispered back, though both of them knew Joy wouldn't do that. Cass hugged her too, and then she went into the master to get ready, Joy left through the front door, and Lauren stood in not-her-house and grinned and grinned as she typed out two texts.

One to her Supper Club group, who were all anxiously awaiting the news. The other went to Blake, who responded almost as fast as Bea and Bessie.

As she left Cass's and went down the street to her house to make her popcorn and order her pizza, her thoughts went west. First to Texas, and then further, to California. Maybe she should reach out to her brother and let him know she was making a twelve-hundred-mile move. She wasn't sure why Jess lingered in her mind, and she didn't know how to reach out to him quite yet. Her memory stirred about an upcoming birthday, and once she got home, she checked her calendar. Sure enough, his oldest's birthday was at the beginning of September, and once Lauren texted him about that, she could let him know about the changes in her life.

Chapter Seventeen

Beatrice Turner joined her husband at the back hatch of their SUV and put in the beach tote filled to the brim with paper products—cups, plates, napkins, and silverware.

"Got it all?" Grant asked.

Bea sniffled as she nodded. She let her husband fold her into his arms, unsure why the weepiness had started so soon. "She's not even leaving until next weekend," Grant whispered. "You still have Supper Club."

"It's not just her," Bea said. On the same day she was driving to Charleston with Joy and Lauren, Grant was taking Shelby back to her mother. She'd moved once again and now lived near Birmingham, and she was going to be in Atlanta next weekend for something Bea didn't quite understand. A fair, maybe?

Grant would be driving her to meet her mom, and then Shelby would be gone. "I love her," Bea said. "I know it makes no sense, but I do. She's fun to have around." She stepped away from her husband and wiped her eyes. "I don't know how you do it."

He turned away from her. "I don't either." He sounded emotional too, and Bea wondered if he'd ever considered asking his ex-wife for a swap in schedules. Now that he was married, Bea could help so much with Shelby during the school year. When she'd met and married Grant, the girl had been thirteen, and she was now closing in on sixteen.

She'd been on the honor roll every term this past year, and Bea texted with her constantly. She knew her mother wasn't home all the time, and she simply wanted the best for Shelby. Something told her not to bring it up—and not to ruin Beach Day by starting it out with crying.

He reached to close the hatch with the press of a button, and he gave her a smile. She saw the pain masked behind the action, and she cradled his face in a single palm. "Thank you," she said.

"Have a fun day," he said. "Call me if Cass forgot something you really need." He gave her another grin and leaned in to kiss her.

Bea gave him a smile and got behind the wheel. He hadn't met Cass if he thought she'd forget something, but she couldn't just run back up to her house if she did. Bea had wanted and organized a ladies-only day on the beach at Lighthouse Point, and as she drove to the destination alone, she wondered why she'd been so lonely for her friends this summer.

She'd been the one to start this domino effect of their

Supper Club leaving their small town along the Gulf Coast of Texas. She was the one who'd fallen in love in a single summer—heck, in ten days—while a tourist on the island.

She'd been the one to encourage Cass to start fresh here in Hilton Head, and she and Harrison had taken almost a whole year to fall in love and get married. But they'd settled here, not there.

She'd been the one to beg her friends to come for the summer, and while Bessie couldn't do it for too long, she'd come when she could. Joy and Lauren had been here for months, and Lauren was now staying.

Bea smiled at that, because Lauren deserved every single good thing in the world. She'd dedicated far too much of her life to her career and her company to have everything fall apart the way it had. She'd not seen her and Blake together yet, but Joy said they were an "adorable couple."

She pulled into the parking lot, surprised to see Blake emerging from his dark-colored SUV too. "Don't worry, Bea," he said. "I'm just here to help you unload. Lauren suggested it last night, and well, here I am."

Bea raised her eyebrows at the tall, sandy-haired man. He was charming and good-looking. Broad shoulders and tight muscles across his chest and in his legs. He opened the back of her car and started pulling out the heavier objects like the cooler and the box of cookies, crackers, and candy.

"I can get the paper products," she said.

He flashed her a smile and waited for her to reach into the car and get the tote. She also shouldered her bag with her eReader, her suntan lotion, and her towel, and then she faced the beach.

"I'm following you," he said. "I can get your chairs and umbrella set up too, okay?"

"Yes, that would be wonderful," she said. She had no problem letting someone take care of her, and she found it romantic and cute that Blake was here doing it.

She followed the sidewalk until it ended, and then she squished through the sand until she found a suitable place. "I think two rows," she said. "So we'll put up the shade in the front and angle it down, and the umbrella can go back here," she said. She set down the tote with the plates and cups.

"Yes, ma'am," Blake said. He put the cooler next to her bag and left to go get more. Bea tilted her head back and took a long, deep breath of the beachy air. She loved the sun. The sand. The ocean. The breeze. All of it.

"Right here, hon?"

Her eyes snapped open at the sound of her husband's voice. Her eyes took a moment to adjust, and sure enough, they saw both Harrison and Grant. They carried the shade and the umbrella, and Bea could only stare as they started to set it up.

"What are you doing here?"

"Getting you ladies ready for Beach Day," Harrison said.

"You call me when you're about done," Grant said. He grinned at her and handed Harrison a rubber mallet. He faced her and brushed his lips along her cheek. "Ya'hear, Bea? I'll come help you take it all down."

"I have a meeting with a client," Harrison said. "But if it's before or after that, I'll come too."

"Thank you," Bea murmured. Blake returned with her chair and the box of snacks, and within minutes, the perfect spot for the perfect day on the beach was set and ready to go. Voices came her way, and they could've belonged to anyone. Another family arriving. A group of teen girls.

They were Bea's friends, and her heart swelled with love for them. To her surprise, Lauren led the way, and her whole countenance brightened when she saw Blake standing there. "Well, well," she said, plenty of flirt in her voice. "What's a man like you doing here?"

He laughed and slid his arm along her waist, pulling her right against him. "Waiting for you." He leaned down and kissed her right there in front of everyone, and Bea pressed one hand to her pulse as if getting ready to recite the Pledge of Allegiance.

"Wow," Cass said. She sucked in a breath as her eyes moved past Lauren and Blake and caught sight of her husband. "You big, fat liar."

Harrison chuckled and shook his head. "I didn't lie. I *am* going to Gourmet Goods...right after this. Isn't that right, Grant?"

"I'm dying for some of their chocolate coffee," he said in an over-exaggerated voice.

Cass kissed Harrison quickly too, then set up her chair right next to Bea's. The other ladies did as well, and it was Joy who bumped Lauren and said, "Oops," in a loud voice, as she was still kissing Blake.

Bea looked away as the men left, and once everyone had gotten a favored beverage and found a spot to sit, she started spraying on her sunscreen. The others did too, except for Sage, who wore a tank top and a pair of shorts and said she never wore sunscreen, and she'd be fine.

"All right," Bea said. "We need updates. Lauren is obviously all the way to making out with her boyfriend in public." She gave the dark-haired woman a semi-sharp glare.

"I..." Lauren shrugged and said nothing more.

"Wow," Cass said.

"Yeah, wow," Lauren said back. "You start with your honeymoon, which none of us have heard more than three words about." She cocked her eyebrows, and Bea's attention zeroed there, because she'd love to hear more about Cass's adventures in Europe. Lauren was right; Cass had barely said anything about it.

"It was really amazing," Cass said. Her voice took on a wistful quality. "Such old history there. Buildings from the eleven hundreds, when we were nothing here." She smiled around at everyone and took a sip from her can of ginger ale. "Beautiful architecture. Great sight-seeing tours. Wonderful food. In Italy, we had the best pizza I've ever put in my mouth. I can't describe how it was different, only that it was."

"It's the cheese," Lauren said, her eyes out on the constantly moving water. "They have incredible cheese in Italy." She glanced around at everyone. "In Belgium too."

Cass smiled at her and talked about a winery tour in the south of France that had Bea's jealously kicking into a new gear. She'd been competing with Cassandra Haslam for as long as she could remember, and Bea reminded herself she didn't need to do that. She could be thrilled for her friend and still enjoy her own life.

"All right, that's all," Cass said, and Bea covered her hand and squeezed it. She met Bea's eye, and Bea gave her a smile that she hoped conveyed to Cass how much she loved her.

Cass squeezed her hand back, so she thought it did.

"What other news?" Bea asked. "Joy? What's going on with you and Chester?"

"Oh." Joy took in a full breath, her chest rising in her cute pink and white striped swim tank. "I broke up with him last night."

"What?" Lauren barked. "Why?" Bessie had caught up to her then, and she asked the second question at the same time Lauren did.

"Because," Joy said, her voice semi-annoyed. "I don't live here, and he does. I'm going to be gone for nine months, and I'm not that interested in him to maintain the long-distance relationship."

Bea caught her saying she'd be gone for nine months, not for good, but she catalogued it away for later.

"Plus, there's your backup boyfriend," Lauren said.

"He is not my backup boyfriend." Joy shot her a death glare, and Bea leaned forward.

"Who?" she asked.

"Scott Anderson," Lauren said.

"Lauren." Joy shook her head, clearly annoyed. "He's not my backup anything. We've never been out."

"He asked," Lauren said.

"Yes," Joy said. "Two months ago, and no, I didn't go out with him. He's not interested, and frankly, I'm not. Doesn't anyone remember that I live in Sweet Water Falls?" She glared Lauren into silence as she opened her mouth yet again, and Bea was impressed by that.

"Scott Anderson," she looked at Cass. "He's the guy who bought Harrison's landscaping company from him, right?"

"Right." Cass didn't say anything else, and Bea found that interesting.

"I'm going to look for something to rent here," Sage said. "My house in Texas is too big, and I've already asked my kids if any of them want the hobby farm."

All attention flew to her, and she raised one hand. "I don't want a bunch of questions. Joy, don't look at me like that. You know you're going to end up here too."

"I do *not* know that," Joy said. "My house is there. I've lived in Texas my whole life. I don't *want* to leave."

She did want to be happy, however, and Bea suspected she wouldn't be if she lived in Sweet Water Falls without the Supper Club. Without someone to love.

"What are you going to do here?" Cass asked Sage, who gave her a wry look.

"I just said I don't want to answer questions." She stood and adjusted the towel she'd spread across the seat and back of her chair. "I don't have the answers right now, and you know what? I'm getting quite the alimony payment, so I don't *need* to have the answers right now." She sat back down and looked at Bessie. "Your turn."

Bea hated being on the outside of news, but she couldn't be in the inner circles anymore. Grant came first, and she'd so enjoyed her summer with him and Shelby. Her friends too, but that meant that Sage knew Bessie's news before everyone else, when that role usually fell to Bea.

"I talked to Wynona," Bessie said. "She said she thought opening a bakery would be really fun, and she's willing to talk to me more about it once I get home." She looked extremely apprehensive, and Bessie wouldn't do anything in a short amount of time. She needed to examine things from every angle, make charts and lists, and then talk to as many experts as possible.

"That's amazing," Joy said. "You and Wynona running the bakery. Does she not want to work with animals anymore?"

"She said there are farms and ranches here." Bessie licked her lips and reached for a bag of sour cream and onion potato chips. The plastic crinkled and crackled as she poked her hand inside. "She'd help me run it on the administrative side, the way Cherry does for The Bread Boy in Sweet Water Falls."

"What about Cherry?" Bea asked. She'd come to their Supper Club several times, but not the ones here on the island, and a twinge of regret fired through Bea that the whole thing was basically going to disband before Cherry really got started.

"I've talked to her," Joy said. "She said she's okay. She

said she might try to find a group of ladies to do a Supper Club with. She's got three sisters-in-law, and her sister, and that's five people right there."

Bea nodded and looked at Cass, but all the eyes on the beach came to her. "Your news?" Cass asked oh-so-coolly.

"Oh, I don't have news." Bea waved her hand. "Nothing ever changes with me."

"That's not true," Lauren said

"False," Joy said.

"Liar," Bessie coughed under her breath.

Sage said nothing, and Bea stared at Bessie. "I am not a liar."

"Then tell the truth," she challenged.

Bea didn't know how to let the precious things inside her mind come out. She shook her head as her chin started to tremble. "I'm going to miss Shelby terribly," she said, not caring that her voice came out like a cartoon chipmunk. "I love that girl and having her leave this year is very hard for me."

No one said anything, but Lauren wore compassion in her eyes, and Cass nodded.

"You know what you should do?" Bessie asked.

"What?" Bea wiped quickly at her eyes, being careful not to smear sunscreen in them.

"Bring her to Supper Club on Thursday." Bessie carried a joyous glint in her eyes. "Let her see what we do."

Bea's mouth opened and she stared at Bessie. "I don't know about that."

"Just because Grant thinks our Supper Club is a giant pillow fight doesn't mean it is," Lauren said.

A few women laughed, Bea included. "He doesn't really think that." She looked at Cass and then Bessie again. "I don't know. I like Supper Club, because I get to say and do whatever I want. If Shelby was there…I might not feel like I can do that."

"Something to think about," Bessie said.

Yes, it was, and Bea nodded that she'd do just that.

"Let's talk about Supper Club moving forward," Cass said, just as Bea had hoped she would. "We're taking December off, and Bessie, you're up in September."

"Yes," she said. "I don't mind if we do a half-video call and half-in-person call. I can order dinner and send it to someone's house. Lauren's?"

That sounded good to Bea, and she agreed. She'd just done Supper Club in June, and Cass had done it in July. Joy was doing August, which meant Lauren was in October and Sage in November.

"So we'll just do video calls for now," Cass said. "If one of us is in Texas, we can join in there. If you're here, you can join in here."

"Good plan," Bea said.

"What about next summer?" Lauren asked. "Joy? Are you coming back?"

Joy's jaw hardened and she shrugged. No vocalization meant she'd more than likely be back, and Bea kept her smile to herself. If Sage moved here, and Bessie was already talking to her daughter about the bakery franchise...it was only a matter of time before the six of them would resume their regular in-person Supper Club—in Hilton Head instead of Sweet Water Falls.

The thought brought Bea so much happiness that she almost started weeping again. She contained herself and let Lauren start reading job descriptions from the want ads, as she hated her job and needed a new one already.

Chapter Eighteen

Joy put the perfectly spiced pork loin on the table, enjoying the way the skin still sizzled and the juices ran clear. She'd slice it moments before they ate, and she turned back to the grill. Harrison had taught her how to use this appliance, and she could see why he enjoyed cooking outside so much.

The corn on the cob had a certain char that made her mouth water, and she pulled it from the rack and put it in the pan she'd prepared with melted butter, garlic, salt, and pepper. She rolled it around in there, making room for all the pieces, and then she put it back on the upper rack and closed the lid.

She'd wrapped potatoes in foil and put them on the grill almost an hour ago, and she had toppings on the table already. Shredded cheese, homemade bacon bits, sour cream, butter, ranch dressing, broccoli, and salsa. That last one was for Sage only, as she was the only person Joy had ever met who put salsa on her baked potato.

"We're here," Bessie called, and she, Sage, and Cass came outside from the kitchen. "Wow, this is what we can smell from Cass's house." She smiled at Joy and stepped into her to hug her. "I'm so glad we're going home together." She pressed her forehead to Joy's, and Joy smiled too.

"Me too." She'd had time to think since Beach Day, and while she hated the questions that had been posed to her, she suspected her friends were right. She wouldn't stay in Sweet Water Falls if they were all coming here. They were her support system. They were all she had, and it was just an address.

Her two sons were out of the house, grown, and on their own. She didn't have a tether to Sweet Water Falls anymore, even if Cherry Forrester lived there and Joy liked her a whole lot. She worked in a fourth-grade classroom, and Hilton Head had three elementary schools. There were plenty of jobs here she could get, and if she went back to school and got her teaching certificate, she could teach here instead of helping kids with their undone math homework or working on reading skills two grade levels below them.

She hated this fissure inside her, as well as the love she had for Texas. She'd been right when she'd said she'd never lived anywhere else. She hadn't, and she'd never wanted to.

Bea entered, and she carried a cake pan. "Here's the custard cake," she said proudly.

"I love you," Joy said. "Can we have dessert first?"

Bea laughed and shook her head. "I'm just putting it in

the fridge." She backtracked into the house to do that, and Lauren stepped outside in a pair of cutoffs and a tank top that barely covered her small chest. She looked like she'd just woken up from a nap, and Joy happened to know she had.

She didn't wear shoes, and Hilton Head had relaxed her in a way Joy was extremely happy about. Lauren had always worked too hard, and she'd told Joy that part of her strategy this summer was to find new ways to relax.

"I fell asleep," she said. "You were going to wake me at five-thirty."

"You looked too peaceful," Joy said. "Did the doorbell get you?"

"All the alerts that someone had entered the house." She smiled and looked around. "What do we still need?"

"Nothing," Joy said. Just because Lauren lived here with her didn't mean she had to help with Supper Club. When it was Joy's month back home, no one helped her get the food on the table. "We're ready," she said louder. "Find a seat, and let's get started."

They'd no sooner done that when the sound of a lawn mower filled the air. She met Lauren's eye, and they both looked toward the front of the house. "Seems kind of late for a grass clipping," she said casually.

Joy got to her feet. "I'll go tell him to come back tomorrow." She didn't care that this was Harrison's house. The grass barely needed to be cut, and Scott certainly didn't need to come every blasted week. She hadn't seen him again since that first time, and he hadn't needled her with texts or calls.

She found him coming toward her down the narrow

strip of grass, and his whole face lit up like the sun when he saw her. Unlike Lauren, Joy had gotten ready tonight, and she wore makeup, earrings, and a cute denim jumper that showed off all her best qualities—her larger chest and the waist that narrowed from it.

"Joy," he practically yelled as he cut the engine on the push-mower and removed the sound-canceling headphones he wore. "Good to see you again."

"You're yelling," she said into the sudden silence. "We don't need you to cut the grass. I'm having my Supper Club on the patio, and you're interrupting us." She gestured back the way she'd come, and she glanced that way too. All five of her friends stood at the edge of the patio, smashed into the narrow strip of cement behind the grill. Unbelievable.

She didn't linger on them and looked back at Scott. He was strikingly handsome, and Joy lost her breath for a moment. She'd only felt like this a handful of times in her life, the last time when she'd been thrown from a horse.

He's not that good-looking, she told herself. But she was lying, because with his reddish-brown-blonde hair with those errant blades of grass in it, and those blue eyes...he was male perfection sent from above.

"Can you—?" Her mind misfired as the edges of his eyes crinkled. "Can you come back tomorrow, please?" She wasn't working, as she'd be doing laundry and packing and cleaning up the house before she left the island for good.

"Oh, I don't know," he said in mock seriousness. "I have a full schedule tomorrow." He stepped around the mower and almost reached for her. He seemed to realize what he was doing, and his hand flinched back to his side. "Especially if a woman as beautiful as you will grab coffee with me in the morning before work."

Joy wanted to reach up and pat her hair like he'd just paid her the best compliment in the world. Chester had called her pretty, and while Joy didn't really believe him, it had been nice to hear.

Beautiful was better than *pretty*, and Joy finally allowed herself to smile. She'd found her wits too, and she stepped into Scott and put her palm against his chest. Instant heat shot into her, and her eyes widened. Could he feel that too? The way the ground beneath her feet shook? The way her heartbeat pounded through every cell in her body? The instant crackle of electricity through the atmosphere?

His smile slipped away, and he gazed at her in a brand-new, intense way, and Joy had the distinct feeling that yes, he felt all of that too.

"Honey, if that's your way of asking me out, I don't like it."

"No?" he asked, matching her flirty tone. "Why not?"

"You feel...fake to me, Mister Anderson. Like you're playing a game with me, and once you get your way, you'll toss me aside." She stepped back and dropped her hand. "I don't like that. I'm too old for games."

He swallowed and licked his lips, his eyes dropping to her mouth. Joy wondered if she should just let him have his fun—it could be fun for her too—and be done with it. She immediately rejected the idea, because that wasn't what women Joy's age did. She wasn't interested in a good time without commitment, and Scott Anderson didn't strike her as a man who committed.

"Me too," he said. "No games."

"I'm leaving for Texas on Saturday," she said. "I broke up with my other boyfriend." Why had she said "other," as if Scott were one of them? She gave herself a mental shake. Lauren and Cass were getting to her. "So I don't think coffee in the morning is a good idea."

He nodded, his eyes bright again despite the shade where they stood. "Can I call you? Text you?"

Her eyebrows went up. "While I'm in Texas?"

"Yeah," he said. "While you're in Texas."

She half-expected Lauren to answer for her, but it stayed quiet in the peanut gallery. Joy didn't know what to say to him. Why couldn't he call and text her?

The fact that you'll be separated by six states?

The idea that you and Scott will end before you ever get to go out with him, hold his hand, is terrifying?

Tell him you're not interested in long-distance dating.

But maybe she was.

"Maybe," she said, and then she turned around. "I'll tell Harrison you're going to skip this week."

"I'll come back tomorrow," he said, and Joy smiled to herself as she walked away. She one-hundred percent added some sway to her hips, sending the skirt of her dress flipping and flapping from left to right as she moved.

She rejoined her friends on the patio, and they all stared at her from their proper spots at the table. "What?" she asked. "He's going to come back tomorrow." She took her seat and pulled it up to the table. "Okay, so the pork loin is a honey sriracha."

"You totally flirted with him," Bea said. "You said you two were nothing."

"We are nothing."

"Oh, honey." Bea shook her head. "That was anything but nothing."

Lauren grinned and ducked her head while Bessie nodded emphatically. "He couldn't look away from you," Bessie said. "I was jumping up and down and waving my arms, and nothing."

Joy rolled her eyes. "That's not true."

"She stomped on my foot," Sage said crossly. "It's absolutely true."

She didn't want to tell them that she'd said he could "maybe" call and text her, nor about the breakfast invitation he'd issued. He'd done that before she'd told him about her break-up with Chester, so for all he knew, she was still seeing him.

No, he was cocky and arrogant, yet with a sweet Southern charm that Joy couldn't dismiss only because of his obvious flirting.

"So what?" she asked her friends. Maybe they'd tell her what to do if she phrased it right. "What am I supposed to do about him? I don't live here."

"Just don't close any doors," Cass said. "You have a phone and a computer. I'm willing to bet he does too, and you'll be here next summer." She raised her eyebrows and nodded. "That's all."

"Options open," Lauren said.

"All options open," Bessie agreed.

Joy nodded, because simply leaving her options open sounded like a blueprint she could get on board with. "All right," she said. "Now, can we eat? The pork was perfect, and now it's probably cold."

Chapter Nineteen

Blake looked up from his phone as Tommy came out of the dressing room. His grin said everything it needed to about the burnt orange shorts he wore. "These are so cool, Dad." He put his hands in his pockets and struck a pose while Blake grinned and got to his feet.

"Finally," he said. "One winner." He'd brought his son school shopping today because Tommy had refused to go with his mother. She'd tried buying him a few things online that he'd then deemed "grotesque," and he'd called Blake.

They'd gotten lunch on the way to Charleston, and they'd found plenty of winners already. T-shirts. A couple of button-up shirts that made Tommy look more grown up than Blake liked—or than he actually was. His son wasn't tripping nearly as much lately, but he was still goofy and gangly. Just the way Blake liked him.

"Let me see what other colors they have. Do you like gray? Khaki?"

"Black if they have them," Tommy said. "They're a thirty, Dad."

"Yep." Blake knew how skinny his son was. Tall, skinny, and strong, that was Tommy. Jacinda had texted to say he'd asked her to start calling him Tom instead of Tommy, but Blake hadn't heard that request yet. He was going to keep doing what he did until his son asked him to do something different.

He pulled a black pair and a light gray pair of shorts off the rack in the right size, and he went back to the dressing room. Tommy had tossed the burnt orange pair over the top of the door, and he snagged those too. "I'm going to go buy these," he said. "Then we'll head down to the shoe store."

"Maybe they'll have athletic shorts that don't cling," Tommy called back.

"Maybe." Blake would be surprised if they didn't, and he'd just tucked his card back into his wallet when his son joined him at the cash register. He looked at his boy and grinned. "You've got lots of shirts now. New shorts. Pants? Jeans?"

Tommy made a face. "I hate wearing pants."

"Same." Blake led the way out of the store, and they went to the mecca of shops for men: the athletic shoe store, Birmingham's. Blake stepped inside and just took a deep breath. Leather, cotton, and perfection, that was what he got.

He gazed around, his smile seemingly permanently etched on his face. The business casual shoes sat near the front, with the basketball shoes, running shoes, and other athletic gear near the back. Blake loved shoes, everything about them, and as he wore a pair of slacks and a tie to work every day, he had a reason to buy the fancy dress shoes in the front of the store.

"Come on, Dad," Tommy said, and Blake tore his gaze from a gorgeous pair of almost red leather shoes with intricate designs carved into them.

He followed his son back to the further half of the store, and he leafed through a rack of silky basketball shorts while Tommy beelined for the shoes. "Try them both on," he called after him, and he pulled a size medium short from the rack in a royal blue. It wasn't quite the same hue as North Carolina—too dark—but Tommy loved watching them play basketball every year. Blake did too.

He took those with him toward the shoe aisle where his son stood, bent over trying to find the right size. He held another box already, and Blake reached for it.

"Look at these sick yellow ones," Tommy said, and Blake wondered when the bright colors had become so popular. He found them a bit garish, though he did like the white high-tops with light pink and blue only a couple of feet away.

He'd never wear something like that—at least he couldn't think of a situation where he would—but he did like them. Tommy picked out four pairs of shoes before he retreated to a metal bench to try them on.

Blake had a feeling he'd like all of them if they were the right size, and sure enough, by the time he'd put on each pair, both shoes, and walked around in them, three of the four pairs sat in the "buy" pile. He looked at them, and he looked at his son's hopeful face.

"You can get two pairs," he said. "You have to eliminate one."

Tommy nodded, his smile huge. "Thanks, Dad." He plucked out the pair of matte brown leather ones and moved them to the "not buying" pile. Blake picked up the two boxes and turned toward the shorts again.

"Did you need to try those on?" he asked.

Tommy held them up to his body. "I think they're fine." He hated trying on clothes, and Blake would be lucky if he got him into another changing room.

"Socks?"

"Yeah, I need socks."

Birmingham's always had a BOGO sale on socks, and Blake ended up getting a few new pairs too. With the big black bag filled with the two pairs of shoes, three pairs of athletic shorts, and dozens of socks, Blake looked at his son.

"Are we done?"

"Hats?" Tommy asked, his eyes once again round and hopeful. "Urban Economy has the coolest snapbacks you've ever seen."

"You're down to fifty bucks," Blake said, making up the number on the spot.

Tommy grinned and said, "It's over by where we parked."

The only good thing about shopping in Charleston was the fact that Tommy didn't run into someone he knew every five feet. Not that the boy had dozens of friends, but Carter's

Cove was a small community. All of the kids knew one another, and Blake didn't like watching Tommy either shrink from the teens he knew and didn't like or take forever to get through buying candy bars and ice cream because he saw ten people he wanted to talk to.

At Urban Economy, Tommy found half a dozen hats that he liked, and he whittled it down to three, as they were having a three-four-five sale, and forty-five dollars came under his fifty-dollar limit.

"Thanks, Dad," he said as they paid for the hats.

"None of those are porn?" he asked for the third time. He looked from Tommy to the clerk, who glanced up from the credit card machine. He shook his head, and Blake nodded to the twenty-something.

"Dad." Tommy scoffed and turned away. "You're so embarrassing."

Blake grinned, signed his name on the receipt, and picked up the bag of snapback hats. "Thanks, man."

The other guy grinned and held out his fist. "You're a good dad."

Blake bumped his fist to the clerk's and said, "Thanks," before turning to follow his son back out into the main halls of the mall. Tommy looked at him with wariness and semi-disgust, and then rolled his eyes.

"What?" Blake asked. "I don't know what's what. You got a hat with a Sasquatch on it and seemed like it was the greatest thing in the world. How do I know what that means?"

"It's from a TV show," he said. "Not porn. Jeez."

“Again, I don’t know that. It’s my job to ask.” He handed his son the hats. “You carry the non-porn hats then.” He grinned, but Tommy only rolled his eyes again. “Home?” he asked as they pushed out of the doors of the mall and back into the muggy heat.

“Yeah,” Tommy said. “Can we go to the beach?”

“Do I ever say no to the beach?” Blake gave his son a smile. “I do have one condition this time.”

His son gazed at him. “A condition?”

“I need to know who that girl was you held hands with a couple of weeks ago.” He deliberately wouldn't look at his son. “The first time Lauren came with us.”

“Oh, uh, let’s see...” Tommy acted like he didn’t know the girl’s name, and that certainly didn’t settle Blake’s gut.

“You hold hands with so many random girls on the beach, you’ve forgotten her name?”

“No,” Tommy bit out. “Her name is Kathy. She’s, uh, older than me by a few years, and I don’t know. We talk.”

Blake wanted to keep it cool, and he remembered Lauren’s palm against his chest. He wanted his son to talk to him. “Talk about what?”

“Her mom, sometimes,” Tommy said. “Her dad was killed in the military a couple of years ago, and they’ve had a hard time.”

“Oh, that’s too bad.”

“Yeah,” Tommy said. He fell into silence then, and if Blake wanted more from him, he’d have to prompt him. He let the conversation fade, because Tommy hadn’t turned bright red, and they’d talked about girls before.

"Do you want to invite her to the beach?"

"No," Tommy said. "If she's there, she's there. I have her number."

"Oh, you do?" Blake grinned at his son then.

Tommy grinned back, his face remaining perfectly happy as he asked, "Are you going to invite Lauren?"

Surprise filled Blake. "Should I?"

"Dad, I told you to have her over while I'm here on the weekends. You don't need to hide her from me."

"I'm not hiding her from you."

"I mean, Cason lives with us," he said. "Mom doesn't seem to care at all." He carried something strange in his tone, and Blake studied the side of his face, trying to figure out what he meant by that.

"Son," he said. "I'm not hiding Lauren from you, or you from her." They reached his SUV, and he clicked the key fob to get the back open. "I value my time with you, and I don't get to see you much. Even less now that school's about to start. I didn't want you to feel like you have to compete with her for my attention." He put the bags he carried inside, then stepped out of the way so Tommy could load in all he held in his hands.

Their eyes met once the purchases had been placed inside, and Blake raised his eyebrows. He'd let the other conversation end on his son's terms, but this one needed to continue. "I need a response here."

"Dad, I know you love me," he said.

"Your mother loves you too," he said quickly.

"Cason's moved a lot of his stuff into Mom's bath bomb

studio," he said. "So she started storing some of her bins in my room." He mumbled the last few words and started around the car to the passenger side.

Blake blinked for a couple of seconds, then reached to close the back and went to get behind the wheel. He couldn't believe Jacinda would displace their son from his bedroom. They'd lived in that house for a decade, and yes, it was small. Most houses on Carter's Cove were. Cason had only moved in, oh, Blake couldn't remember. Within the last year, he knew that.

He got behind the wheel and glanced over to Tommy, who now had his arms folded, his gaze stuck out the side window. Blake started the car, his mind spinning. "Son, this is one of those times you're going to have to tell me everything," he said slowly and carefully, trying not to scare away the frightened teen.

"I just feel...I feel like he's taking over the house," Tommy said. "And Mom doesn't have anywhere to expand but my room, and I'm not always there, so why not store a few bins in my room, you know?"

"But it's your room." Blake backed out of the parking spot, and since they'd already eaten, they only needed to drive south to Hilton Head. "She has a studio in her shop. She shouldn't need to store anything in there."

He'd talk to her about getting a shed if she really needed it. She had a little backyard with a nice deck that stayed shaded in the hottest parts of the afternoon and evening.

"I feel like maybe I'm a nuisance to her," Tommy muttered.

Blake swallowed. He had an open relationship with Jacinda, and she'd likely be horrified to know her son felt this way. He didn't want to tell her, but he couldn't keep it to himself either. "Do I make you feel like that?"

"That's my point," Tommy said. "No, you don't. I know you like Lauren, and I actually like her too. So if you want to invite her, don't not do it because of me." He frowned and looked over to Blake. "Does that even make sense. Don't not do it...?" He sighed. "I'm saying, invite her. You don't have to think you can't because I'm around. That's the last thing I want, actually."

"Great," Blake said coolly. "I'll call her right now and see if she can meet us at the beach."

"She told me about her new house," Tommy said. "Has she moved in yet?"

Blake's eyebrows show up. "She told you about her new house? When?" Lauren had only gotten the house about a week and a half ago. As far as he knew, she hadn't seen Tommy in person since then.

"She has my number, Dad," he said. "She texts me sometimes."

"She does?" This was news to him, and Blake honestly wasn't sure how he felt about it. "Can I see the texts?"

"Sure." Tommy started swiping. "Do you want me to read them to you?"

"Yep."

"She's only texted a few times, and she first asked me the name of that game I was playing with Ryan. I told her it was SquareSpaces, and she acknowledged that. Then she asked for the name of Ryan's uncle's chocolate shop, and I had to text him to get it, and then I sent that to her. Then nothing for a little bit. I sent her a meme about making the drive into Charleston when you told me she started her job there."

Blake looked over to his son, surprised he'd done that. It wasn't only Lauren making the connection between them, and he really liked that.

"Then she told me that she'd bought a new house, and it was 'so cute' and she sent me a picture of it." He turned his phone toward Blake, but he couldn't look at it for long, as the light turned green in front of him, and he had to drive.

"I can invite her," Tommy said, pitching up the last word into a question.

"Sure." Blake swallowed. "Tell her we're at least two hours away. We have to drive home, take everything inside, and then get packed up."

"Yep," Tommy said, and he sounded just like Blake. His thumbs flew across the screen, and he looked up only a few seconds later. It didn't take Lauren long to respond, and he read, "She said, Just let me know where, and I'll meet you."

"We can just go pick her up," Blake said. "We could go to Harrison's private beach." He looked over to Tommy, who clearly didn't like that idea by the sour look on his face. "Or not. I guess Kathy won't be there."

Tommy rolled his eyes, and Blake chuckled. "Tell her we'll text her where when we decide. You like Library Downs the most, but it's Saturday and it'll be packed. We'd be better to go to Lighthouse Point or just somewhere along the highway."

"I hate the highway beaches," Tommy complained. "It's noisy, and the waves aren't good for body surfing."

"All right," Blake said. "Pick one then. I don't care."

"There's three of us," he said, his fingers tapping away on his phone. "We'll be able to find a place at Library Downs. It's a huge beach."

Blake repressed his sigh, because his son was right and he didn't truly care where they went to hang out for the afternoon. He was just glad Tommy would be out of the house, off the video games until tonight. He was getting better at body surfing, but by the number of texts he received and sent, he was inviting more than Lauren to stop by the beach.

Blake told himself that was fine. He wanted his son to have friends, and he'd rather know who they were than be kept in the dark. His mind wandered to Lauren and what her swimming suit would look like today. She'd once told him that she owned several, though she never really got any of them wet.

She liked hot tubs, not lakes, the ocean, or pools, and of course, a suit was the lightest, coolest garment to wear at the beach—according to her. Blake smiled just thinking about her, and he couldn't wait to ask her how the job search was going, and how she'd fared for the first full week in Harrison's house alone now that Joy had returned to Sweet Water Falls.

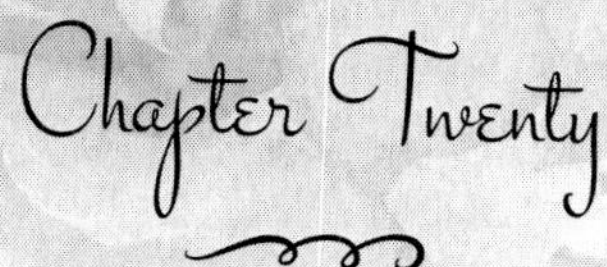

Chapter Twenty

Lauren couldn't stop herself from driving through On The Rocks and getting drinks for herself, Blake, and Tommy. Then she stopped at a Lowcountry store and dashed inside to grab some candy. She simply couldn't go to the beach without licorice, sour gummy worms, or chips. Or apparently, all three.

Tommy's favorite candy was a caramel Twix bar, and she got a king sized one. Blake would have a cooler, and she could put it in there until the teenager came in from his boogie boarding. She saw a Frisbee by the checkout counter, and she grabbed it while she waited for the person in front of her to finish up.

She bought everything and headed to Library Downs, which was where Blake and Tommy seemed to always end up. This time, Blake had said he'd text her when they had a spot, because it was really crowded today.

Lauren saw what he meant, as she couldn't find a

parking spot in the public pay lot. She started driving up and down the residential streets, but they all had "no beach parking" signs posted. Frustration tickled the back of her throat, and she made the circle again.

This time, a small sedan was leaving the pay lot, and Lauren put her blinker on and waited. And waited. And waited. The man seemed to simply be texting on his phone, and the stubbornness inside Lauren refused to leave. She stared at the man and his wife sitting in the passenger seat like they had nowhere else in the world to be, like there weren't at least a dozen cars trolling this lot looking for a spot.

He finally pulled out, and Lauren took the space. She wasn't sure which beach Blake had ended up on, but she'd learned they weren't that far apart. She could walk for a couple hundred yards and go from beach four to beach five, so she simply started putting all of her purchases into her beach bag. She'd shoulder that, carry the chair over her forearm, and then support the drinks with her other hand.

Beach three, Blake finally said. *It's insane here. I tried to get Tommy to go somewhere else, but I think he invited that girl he was holding hands with last time, so that was a no-go.*

Lauren was actually close to beach three, and she responded with a quick affirmative, and got out of the car. She soon learned that it wouldn't be as easy to spot them as it had been last time. The sheer number of people made her want to turn around and go right back to the car. She had a private beach off the steps of the house where she lived.

She'd been out there sipping her morning coffee a few hours ago, and she hadn't seen a single soul.

On this last Saturday before school started here on the island, it sure seemed like every man, woman, and child felt the need to get one more day of sun, sand, and surf. She didn't get that. They lived here. They could literally come next weekend too. It wasn't like it would be cold or the kids would have school.

It was probably thirty yards from ocean to the grasses that grew at the back of the sandy beach, and Lauren couldn't possibly wander around, searching under every umbrella for Blake and Tommy. She dialed him and put down her beach chair, resting it against her thigh, as the phone rang.

"Howdy, sweetheart," he drawled, and Lauren's chest caved in. She craved his touch when she felt hollow like this. She hadn't seen him enough this week, and she wasn't even sure why.

She told herself that wasn't true—she knew why. She'd disappeared inside herself again, because Joy had left the island. Lauren lived in that huge house alone now, and she couldn't wait to move into her new, smaller house.

"I'm on beach three," she said. "But it's going to be impossible for me to find you."

"Where you at?" he asked, and she recognized the Southern slang. It made her smile, and she glanced up to the lifeguard tower.

"I parked in the public lot by the big lifeguard tower."

"I'll come grab you," he said.

"Good," she said. "Because I have too much stuff to carry very far."

"You went to the Lowcountry again, didn't you?"

"It's not a crime to have candy at the beach." Lauren saw a family several feet away who'd brought a freaking grill and were serving hot dogs from it. She couldn't even imagine having a family who gathered at the beach for a Saturday afternoon shindig such as these people did. Her heart felt hollow now, and she didn't understand family as she saw it in front of her on a deep, fundamental level.

Her phone beeped, and she realized Blake had probably said something and ended the call. She lowered her device and tucked it back into her bag, then set it down on the sand too. No need to work so hard if she didn't have to.

It took a few minutes before Blake called her name, and she turned toward him, the three drinks in her hand. He took them in, his smile instant. He jogged barefoot through the last several yards of sand and said, "Wow, look at you."

"I've worn this coverup before," she said, glancing down at the wispy white thing.

"Uh, nope." He ran his hands from her shoulders down to her elbows and took the drink carrier with the three pops in it. "I would remember this."

She also wore a little black bikini, and she knew he could see it through the gauzy fabric of the coverup. It also barely brushed the tops of her thighs, and she sure did like the way his gaze heated as he stared at her.

"You're staring," she teased, and he blinked.

He never wore sunglasses at the beach, and his hair

looked like he'd already dipped himself in the ocean and then ran his hands through it. It wasn't wet though, and neither were his board shorts. He didn't wear a shirt, so they'd been here long enough for him to strip and probably spray his son with sunscreen.

Lauren found herself staring now, and it wasn't until Blake took the chair leaning against her leg that she realized he'd moved. "Talk about staring," he whispered in her ear.

She grabbed onto his bicep with one hand, the heat between them intense. "Kiss me," she said, her voice grinding and growly in her own ears.

Blake obliged, and Lauren couldn't control the pace of it. She accelerated it instantly, and thankfully, Blake knew how to handle her. It wasn't a long kiss, something she didn't choose, but was grateful for when he pulled back and she opened her eyes to see how many people surrounded them.

"Come on, sweetheart," he said, no teasing in his tone now. "Can you get your bag?"

She bent to collect the straps, and she shouldered it and followed him through a messy maze of people to the spot he and Tommy had found. There was room for her, and there was space around them, even though it felt like people were right on top of them.

"You got the Summer Lovin'," Tommy said, grinning. He took his soda pop from the drink carrier his dad held. "Thank you, Lauren."

"Sure thing," she said. "Thanks for inviting me."

"Did you watch that video I sent?" he asked.

Lauren had, so she nodded. She'd had no idea what she'd watched though. "I did," she said. "Pretty amazing how the Loriats got that dragon at the end."

Tommy blinked, so Lauren knew she'd gotten something wrong. She frowned and then smiled. "Wasn't that good? The announcers seemed pretty amazed by it."

"It was a cool kill," Tommy said. "But they still lost."

"Oh." Lauren trilled out a laugh. "I honestly wasn't sure who'd won. That one announcer was screaming about the dragon, so I thought it was good."

Tommy laughed too and took a long pull on his drink. He had been in the ocean, as he dripped water from the ends of his hair. "It was a mega-kill," he said. "The whole screen flashed. That would be awesome to see in the gaming arena."

"We're not talking about SquareSpaces all day today," Blake said, and Lauren glanced up at him. "Rule number one."

"What's rule number two?" Lauren asked, grinning at him with all she had.

He gave her a withering look and turned back to Tommy. "You check in with me every fifteen minutes. There are fifty million people here today, and I can't see the water from here."

"Yes, sir," Tommy said.

Blake looked at Lauren. "Rule three, we want to hear about your job hunt, as well as when you can move into your new place, so you can't just be flirty today."

"Wow," she said. "I thought this was going to be fun."

"It will be fun." Blake sat in his chair, and it wasn't one

of the beach loungers like hers, so he hovered above her. "We just have to have a couple of rules to keep everyone safe."

"I don't see how me not talking about SquareSpaces has anything to do with safety," Tommy said, grinning.

"It does if you want to live," Blakes said. "Otherwise, I might kill you." He raised his eyebrows. "Does that make it a safety rule for you?"

The smile slid from Tommy's face. "Yes, sir." He took another drink, shifted his cup around in the sand until it stood up on its own, and said, "I'm going back in the water. I'll check in in fifteen minutes."

"Thank you," Blake said. "Watch out for girls!"

Tommy didn't look back, and Lauren watched him disappear around an umbrella a few yards in front of them. She looked over to Blake and wrapped her own lips around the bright blue straw of her soda pop. "I can't be flirty?"

"Not when I'm trying to be serious," he said. He looked left and right. "I hate this beach when it's like this. He just *had* to come here."

"Oh, so you're in a bad mood."

"I'm allowed to be in a bad mood," he said.

Yes, he was, and Lauren didn't say anything else about it. She got out her gummy worms, and she'd only taken one bite of the first one before Blake reached over and took her hand in his. "I'm glad you're here," he said, his voice much softer now.

She pushed her sunglasses up, because she didn't really need them in the shade. She carefully undid a couple of buttons on her coverup and pushed it off her shoulders, revealing the sexy black straps of her swimming suit top. "Me too," she said with a sigh. She leaned back in her chair and stretched her legs out in front of her. "It's kind of loud with all the people, but I don't hate it." She turned her head and smiled up at him. "It kind of mixes in with the waves."

He smiled back at her. "I really do want to hear about your job hunt, and I'm going to be totally available on the day you move into your new place."

She nodded, her smile turning soft as his did. "I think I'm going to quit my job," she said. "And start an online marketing consultation business." The idea had been mulling in her head for a few weeks now—ever since her first commute from Hilton Head to Charleston, a drive she hated—and she'd been working on a few things to get it off the ground.

"I have a lot of experience in corporate marketing," she said. "I can take that to small businesses looking to level up or grow. I can do it from home. I can meet online, via video, or travel if I need to."

"Yes, I think you could do all of that."

"I can work when I want," she said, tasting the freedom of the words as she said them. "I think it's a really good strategy for me right now."

"You're always talking strategy," he teased.

Lauren nodded and looked back. She could see the sky beyond the edge of the umbrella, and she closed her eyes. "My seaside strategy was to come here and find myself," she said quietly. "Relax. Figure out what I want. I've got this great boyfriend." She squeezed his hand and smiled, but she kept her eyes closed.

She could almost hear the breeze beyond the mishmash of voices, dogs barking, people calling to each other, and the ocean roaring down the beach. "I'm moving into a fabulous new house in only two weeks, and I have enough savings to tide me over while I start this new business."

Lauren turned toward him again. "In fact, I already put in my notice at my job. Only two more weeks of that too, and then I'm going to start implementing the pieces of my plan."

"What about the house in Texas?" he asked.

"I'm going there next week," she said. "To list it. See what else I want from it. I'm going to have a yard sale on Saturday. Then...then, I'll be back here for good."

He tugged on her hand, but Lauren didn't know what he wanted. She looked at him, and he said, "Come sit with me," in a needy, quiet voice.

Oh, she liked the idea of that, and she stood, her cover-up slipping further down her chest as she did. She didn't bother to adjust it as she took her place on his lap, his hands sliding up under the sheer white fabric and settling on her bare waist. "Mm, you're sexy," he whispered.

She bent down and kissed him, and she liked being higher than him. She felt on top of the world in that moment, but she reminded herself that they were on a public beach—a very, very busy public beach.

He knew it too, and he didn't take the kiss too far. He

pulled away and sighed, and Lauren laid her head on his shoulder. "I sure like Tommy," she admitted.

"I didn't know you'd gotten his number," Blake said.

"Yeah," she said, somewhat surprised. "I thought he told you."

Blake shook his head. "I don't mind; I was just surprised when he told me this afternoon."

"Shopping went well?"

"Good enough," Blake said. "Yeah."

Lauren had always wondered what couples did on a day-to-day basis. Breakfast, lunch, dinner, the beach? Homework and checking up on family members and friends. It had all once felt so boring to her.

Now, sitting with Blake on the beach, on an ordinary Saturday, just talking, it felt like pure perfection to her. She realized life didn't have to be fireworks and events all the time. It could be slow, and subtle, and relaxing, and still be good.

"I've been thinking," she said quietly. "That I need to call Jess and tell him I'm leaving Texas."

Blake perked up then, because Lauren never talked about her family. "Yeah," he said. "That's probably a good idea."

She knew it was a good idea, and yet, she hadn't done it yet. "I don't know how to talk to him," she said. She tore her gaze from the couple packing up their belongings. "Would you, I mean...maybe I could meet your family, and then I'll see how it's done."

"Lauren." Blake shook his head, and Lauren looked

away again. He brought her face back to his gently. "You know how it's done, but I'd love for you to officially meet my momma as my girlfriend, as well as my siblings. Peter and Lindsey are going to love you."

He touched his lips to hers again, and he might as well have said, *Just like I do*. Or maybe Lauren was imaging that part.

"I'm alive," Tommy said, and she looked over to him with a smile. He did spray water everywhere as he bent to get his towel. "Dad, Kathy is here. She's down about thirty feet that way." He pointed to the left. "Can I go hang out over there?"

Blake shifted beneath Lauren, almost like he'd get up with her on his lap. "I don't know," he said. "I can't see over there."

"I'm not five years old," Tommy said.

"Maybe," Lauren said as Blake prepped to say something else. "We can meet her and anyone she's with first." She looked from Tommy's surprised and horrified expression to Blake, who seemed quite happy with her suggestion. "Then, we'll know who you're with, and you can show your dad—or me—where, so we can come get you if we need to."

She let her words hang there, waiting for one of them to agree or disagree.

Chapter Twenty-One

Blake wasn't sure how to answer Lauren. He wasn't sure he liked *her* taking charge of the situation with his kid. He watched Tommy for his reaction, but his kid looked at him to take the lead.

"I'm down with that," he finally said. The tension in their patch of shade leaked away, and until it did, Blake hadn't even realized how high it had been.

Tommy blew out his breath. "All right. I'll go talk to them."

Lauren vacated his lap as Tommy left, and Blake looked up at her. She pulled her cover-up back into position on her shoulders, buttoned it, and fixed her sun hat before she retook her seat.

"Have you ever dated someone with kids?" he asked.

She swung her attention to him, a bag of candy in her hands. "No."

He nodded, his throat somewhat tight.

"You didn't like me interfering with your parenting."

"It wasn't that I didn't like it," he said. But he hadn't loved it. "I don't know how I feel about it."

"What don't you like about me talking to Tommy?" she asked. "I told you I didn't want to be an unknown stepmother. That requires me to talk to him and become someone he learns to trust."

Blake nodded, because all of that sounded really good on paper. "I don't know," he admitted. "I need to think more about it."

"I'm sorry." She reached over and covered his hand with hers. "Really. If you think I overstepped, I'm sorry."

"It's not overstepping," he said. "It's just...I think honestly, I'm already a little annoyed with him, because he's starting school on Tuesday, and our summer is over, and he's off with his friends?" He shook his head, unable to articulate it.

"You miss him already."

Blake just nodded, his heart too big in his chest. So big, it crowded into his throat.

"He's growing up," Lauren said.

Blake took a drink of his soda pop, enjoying the burn that slid down his throat. "That he is."

His son came back into view, and Blake pushed to his feet. Tommy held Kathy's hand right there in front of him, and they led a group of three other teens.

"This is my dad," Tommy said. "Blake; and his girlfriend, Lauren." Tommy gave his dad the briefest of smiles and looked at Lauren as she stood too.

"Nice to meet you," Blake said. He didn't want to embarrass his son in front of his friends, because most of them lived on Carter's Cove, not here.

"Howdy," he said as he extended his hand—and Tommy cringed. He looked at his son. "What's your name?" he asked rather pointedly, and Tommy flinched.

"Oh, uh, this is Kathy—uh—Baker." His face flamed red, and Blake couldn't wait to ask him if he knew the girl's last name or not. "And her brother, Luke. Then their cousin, Jacob, and another friend I just met today. Uh..."

"Rob," Jacob said. "He lives by me."

"Great to meet you all," Blake said. He shook Kathy's hand, then all the boys with them. Lauren did the same, and Blake stepped out of the shade.

"Show me where you'll be, son, and then we'll leave you alone."

"My mom dropped us off," Kathy said. "She's gonna come back though. She just ran to get fried chicken." She smiled at Blake, and he could see why his son was enamored with her.

"That's great," he said. "We'll be here a while. I just want to know where he is, since there's so many people."

"Oh, for sure," she said.

"How old are you, Kathy?" he asked.

"Fifteen, sir," she said. "Luke's just about to turn thirteen. He met Tommy on SquareSpaces, and they figured out they lived on Hilton Head together."

"Tommy's on Carter's Cove," Blake said.

"Dad," Tommy said.

He swung his attention to his son. "What? You are, especially now that school is starting up again."

"But I live here with you too."

"Also true," Blake said, realizing he'd put his foot in his mouth. "He comes whenever he wants, actually." He gave his son a smile.

"We're right here, sir." Kathy indicated a patch of multicolored beach towels, a small cooler, and an assortment of T-shirts that had been discarded.

"We're gonna play spikeball," Luke said. "Right, Tommy?"

"Yeah, right." He dropped Kathy's hand and walked over to the black mesh bag holding the game.

"Okay, well, we're right over there." He and Lauren would be maybe fifty feet away, and if everyone would clear out and go home, he could spy on his son easily.

He looked at Tommy and muttered, "Don't hurt yourself, okay? You start school in three days, and you don't want to do it on crutches."

"I got it, Dad," he mumbled, his face burning a little redder than normal.

Blake went back to Lauren, who now held a Frisbee in her hand. He cocked one eyebrow at it and stayed in the sunshine. "What are you doin' with that?"

"I bought it at the Lowcountry," she said. Her smile tickled his hormones in all the right ways. Or maybe that was the black bikini that shown like a neon sign beneath her cover-up. "Have you ever tossed one of these around with your friends?"

"Have you?"

"Nope." She popped the P, her grin playful and flirty now.

"Well, you *throw* a Frisbee," Blake said. "You *toss* a football." He ducked under the umbrella. "If we're gonna be out in the sun, I need to spray myself first." He did that, and then he snatched the Frisbee from her. "Let's go."

He jogged away from their spot and down to the hard-packed sand. He positioned himself so he could see Tommy and his new friends, and he waited for Lauren to join him. She stood too far away, but Blake had thrown a Frisbee before, and he had no problem gliding it toward her.

She got nowhere near catching it, and while she wasn't particularly athletic, she was graceful. She came toward him and picked up the disc, then threw it about as hard as she could.

He laughed when it went zipping straight out into the ocean, and he looked at Lauren, with double hands clasped over her mouth. She wasn't going to go get the Frisbee, that was for dang sure.

Blake high-stepped it out into the water, collected the floating red thing, and threw it back to her. Water droplets whisked off of it as it went, and she held out two hands and clapped them together in sheer desperation. She had her eyes closed and everything.

He hadn't stopped laughing over her throw, and watching her try to catch was even more hilarious. "Honey," he said as he left the ocean. "I don't think this is for you."

He looked up the beach to where the kids were, and he

found the four boys playing spikeball. Kathy lay on a towel, her phone held above her in the air.

Her mother hadn't arrived yet, and Blake's mental alarm started ringing. Then Lauren arrived and she slapped the plastic disc against his chest.

"Ow." He placed both hands over it to keep her from pulling it back and swatting him again with it. He grinned at her. "Frisbee's not your sport, sweetheart."

"I don't have a sport," she said. "Unless getting dressed up right for the beach counts."

He was aware of where they stood, so he didn't wrap her up and kiss her in front of literally thousands of beach-goers. "What about walking?" he asked. "Do you do that on the beach?"

"Sure." She laced her fingers through his, and he tucked the Frisbee into the back of his board shorts. He cast a look at Tommy, wondering if he needed to let his son know where he was going. "I don't have my phone," he said.

"I do." She looked over to him, her eyes barely visible through her sunglass lenses.

"Will you text Tommy and let him know we're going for a walk?"

"Yep." She did that, and Blake took her hand when she finished. He could kiss that in front of others, so he did. They started down the beach, and Blake once again checked for Kathy's mom.

"You know," he said. "I don't think Kathy's mom is coming back with fried chicken."

Lauren looked up the beach and slightly back over her shoulder. "Maybe not."

"Why would she lie to me?" Blake asked, a sour pit opening in his stomach. "I didn't even ask about her mom."

"Maybe she was nervous," Lauren said. "You make women nervous."

He rolled his eyes. "She's fifteen."

"And your son's girlfriend," she said.

"I'm just saying, I don't make her nervous for the same reason I make you nervous."

"Who says you make me nervous?" She gave him a high-flirt smile, and Blake grinned at her.

"You know I can pick you up and haul you into the ocean, right?" He tightened his grip on her fingers, and her eyes widened as she tried to pull her hand away and couldn't.

"Blake Williams, I will never talk to you again," she said. "This is my *gauze* cover-up."

"I don't know what that means," he said. "It's sexy, though."

"It isn't meant to get wet."

"Maybe you should take it off." He lifted his eyebrows, and she looked away from him.

"Why?" she asked. "You can see through it."

Blake chose not to answer, and instead he enjoyed the sun on his back and the wind in his hair as he walked this beautiful beach with the world's most beautiful woman. They walked for several long minutes, and then Lauren wanted to turn back.

He happily obliged, and by the time they got back to

their section of the beach, he expected to see Kathy and Luke's mom. After all, he and Lauren had been gone for at least a half-hour, and it didn't take that long to get fried chicken.

She wasn't there. In fact, the spikeball had been left out, and none of the kids were there. Blake's heartbeat picked up speed, and he immediately turned toward the water. His adrenaline cooled when he found Tommy there, laughing and splashing with the other teens.

They shouted to one another, and he frowned at the crude and foul language they used. "I don't like this," he murmured, his dad-radar going off strongly now.

"What?" Lauren asked.

He turned toward her. "These new friends of Tommy's. They don't seem like...him." He watched his son for another few moments, and he never heard him curse. But the kids he was hanging out with did, and Blake had never known his friends to do that.

He's growing up, he thought, but something inside him told him it was more than that. What, though, Blake didn't know.

"I'M JUST ASKING," BLAKE SAID. "I'M NOT accusing you of anything." He really didn't want to be having this conversation with Jacinda at all. He, Lauren, and Tommy had been back from the beach for a couple of hours now.

He'd ordered pizza while Tommy had showered and then said he was going to "run down to Ryan's for a minute," and Lauren currently sat on his couch on her phone, talking to Joy. He'd stepped into his bedroom to call his ex and ask her about Tommy.

"He didn't say anything about the bins bothering him," she said. "They're under his bed, Blake. How can they bother him?"

"I think he feels like he doesn't have a space," Blake said. He sat on the edge of the bed and rubbed the stubble on his face. He needed to shave before his meeting on Monday morning, and he couldn't believe he was thinking about this right now. "I think he's feeling like he's in your way."

Jacinda sighed; she didn't deny it. Blake didn't know what to make of that, and his mind shouted at him to ask about Tommy's friends.

"We got all of his clothes," he said instead.

"Great," Jacinda said. "Thanks for doing that. My orders have been insane."

"I'm glad it's going well," Blake said. "Has he said anything about a girlfriend?"

"No." Jacinda drew out the word. "He has a girlfriend?"

"Yes," Blake said. "She...she lied to me today. She said her mother was coming, and she never came." He looked up and watched the door, though it was closed, and no one would come in without knocking. "He's got these new friends here, and I'm not sure about them."

"He hasn't said anything about new friends or a girlfriend." She paused for a moment. "He hasn't been hanging out with Gwen very much either…" She sounded like she was just now connecting the dots.

"Blake," she said next.

"Yeah?"

"What do you think about having him come to live with you?"

He blinked, not sure how this conversation had gotten there so quickly. "I've been thinking the same thing," he said. "He'll likely want to stay at one high school." That didn't start until next year, so the decision didn't have to be made right now. "I don't know, Jace. School starts in three days. He's registered for his classes already. He's not going to want to move in a week or two."

"It's something we need to perhaps start talking to him about." She sighed. "I'm sorry about the bins. I'll move them out and make sure he knows he has a space here."

"He'll be mad I mentioned it to you," he said.

"I won't make it a big deal."

"Thanks," Blake said. His doorbell rang, and he wasn't sure Lauren would answer it. Knowing her, she would. The woman wasn't afraid of anything, and Blake sure did like her nerve and her strength. "I have to go. Dinner's here."

"Yep, we'll talk soon."

The call ended as Blake opened the door and went into the hall. He rounded the corner and found Lauren standing there. "I'll check," she said, turning back to him.

He thought he'd find the pizza boy standing there, holding their dinner. It wasn't anyone like that, but Ryan

Shaffer from down the street. Lauren wore concern in her eyes. “Is Tommy here? I thought he...”

Blake came to a stop. “He went to Ryan’s.”

But he obviously hadn’t gone to Ryan’s. So where was he?

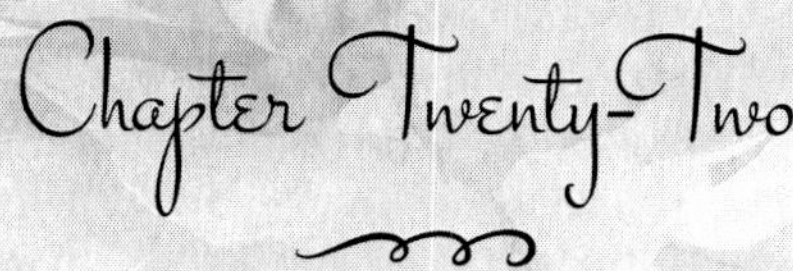

Chapter Twenty-Two

Lauren kissed Blake and said, "It's fine. I have dinner. Cass said Harrison is at a City Council meeting for some zoning issue, and she's waiting for me at her house."

Blake said nothing, which meant the words were piling up inside him. Lauren guided his eyes back to hers. His glare was being wasted on Tommy, who'd put his head down on the table and turned his face away from the front door, from his father.

"Call me later?"

He nodded and finally *saw* her. "I'll call you."

She gave him a smile and touched her lips to his again. He did kiss her back this time, and Lauren took her box of half a pizza and ducked out the front door. Blake had called Tommy three times before his son had answered and said he was on his way home.

Blake hadn't let Ryan leave, and the moment Tommy had rolled up on his bike and seen the boy he was supposed to be with, the tension had spilled out. Blake was not happy. Tommy wasn't happy. Ryan was finally dismissed, and Lauren had taken the pizza when it had come, quietly separated a few pieces for herself, and said she'd catch up with the two of them later.

She really wanted to stay and make sure Blake was okay. She really wanted to stay and make sure Tommy was okay. Her maternal instincts for the boy surprised her, and the strength of her feelings for Blake did a bit as well.

She'd let them get really close to her, and panic built beneath her tongue on the way to her car. She'd managed to dismiss the feelings and accept that Blake and Tommy were important to her, the same way she'd done for her Supper Club ladies.

She wanted them in her life for a good long while, and as she drove from his house to the gated community where she'd live for another couple of weeks—as well as Cass and Harrison's house—she pondered the idea of being in love with Blake Williams.

Was she?

She'd loved so few people in her life, and romantic love seemed to have eluded her almost completely. She didn't know the answer, couldn't puzzle it out, in only fifteen minutes, and when she rounded the car with her box of pizza, Cass waited for her on the porch.

"Hey," she said.

Lauren smiled and moved up the few steps and into Cass's arms. She didn't say hello, but she didn't need to. Cass hugged her. "What's the matter?"

Lauren didn't know how to answer. She felt herself shutting down, but Cass wouldn't let her do that. She pulled away and wiped her eyes. "I might be in love with Blake."

Cass smiled at her, no wide eyes in sight. "Oh, honey, that's great." She turned back to the house and opened the door. "Come in and tell me about it."

Lauren followed her as she said, "I don't have anything to say."

"Right." Cass laughed in a lighthearted way. "I believe you."

"I don't." Lauren closed the door behind her and went into the kitchen. "It's just tense right now with them, and I wanted to be there. I wanted to stay and make sure they were both okay." She looked at Cass. "How do you know if you're in love?"

She felt odd asking her friend this instead of her mother or sister. But she didn't have a mother or a sister to ask, and while she and Cass hadn't always been best friends, Lauren had always respected her. Though they were close to the same age, she'd always possessed a wisdom in a different type of way than Lauren did.

"It's hard to say," Cass said. "It's just this feeling you have. You want them to be happy, which it sounds like you do. When you think of them, they make you smile. When they hurt, you hurt. When you imagine your future, they're in it. When you try to find another emotion to describe how you feel about them...you can't. That's love. That feeling." She touched her fist to her chest. "Is love."

Lauren teared up again and nodded. She flipped open

the pizza box, trying to get control of her emotions. "Okay," she said. "This is the gourmet pepperoni pizza from Avenue Three-Fifteen. It's got the spicy marinara sauce on top, with extra cheese." She picked up one of the square pieces and took a bite of it straightaway.

Cass only watched, her smile wide and genuine. "I'll get out some wine, and we'll sit on the back deck and listen to the ocean talk to us."

"Thank you," Lauren said. She didn't want to talk tonight, but she didn't want to be alone either. She wanted to sit in her feelings and start naming them, so she could decide if she came to one that she couldn't identify and then she'd know it was love.

"It's great to meet you," Lauren said, striding forward. She shook the shorter man's hand, smiling as she did. "Cassandra says such amazing things about you."

Miles Pince shook her hand with vigor. "I'm glad. Thanks for callin'." He spoke with the strongest Texas accent Lauren had heard. Or maybe she'd been in South Carolina for too long. "So this is it." He dropped her hand and gazed beyond her to the house.

She turned back to it too. "Yes," she said. "I'm afraid it might be a bit dusty and drafty. I haven't been here in a few months, and I just got in Friday night."

"I can have a maid service come through," he said. "But you've cleaned out what you wanted?"

"Yes." Lauren nodded, her back and shoulders testifying of the work she'd done yesterday to get the house ready for Miles to look at today. She'd moved out furniture, sold it, packed more boxes to take with her to Hilton Head, and much more.

She hadn't had enough time or energy to clean completely, and she'd gotten up early to start on that. The house needed more, she was sure, and she'd gladly take advantage of a maid service.

"Let's go take a look," he said.

She led the way up her steps to the porch, and Miles paused there. "Nice porch," he said. "Looks thirty-foot wide." He looked at her, and Lauren finally felt prepared.

"It's forty-two feet," she said. "I have the blueprints inside, along with the original square footage."

He scratched the dimensions out on his clipboard, and they proceeded through the house. Lauren answered his questions about when the carpet had been laid, and if the windows were double-paned or not. When the walls in the bedroom had been painted, and how much the HOA fees were.

"All right," he said. "I'm not sure how much you're hoping to get for the house, but this is a beautiful home. I think we can list it at five-ninety easily, and I think I'll go in at five-ninety-nine." He looked at her with questions in his eyes and cocked eyebrows. "Does that give you what you need for your next place?"

Lauren swallowed, because it was more than enough. Far more. "Yes," she said. "Five-nintey-nine? Really?"

Miles smiled. "I think it'll sell quickly too. I'll get my girls in here to clean, and then Josh will come get pictures. We'll use a drone on the property, and I'll make sure they do the video tours. Those are pretty great for out-of-towners looking to relocate. Sound good?"

"Yes," Lauren said. "Thank you." She signed the necessary paperwork for Miles to do all he'd said, and he left.

She stood in the house she'd lived in for the past fifteen years, the weight of it lifting from her shoulders inch by inch. When it finally dissipated completely, Lauren smiled. "This is the right thing to do."

She did walk back into the dining room behind her and trail her fingers along the table and chairs she was leaving here. Eight people could enjoy a meal here comfortably, and she'd hosted Supper Club here many times.

The laughter of her friends, the sniffles when they'd cried, the tense moments when they'd argued, all assaulted her, and Lauren let herself weep for the past. Weep for the woman she'd been then, and the hard work she'd done on herself to get better and better and better.

When she tried to name how she felt about the five women in her Supper Club, it always came back to love.

"Lord," she prayed. "Bless Joy and Bessie." She didn't know what else to say, but she couldn't imagine Supper Club—or her daily life without them, and she wanted everyone to end up in Hilton Head. It would be crazy and Lauren didn't understand how changes came about sometimes, but she could imagine her friends gathered round a new table, this one on the beach, in her new house, with

Blake and Tommy retreating to their rooms so she could host Supper Club.

It was a good fantasy, and Lauren left her house with a smile on her face.

Blake reached over and took her hand from her mouth. "You're so nervous, it's making me nervous."

She looked at him, wishing she could internalize his calm, relaxed smile.

"Part of your seaside strategy," he said. "Is to relax more. Do what you do. This is just dinner with me."

"And your family," she said.

He'd put together a meal that included everyone in his family, from his momma to his nieces and nephews. Lauren was the only one who hadn't been through this before, and she couldn't stop chewing her nails as the downtown buildings in Charleston kept growing and growing and growing.

"They're going to love you," he said. "Really. I've been talking you up." He smiled at her, but that only made Lauren feel worse.

"Great, then I'll be a disappointment." She couldn't help feeling the way she did when her mother had packed up and left Texas. She hadn't been good enough then, so why should she expect this to go well?

She tried to banish the thoughts, and she succeeded for a few minutes. By then, Blake was turning away from the city and starting through the more suburban areas of Charleston.

"You missed the road, Dad," Tommy said.

"That one's closed," Blake said. He'd told her about the conversation with Tommy, and Blake had him on watch-dog mode now. He could track his phone at any moment, and if he tapped a button on the app, and Tommy didn't respond within sixty seconds, Blake would literally get in his car and go find him.

The boy was so good, and he'd been so apologetic. Blake said he'd hated disciplining him, and that he and Jacinda were talking about having him come live with Blake for his high school years.

"Tommy." She twisted in her seat. "Tell me how that art project went." She gave him a smile and watched his face light up. The boy could draw, and she'd found one of his notebooks at his father's place and then texted him to ask if she could look at it. They'd been talking about art and design since, as Lauren did a bit of that with marketing.

"I'm still working on it," he said. "But it's fun. Mister Thompson lets us use any media we want, so I've been using paper and glass."

"Is that the dragon, bud?" Blake asked.

"Yep." When he said that, he sounded just like Blake, and Lauren once again smiled at him.

"That's awesome," she said.

He cut a look to his dad, and then he asked, "How's the new website coming along?"

"Good." She'd been building it herself, and she added, "I'm waiting on the logo, but it should be done next week."

"Did you tell him about your first client?" Blake asked, giving her a side-eyed look.

"No," she said.

"She actually has two," Blake said.

"No," Lauren said as she faced the front of the car again. Her neck ached from twisting it like that. "I don't. Not a single person has actually signed with me yet."

"I'll sign anything you want, sweetheart," he said, and Lauren's heart melted into her ribs. "And you've just got to go down to Island Sweets. Bill's ready to sign too."

Yes, he was, and Lauren was glad for the connections Blake had on the island. He knew everyone, as he'd lived here for a while, and he'd spoken to Ryan Shaffer's parents first about Tommy and his concerns there, and then Lauren's new marketing firm.

Bill Shaffer had called Lauren himself, wanting ideas and a marketing strategy to keep their sales going now that tourist season had ended. Lauren had been talking to him, getting the details, and preparing contracts for her new business, but she hadn't officially launched anything yet.

Cass was helping her with permits, licenses, and all the legalities of working from home, something Lauren wanted to make sure was in place before anyone signed anything. Plus, she'd been dealing with her house in Texas—which had sold the day it had been listed—and trying to support Blake as he dealt with new obstacles in Tommy's life.

As if all of that weren't enough, she'd had to keep

making the drive to the job she hated, and she'd been working on her new marketing venture in the evenings. Afternoons, mornings, whenever she had a spare bit of time.

"Look," Blake said, and Lauren pulled herself out of her thoughts. "Aunt Lindsey put in the bushes she's been talking about."

"They look nice," Tommy said, completely disinterested.

Blake pulled into the driveway of a classic, well-taken-care-of house, and Lauren's anxiety grew. "I really don't do families," she said.

Blake took her hand again. "Honey, this is why we're here." He met her eyes, some nervousness in his now. "You want to have your own family...right?" He glanced into the backseat as Tommy got out.

Once the door slammed, he leaned toward her. "I mean, if we're not going to be a family, and work on building a family, what *are* we doing?" He searched her face, and Lauren started to calm. "I thought this was part of your seaside strategy. To find yourself and what you wanted—and you said you wanted those close family connections."

Lauren nodded. "You're right. I do." She took a deep breath. "I'm so bad at this, Blake."

He gave her a kind smile and touched his forehead to hers. "You can't be good at everything, Lauren. But now is not the time to retreat, okay?"

"Yes, okay." She touched her lips to his quickly, stealing some strength from him before she got out of the SUV.

Tommy disappeared through the dark brown door, and Lauren took another breath of fresh air outside Blake's sister's house. A little girl ran out of the still-open door, calling, "Uncle Blake! Uncle Blake, come see my new bunny!"

The blonde child flew toward Blake, who bent, braced himself, and lifted her into the air. He laughed with her and set her back on her feet as she was far too old for him to hold on his hip.

Lauren wondered what he would look like with a baby in his arms, and her heart softened completely. She might not be able to ever be a mother, but she could be an amazing step-mother and aunt, and she grinned at the girl and Blake as he turned toward her.

"Jilly," he said. "I have to introduce my new girlfriend around first." He extended his hand toward her, and Lauren hurried the few steps to him and slid her fingers between his. "This is Lauren. Isn't she so pretty?"

Jilly curtsied and said, "She sure is. Nice to meet you."

"And you," Lauren said, nodding her head as if meeting a princess.

"Mama says we only have a few minutes before dinner," Jilly said. "So hurry, Uncle Blake." She actually moved around behind him and started pushing him toward the house. He laughed, as did Lauren, and she calmed as they moved into the house ahead of the little girl.

Conversations filtered to the front door from the back of the house, where the kitchen was filled with people. Blake's brother and sister, plus their spouses, children, and his momma.

Lauren had technically met her before, but not as Blake's significant other. Not really. They'd been in test mode then.

He took her past a clean, obviously new sectional, the huge hearth, and toward the dining room table which had been set for twelve.

Twelve.

Lauren swallowed, and the walls of her throat stuck together.

"Blake," his brother boomed. "You finally made it."

"We're not even late," Blake said, and he released Lauren's hand as he moved into Peter and hugged him. They did laugh together, and Lauren wasn't sure how often they got together, but it wasn't every week or anything.

"Pete, this is Lauren," he said, stepping to his brother's side. They both faced Lauren, and she could see how they belonged to each other. His wife stepped between Blake and Peter, her arm sliding around her husband with his doing the same to her.

They belonged together too, and Lauren yearned for that. Whispers filled her mind that perhaps she could belong here too. To Blake. To Tommy. To his brother and sister and momma.

"This is his wife, Ruth," Blake said.

Lauren put her hand out and shook Peter's. "It's so great to meet you. Blake's been telling me so much about everyone."

Ruth smiled at her, her own dark eyes and hair shiny and happy. She took Lauren's hand and pulled her forward into a light kiss on the cheek.

"Nice to meet you," she said to Lauren, and Blake took her hand again. Tommy went out the back door with a couple of other teenagers, and he said, "Those are Peter's boys—Cardon and Aaron. Lindsey's kids are Carl, Susie, and Jilly." He glanced around. "I don't see her husband."

"He's on the grill," a pretty woman with redder hair than Blake's said. She grinned like it was all her face knew how to do, and Lauren felt she had no other option but to return the smile.

"My sister, Lindsey," Blake said. "Linds, this is Lauren Keller." He leaned toward her, almost like he'd kiss her. He didn't, and Lindsey pulled her away from him in the next moment.

"Oh, it's great to meet you."

"Lindsey," Blake said.

"You know, he hasn't brought anyone home in such a long time?" She picked up a bowl of macaroni salad and started toward the table. "Lindsey," he said louder.

"Years, I think." She put the bowl on the table and turned toward the kitchen again. "Oh, there's Sterling. Sterling, this is Blake's new lover, Lauren."

"Lindsey, I'm going to kill you." He lunged toward his sister. "Lover? You're impossible."

She shrieked and giggled as he wrapped her up in a big bear hug. Lauren wasn't sure what to say or do. Her eyes couldn't get any wider, and she gaped at the two of them.

If she ever got in the same room as Jess, there wouldn't be any hugging. Or laughing. Or embarrassing exchanges, at least not like this. There would be plenty of tension and awkwardness, but only because they were complete strangers.

Sterling rolled his eyes and held out his hand. "Ignore my wife. She likes to tease her older brothers. Calls it payback for all the 'torture' they put her through growing up."

They shook hands, and then the back door opened again. The teens entered, carrying plates and platters of steaming, grilled food. Hamburgers, hot dogs, corn on the cob, and even watermelon.

Tommy brought up the rear, and he said, "Guys, this is my dad's girlfriend, Lauren."

"Hey," the two boys said, but they'd already gone by her to the table, where they put the food.

"Time to eat," Lindsey called. "Stop it, Blake. It's time to eat. Let me go."

He did, and Lauren put her hand on Tommy's forearm. He paused to look at her. "What? Did I do it wrong?"

"No." She shook her head. "You did it exactly right." She gave him a smile. "Thank you for introducing me to them."

A quick smile came to his face too, and he nodded. "We better not dawdle," he said. "Aunt Lindsey doesn't like it." He nodded over to her. "Look. She's already gone into battle mode."

She pointed to her kids, at Peter's, and then the piles of food she had on the counter—buns, sliced tomatoes, ketchup, mustard, mayonnaise, more bowls of salad, sweet tea, and more—got put on the table. Lauren wasn't sure how any people could squeeze in with their plates, but she figured they would.

"Ah, Tommy," an older woman said. "Introduce me to Lauren."

Tommy turned toward his grandmother, and he said, “Gramma, this is Lauren Keller. Dad says you’ve sort of met her at the fireworks a couple of times.”

His gramma grinned and said, “That I have.” She leaned in and brushed her lips across Lauren’s cheek.

“Sally, right?” Lauren asked.

“Oh, right,” Tommy said. “My gramma, Sally. I always forget that part.”

“You did good, baby,” Sally said, and Lauren agreed.

“We’re eating,” Lindsey said, her voice getting closer and higher-pitched. “Momma. Everyone’s waiting for you.” She flicked a glance to Lauren, her eyes still in “battle mode.”

“It’s a family picnic, Lindsey.” Sally rolled her eyes. “I’m an old woman. No one cares if we’re delayed by ten seconds.”

Tommy stifled a laugh and turned around. “I’m on my way, Aunt Lindsey.”

“Me too,” Lauren said. “Come on, Sally. I don’t want to be in trouble on my first time here.”

His gramma chuckled, and Lauren felt like she’d won a great war by getting that from her. Then she joined Blake at the table, where he waited for her beside her chair. He pulled it out for her, and Lauren exchanged a flirty glance with him.

As the meal continued, Lauren realized how amazing having a family could be—and she did want it for herself.

Chapter Twenty-Three

Blake checked his son's location and found him in his bedroom at his mother's. Of course he would be, as it was a Thursday evening and he had school in the morning. Blake hadn't said anything to Tommy about coming to live with him. Not yet, at least.

Jacinda hadn't either. She'd taken her bins out of Tommy's bedroom, and Blake had been handling the girlfriend and friend issues here on Hilton Head.

Since Jacinda hadn't had anything to do with it, she'd not said much to Tommy about it.

Blake had said plenty. He'd confiscated Tommy's phone. He'd put a parenting tracking app on the device, and he used it just to make sure that Tommy knew he would. He was serious about knowing where his son was and who he was with at all times.

Thirteen-year-olds could get into some serious trouble otherwise. Blake loved his son. Adored him. He'd do anything for him. Anything. And that included coming down hard on him when he lied and concealed things from him—both of which he'd done.

They'd had an agreement that Tommy wouldn't delete his messages and texts, and he had. He'd been hiding his conversations with Kathy, who Blake had poked at his contacts around the island to learn more about her.

Her father had indeed passed away during his military service, and her mother did work two jobs to cover their expenses.

She had two children, but Kathy wasn't the oldest. Luke was older than her, and when Blake had told Tommy, his son had been livid.

Accusations had been made, and Blake had told him then that he'd do whatever he had to in order to ensure his safety. *Whatever* he had to.

"There's trouble you don't understand," he'd told his son.

"You don't get teenagers," Tommy had shot back.

Maybe Blake didn't, but he didn't have to. Tommy's girlfriend had lied to him, and Tommy had lied to Blake. That was all he needed to know.

He got out of his SUV and walked toward Lauren's new house. She'd moved in last month, and she texted him every single day about something new and amazing she liked about the house. He smiled as he walked up to her front door and rang the bell. He went in a moment later, calling, "It's just me."

"I'm in the yard." Her voice echoed back to him from

outside, and he closed the door and started toward the back of the house.

She had no back door, so he'd have to go around, or through her bedroom, and she lifted one gloved hand as he peered through the window. "I'm coming in." She bent again and gathered up the produce she'd just harvested, and several seconds later, her footsteps came down the hallway toward him.

"You're early," she said. "I haven't had time to start the soup." She gave him a smile and barely met his eye.

He'd caught her retreating from him a couple of times in the past month or so, and he'd carefully brought her back to him each time. They'd had a great meal with his family, and Lauren had gushed and gushed about how great they were.

They'd done the same, and Blake watched as she went by him with carrots, tomatoes, a couple of onions, and some heads of lettuce in her arms.

"I'm making a minestrone," she said.

"Great," he said. "I thought we were calling Jess."

"We are," she said. "But I need soup to do that." She dumped all of her produce on the counter and looked at him. "Tell me about Tommy."

"Nothing more to tell," he said. "Not since last time. He's still surly all the time. Thinks I'm being unfair. But I can see all of his texts and messages through the app, so he doesn't delete them anymore."

"Is he still with Kathy?" She picked up a peeler and started shaving off the skin on a carrot.

He went into the kitchen with her. "Are you dicing the tomatoes?"

She gave him a flirty smile. "Yes, sir."

He opened a couple of drawers until he found a knife, and then he took the cutting board from the narrow strip of countertop between the stove and fridge.

"I didn't know you cooked," she said.

"I can do it," he said. "I just don't like it. So cereal is easy for breakfast. Or toast and coffee. I grab sandwiches for lunch or go out with a client. I can make breakfast for dinner or get take-out on the way home from work." He shrugged as he cored the tomato. "But I can do a few things."

"Set water to boil?" she asked.

"That's something I can do."

She got out the pot and he filled it with water and lit the big burner on the front corner of the stove. Cooking in the kitchen with her felt very domestic. It felt like something a man would do with his wife, and Blake really wanted to tell her that. He wanted to tell her he loved her.

His pulse beat faster and faster in his chest, in his neck, and as she started telling him about the new campaign she'd launch at the end of the month for Island Sweets, Blake smiled and chopped.

He laughed with her as the soup came together, and once that was boiling, Lauren washed her hands and met his eye.

"You're not going to let me get out of this, are you?" she asked. She wasn't smiling now.

He shook his head. "You asked me not to." He didn't

want to be the heavy with her all the time, but he sensed this was very important to her—and extremely difficult.

"You've got the number?" he asked. "I'll dial. All you have to do is talk. Tell him about your great new house, your new firm and how wonderful it is, and how handsome and hot and simply *amazing* your new boyfriend is." He grinned at her, and she did crack and shake her head with a small smile in place.

"Fine," she said. "Dial. We have ten minutes until the soup is done."

"Will you talk that long?" he asked.

She handed him her phone and shrugged.

He took the device and tapped until he found Jess's name. "Video call?"

"He won't answer if it's not a video call," Lauren said. "He works in film, and he says he's so visual, he likes his calls that way too."

Blake nodded, his adrenaline firing again. Not because he'd realized he might be able to tell her he loved her, but because he hadn't met a woman's family in a very long time. Years, Lindsey would say.

The line rang once, then twice, and then it *beep-beeped* as it connected. The video image flared to life, and a man with Lauren's straight nose and dark hair filled the screen. Silver salted his hair in his beard and sideburns, and he definitely looked like someone who lived around actors, movie sets, and year-round sunshine.

"Lauren," he said with a laugh. "Wow, I haven't heard

from you in a while." He peered closer to his phone. "And you're not Lauren."

She crowded in beside him as Jess's smile slipped away. "I'm right here, Jess." She grinned at him, and Blake straightened so he wasn't in the frame anymore.

"I wanted to..." She cleared her throat and glanced over to him.

He'd leaned her phone up against her recipe stand, but she picked it up and held it in front of her face now. "I, uh, how's California?"

"Still hot," he said.

The conversation stalled again, and Blake could see how awkward this was. She could ask about his children, but she didn't. He could ask her about literally anything in her life, but he didn't.

She swallowed, and Blake pressed in close to her. She leaned into his body heat, and Blake felt her taking something from him. Strength, warmth, whatever she needed, and he'd gladly give it to her.

"Tell him," he whispered.

"I'm seeing someone new," Lauren said. "Well, it's not really new anymore. We've been dating since July."

"That's only a couple of months, Lauren." Jess laughed, but Lauren didn't even smile.

"His name is Blake Williams," she said, and she held the phone further from him. "Blake, this is my older brother, Jess. It looks like he's at work."

"Great to meet you," Blake said. "Lauren's told me a lot about you."

"Has she?" His eyebrows went up, as if Blake said something truly shocking. "I can't imagine what that would be."

"I know what you do, Jess," she said. "Anyone can look you up online. I can't believe you worked on the latest Sandra Bullock romcom and didn't tell me." There was no playfulness in her tone, though Blake knew she loved Sandra Bullock and any romcom with or without her.

"I'm pretty busy with all sorts of projects," he said.

Lauren sighed and nodded. "How's Rena?"

"Good," Jess said. "Are you going to marry my sister?" He switched his eyes to Blake.

"Jess," Lauren said. "Don't ask him that." She turned to Blake. "Don't answer that." She wasn't happy, and Blake wondered if this call had been a good idea. He had no clue what the conversation would be without him there, he knew that much.

"How's Bella?" Lauren asked, obviously trying to get the topic off Blake.

"Oh, she died," Jess said with a sigh. "Louisa and Eliza cried and cried." He shook his head. "Now Rena's talking about getting another dog."

Lauren pulled in a breath. "Bella died? Why didn't you tell me?"

Jess gazed evenly into the camera on his phone. "Because, Lauren, she wasn't your dog."

"I loved that dog," Lauren said.

Blake put his hand on her lower back, out of sight, hoping to infuse her with strength.

"Sorry," Jess said without much apology in his tone. "I

was dealing with a lot at that time." He let a beat of silence go by. "Have you heard? Hillary had a baby, so we have a new baby niece."

"Sort of," Lauren said. Blake had no idea who Hillary was, as that wasn't a name he'd heard Lauren say.

"She's Mom's granddaughter," Jess said. "That makes her our niece."

"Sort of," Lauren said again.

"I'm not arguing about it again," Jess said with a sigh. "Did you need anything? I've got a contract to finish up before the day ends."

Lauren shook her head, her jaw set tight. "No, I just wanted to let Blake meet you."

"Great to meet you, brother," Jess said.

"You too," Blake murmured, and Lauren said she'd talk to him later.

The call ended, and Blake saw that it hadn't even lasted five minutes. Lauren set her phone on the counter and walked away from it.

"It's okay," he said after her, but she clearly wasn't. He could physically feel her withdrawing, and Blake knew then that Lauren would never have the familial relationship with her brother that he had with his.

They lived on opposite coasts now, and Blake had a close relationship with his family. Lauren could become one of them.

He glanced at the timer on the stove for the soup and made a snap decision. He flipped off the burner but left the pot on the hot grate. It would finish or it wouldn't, and he could check on it later.

He canceled the timer and strode after Lauren. She'd gone into her bedroom, but she hadn't closed the door.

He'd never been inside this room, at least after he'd helped her set up her bed when she'd moved in. Today, he only hesitated for half a step, and then he entered.

Lauren loved things neat and clean, crisp and fresh, and her bedroom was no different. She'd laid down on top of her comforter, her back to him.

"Hey," he said, sure she'd heard his footsteps. "I'm coming in."

She said nothing. Not even a sniffle met his ears. She'd discarded her shoes in the kitchen during the soup-making, but Blake kicked his off beside her bed.

"I'm laying down by you," he said.

She scooted further into the middle of the bed, and Blake climbed into bed with her. He pressed his chest to her back and slid one arm under her head and the other he laid over her arm and side.

He had no idea what to say. "Listen," he said. "I don't care if he likes me. I got to meet him, and that's all I wanted."

"It's not all I wanted," she whispered.

"I know, baby." He pressed his lips to the back of her neck, the moment between them tender and sweet and memorable.

He decided he didn't need to say anything else, and he simply held Lauren so she wouldn't have to be alone. After a few minutes of peaceful silence, she did sniffle and turn into him.

He held her closer to his heart, her face pressed against his chest, and stroked her hair. "Hey, it's okay," he murmured. "I'm right here, and we have something so great. Okay?"

She nodded, and Blake just let her cry softly for several more minutes.

Then he said, "I'll get you some soup and be right back."

"Thank you," she whispered, and while Blake didn't want to leave her alone in the bedroom, and he was really enjoying holding her on her bed, he slipped away and padded down the hall to the kitchen.

He tasted the soup and found the noodles and carrots tender the way he'd suspected they'd be. He found the bowls easily, as he'd helped her unpack and put those away, and he dished up their dinner.

Everything about tonight hadn't gone right, Blake knew. But so many things had. So many things aligned inside him as he moved about this house, knowing where things were and working together with Lauren.

He paused as he took out the spoons, because he'd just had a thought. This house wasn't as large as his—only two bedrooms. Lauren loved it so much, and Tommy could still live here with them.

They hadn't talked too terribly much about getting married, which was why Lauren had shut down Jess's question. He'd pointed out that they'd only been dating for two months too.

It was almost three, and Blake had been trying to start something with Lauren for much longer than that. Jess simply didn't know that, because he didn't know anything about Lauren and her life here.

Her very good, very amazing life here, in this amazing house that she loved so much.

She was a strong, talented, smart woman, and as Blake lifted two spoons from her utensil drawer, he knew he was in love with her.

It didn't feel like the right time to tell her, those words not something she'd want to absorb after the disastrous phone call she'd been hoping would go better. Or different. Or something.

Still, he smiled to himself, and he put it on his relationship to-do list to start asking her about her ideal wedding, and where they should live once they got married, and how they wanted to build their family life together.

He took the soup down the hall to find Lauren's bed empty. She came out of her bathroom a second or two later, and he held up one bowl for her. She owned bowl cozies, so she could take it without burning herself, and she did with a soft, grateful smile.

She'd changed out of her gardening clothes and into a pair of soft black pants and an oversized sweatshirt. She tucked her legs under herself as she sat on the settee against the wall that faced the bed, and Blake lowered himself to the remaining seat beside her.

He stirred his soup and lifted a steaming bite to his lips.

"This is going to be incredible with the veggie from your garden."

"It's too hot," she warned, but Blake put the soup in his mouth anyway.

It was entirely too hot, and he grunted as the boiling liquid touched his tongue and burned the roof of his mouth. He swallowed it quickly and coughed. "You were right."

She laughed quietly and continued stirring hers to let the heat out. Lauren looked over to him, everything between them sober now.

"Thank you," she said. "For being here. For anchoring me."

"You do the same for me," he said back, his voice just as quiet and just as serious as hers had been. "You know that, right? You do the same for me."

She nodded and ducked her head. He lifted her chin to look at him, and Blake felt only love streaming inside him, between them. Could she feel it?

"You have me," he said. "Always. You have Tommy. My brother and sister adored you. Momma asks me if I've proposed to you yet every day." He smiled, because it was all true. "We'll be your family, okay?"

She nodded, a single tear slipping down her face. She dropped her chin again and Blake let her this time.

He cleared his throat and started stirring his own bowl of soup. "In fact." He cleared his throat. "I wanted to talk to you about some of that."

"Which parts?"

"Us being a family," he said. "Getting married."

She said nothing, and Blake had to have something to occupy his mouth or he was going to say too much. So hot soup or not, he took another bite. It was easier this time, though still blistering as he chewed the noodles and white beans before swallowing.

"You don't have to say anything," he said. "But let's be thinking about it, okay? What we want. Where we want to live. If you even want to keep this thing going." He glanced over to her, and she did let a small smile lift the corners of her mouth.

"I want to keep this going," she said. "And the rest...I'll start thinking about it."

That was good enough for him, so he nodded, and asked, "Where did you learn to make this soup?"

"It's Bessie's grandmother's recipe," she said, and Blake let her lead the conversation to her Supper Club ladies—who had been her family for so long.

Blake hoped she had room in her heart for him and Tommy, and with how things had gone this summer, he suspected she did. He just needed to be patient with her, and he needed to keep her close even when she wanted to pull away.

Chapter Twenty-Four

Lauren didn't notice much difference between summer and fall in Hilton Head. The sun shone brightly and hotly every morning and all day long. There were less tourists in the fall, and Joy had gone back to Texas. Otherwise, it felt like business as usual on the island.

Blake went to work every day, and things between him and Tommy seemed to get better every single day. Lauren wasn't entirely sure, because she got everything second-hand, mostly from Blake, but sometimes from Tommy.

She walked in from her time at the gym that morning, her phone already ringing. She'd set up a landline here at her house, in the narrow office just on the other side of the wall. She ran down the hall and around the corner to grab the phone. "Keller Marketing Group," she said, and she drew in a long breath to try to tame the panting. She'd already put in five miles on the treadmill that morning.

"Yes, hello, Miss Keller," a crisp male voice said. "This is Agent Toledo. Do you remember me?"

Lauren sank into her desk chair, because how could she forget? An image of the tall federal agent flashed through her mind. "Yes," she said, trying to make her voice as crisp and as sure as his had been. She wasn't entirely sure she'd succeeded. "What can I do for you, Agent Toledo?"

She stared at the black computer screen in front of her, her hand moving to wake the machine. She needed to pick up some new clients, and this wasn't the kind of call she wanted to get at her new firm. A firm of one person. One woman who ran the whole show, from the marketing department to the art manager to the financial secretary to the CEO.

"We've reached a settlement with Simple Solutions," he said. "We're distributing money back to the employees who it was taken from, and I just need to confirm your payment details. Do you have a few minutes?"

"Yes," she said, utterly surprised to hear she'd get any sort of compensation. "Simple Solutions is still out of business, right?"

"Yes, ma'am," he said. "Now, let's go over your current address..."

Lauren gave him all the details he wanted, and he said the money would be in her account by the weekend. The call ended, and Lauren supposed that could count as securing a client without having to do any of the work.

She showered and got back to business. She had two

clients right now, with a possible third on the table. She had a mock-up to do for them, as well as a quote to put together, and then she needed to call Bill Shaffer and find out what he thought about the designs she'd put together for him.

The hours passed quickly, as Lauren loved thinking through sales concepts, looking at and creating creatives for campaigns, and working from home. Whenever her tea got cold, she made more. When she was hungry, she could pad into the kitchen and make something to eat. Her mind whirred during her quieter moments, and she'd often come up with her best ideas while away from the job.

An alarm went off, and that was Lauren's signal to stop working for the day. She sat back from the drawing in front of her, her fingers releasing the pencil they clutched. She'd forgotten how much she enjoyed actually hand-drawing the art. She loved sketching things out by hand, but Simple Solutions had moved to digital tablets and pens five years ago.

A smile touched her face and filled her soul. She'd really done it. She'd moved to Hilton Head with a strategy in mind —and she'd done it.

She was more relaxed. She enjoyed her life so much more, because she got to live it. She'd found who she was, and gone back to roots she hadn't known needed re-watering.

"Blake," she said, and she got to her feet. The pencil dropped where it was, and Lauren knew it would be waiting for her tomorrow. Something always was, and when she was mentally healthy and excited about her tasks, they weren't such a chore to do.

She quickly changed out of her more casual attire and into a little black dress that was sure to make Blake's eyes light up the way they did when he wanted to kiss her. It was their three-month anniversary, and he'd promised to take her "somewhere special."

She'd asked if she'd have to get on another boat with her eyes closed, and he'd promised she wouldn't. Lauren did love a surprise, and she loved how Blake knew that. He took good care of her, and as she tucked her toes into a pair of lemon-yellow heels, she said, "Maybe you should ask him tonight about getting married."

They hadn't talked much about that, but Lauren suddenly heard a huge, booming clock in her head. Tick, tick, ticking away. They hadn't talked about having more kids either, other than Lauren saying she was too old for such things. She'd started to wonder if she was, though, as more and more women had babies in their forties now.

When she finished getting ready, she still had a few minutes to spare, and she quickly tapped out a text to him. *I want to talk about some serious stuff tonight. Is that okay? Or would you rather I waited until another day?*

She sent the message without specifying much else, and she tucked her phone into a jeweled handbag. Blake didn't respond immediately, and he never texted while he drove, so she assumed that was why.

He'd get the message, and he'd respond, either in a text or right to her face. Her heartbeat picked up speed at the thought of that, then immediately quieted when she reminded herself that she *wanted* to talk to Blake about these things. He was her safe space. The one person she could absolutely be herself with, and it didn't matter if she was scattered, messy, crying, or upset. He took all of it for her, held her close, and then brought her soup.

Lauren stood at the back windows and looked out into her yard. Chloe meowed and wound through her legs, and Lauren tore her gaze from the sunshine outside. "I'll feed you," she said. She got fresh water for her cats, called for Oscar who didn't come, of course, and looked at the clock.

Blake was late, and he hadn't texted. Lauren hadn't even realized what time it was. A spark of concern mixed with irritation fired within her. She didn't have Tommy's or Blake's pin on her phone, and she didn't have a monitoring app.

Her boyfriend hadn't responded, and Lauren tapped out another message to him. *Are you okay? On your way? Traffic is bad?*

Traffic should be a non-issue, as it was a weekday. Tommy wasn't with Blake during the week, but he could have some needy clients.

"Not at seven o'clock," Lauren muttered to herself. She didn't hear from him, and she'd employed a personal rule of cutting him off after a half-hour the first time they'd agreed to get together.

This wasn't the first time they'd be going out, and Lauren tamped down her frustration and let her concern rise. There had to be something seriously wrong if Blake hadn't called her or texted her back by now.

She went to her phone, which had seemed like a third hand for so many years. She tapped out a message to Grant, Harrison, and Scott, all of whom knew Blake really well and whose numbers she had.

They all got the same question from her. *Have you heard from Blake recently? I'm trying to get in touch with him and haven't had any luck.*

Of course, she hadn't called him yet either, and the moment the last text was sent, she tapped to do just that. His line rang and rang, and when his voicemail picked up, so did Lauren's pulse.

She reverted right back to the woman who'd been so excited to go out with him last summer. She'd spent time and energy on her makeup and clothes, choosing things with great care and matching her jewelry just-so. She'd then sat at the restaurant by herself, without a single peep from Blake.

She closed her eyes and drew in a breath through her nose. Her call with Jess had not gone well. She hadn't heard from him since. Not even a text.

Her mother rarely texted or called, and usually only after Lauren initiated something. Not a peep from her either.

With her eyes shut, the world was dark, and Lauren was so utterly alone. No one to talk to. No one to share her great day with. No one to love, and no one to love her.

Her chest felt hollow and collapsible, like one wrong breath would do her in completely.

Cat claws sounded on the tile floor in the kitchen, drawing Lauren out of the dark space inside her mind. Oscar lapped at the running kitty fountain, then took a bite of his cat chow, finally gracing them all with his presence. In this house, he really liked the spot under the settee in her bedroom, for a patch of sunlight fell underneath it all afternoon, keeping him warm and comfortable.

Chloe jumped up on the couch next to Lauren, and she stroked her absently. She meowed too, probably wanting to go outside and find some innocent birds to torture.

Lauren didn't move from the couch. She sat there for a long time. Long enough for her stomach to rumble for the want of food. Long enough for everyone she'd texted to say they hadn't heard from Blake. Long enough for the sun to go down.

When it was too dark for her to see much in the house, Lauren got to her feet. She changed out of her dress, this three-month anniversary bad enough to make tears prick her eyes. She didn't let them fall, and she bypassed the card she'd picked up for Blake yesterday.

If he ever called her, she'd find out what was going on.

She switched on lights and started making chicken noodle soup. Her father had made it for her when she was a tiny, tiny girl, and she couldn't believe she still had those memories in her brain. She missed her father terribly, and she couldn't help wondering how different her life would've been had he not died when she was ten years old.

Her mother wouldn't have gotten remarried. She wouldn't have moved north, leaving Lauren all alone, hardly able to take care of herself. Her daddy had possessed a big personality, and he wouldn't have allowed the distance that currently sat between Lauren and Jess.

She'd just ladled soup into a bowl when her phone rang. Lauren looked at the screen, her pulse bouncing along her jawline. It wasn't Blake, but his mother.

She swiped quickly to get the call open. "Sally," she said. "Is everything okay?"

"I'm just wondering if you've heard from Blake," she said. "I've been trying to get him on the phone, and the blasted man isn't answering." She didn't sound happy, and Lauren wanted to tell her to join the club.

"Sadly," she said. "I haven't heard from him either." She didn't go into details, because it wasn't like Lauren to air dirty laundry. She did want to tell Sally that her son had stood her up on their three-month anniversary, and even if she'd been trying to call him, he wouldn't have answered. Because he would've been on a date with her. An important date. A date where Lauren had wanted to open more doors with him.

Now, she wasn't so sure about anything.

Sally griped some more about her son, and Lauren let her end the call. True worry ate through her now, and Lauren called Blake again. This time, when his voicemail picked up, she said, "Hey, I'm worried about you. Where are you? Your mother just called me looking for you, and none of your friends can find you. I hope you're okay. Call me, okay?"

She left the message and took her soup to the couch. She fed chunks of carrot to Chloe while something played on the speaker system in her house, and when she couldn't wait up for another moment, Lauren finally went to bed.

Blake hadn't answered any of her messages yet.

She couldn't sleep, so she picked up the phone and called the hospital. "Yes, hello," she said. She cleared her throat. "I don't suppose you could tell me if you have a patient there, could you?"

Chapter Twenty-Five

Blake looked over to Tommy, who slept on the bed beside him. His heart still pounded, and he glanced to the door he'd shut and locked an hour ago. Olympia Heartwood had been gracious and kind—and discreet. She'd come straight to the check-in counter when he'd requested her, and she'd put him in a room on the second to highest floor, then told her security not to let anyone in who couldn't show their room key.

The Heartwood Inn wasn't as fancy as some of the high-end hotels that required a keycard in order to get the elevator to go up. Anyone could walk in off the beach and get in the elevator and up to guest rooms, and Blake ran his hands through his hair.

He'd just gone to Carter's Cove when Tommy had texted him that afternoon after school. He'd said his mother and Cason had gotten in a fight, and he wanted to come stay with Blake. No problem. Blake had made the trip there and back in a couple of hours before, and he didn't need to get Lauren until seven.

He had no idea what time it was. His phone had been confiscated the moment he'd walked through the door, and Cason had stomped on it with his big work boots. With the steel toe of them, he'd crushed the screen, and despite Blake's protests and threats, he hadn't been able to stop him.

He'd kept a level head while he'd taken in the scattered items in Jacinda's house. It looked like her bath bombs had exploded everywhere, and Blake had known in that split second of time that he needed to get his son out of that house.

He'd offered to do just that, and he and Tommy had spent the next couple of hours in tense silence as they packed everything the boy needed to come live with him. Jacinda hadn't been home, and Cason had glowered at them from the kitchen table, a beer bottle in his hand that seemingly never ran out.

Tommy didn't have his phone either, and Cason had ranted at him about texting girls and running up bills, but Blake had pointed out that he paid for the boy's cell phone. He wasn't afraid of Cason, but Tommy was, and his heart hurt that he hadn't seen it until tonight.

He'd called Gage, who was ex-military and had done some security work, and he'd helped Blake with a cart. There were no vehicles on Carter's Cove, and moving on and off the island was difficult. He and his wife currently had all of Tommy's belongings at their house, and he'd work on getting them off the island and to the house in Hilton Head tomorrow.

Tomorrow, tomorrow, tomorrow.

He didn't have Lauren's phone number memorized, and he had no way of getting in touch with her. He knew his mother's phone number, but he hadn't wanted to worry her, and it was her bridge night besides. She wouldn't have answered, and once she got home and did, she'd be unable to do anything anyway.

He'd talk to her tomorrow too.

He paced in the hotel room, wishing the ferry had been running when Cason had finally told them to "get."

Blake hadn't asked Tommy what he'd done. This wasn't the boy's fault, and Blake simply needed to be his father, his champion, his rescuer. And he would be. Everything and everyone else could wait.

He finally slept, and he woke the moment the sun started to light the day. Tommy didn't, and Blake showered and put on the same clothes he'd worn yesterday. He called his office, as he didn't have his secretary's personal cell phone number memorized either. He kicked himself for living so much in the twenty-first century, but no one memorized phone numbers anymore. It wasn't required, and therefore, he didn't do it.

"Sandra," he said. "This is Blake. I lost my phone yesterday, and I won't be in the office today. Please move or cancel anything I have on the calendar today. I don't have a phone, but I'll try to check in with you throughout the day if there's anything you need."

He hung up, and then he thought better of that. He called back and said, "If possible, could you find and get Lauren Keller's number? She's friends with my friend Grant Turner, Harrison Tate, and...yeah. Try those two. They have her number, and I'm sure they'll give it to you. When I call back in a bit, I'll need it." He took a breath, because while Lauren wasn't the same woman she'd been last year, he'd still stood her up—on their three-month anniversary no less.

He hated thinking about her with her makeup on, and her heels, all dressed up and wondering where he was. Pushing aside the image and all the emotional damage that would do to her, he looked at his son again.

"Tommy," he said as he touched the boy's ankle. "We need to get goin', son."

He wanted to be off this island, and the first ferry would be running in half an hour. Gage had said he'd call in a couple of favors, and the man slept less than any other human Blake knew. "I'm going to go downstairs and get some breakfast, and I want you up and ready when I get back."

"Okay," Tommy said. He rolled over and didn't move again, and Blake watched him for a moment. He really didn't like thinking of him living in that house, with all that tension and fear, and he wondered how long it had been going on.

Even one day was too long.

He wanted to wake him again and tell him to latch the door behind him, but he didn't really think Cason would follow them here. Downstairs, only a few of the early bird guests had found the breakfast room, which made it easy for Blake to load up two plates with eggs, bacon, and biscuits. He took the food upstairs, stuck the card into the door, and entered the room.

Tommy was awake, and that surprised Blake. He'd fully expected to find his son still snoring. He'd brought a backpack to the hotel with him, and he glanced over to Blake as he put one plate on the built-in desk in the room.

He handed the other one to Tommy. "Eat and let's get going."

"Dad." He took the food in one hand and finished pulling down his sweatshirt with the other. "I—I didn't know he was going to freak out like that."

"It doesn't matter," Blake said. He pressed his lips into a line. "You didn't do anything wrong." He still didn't know what Tommy had done at all, but as he'd said, it didn't matter. "He's the adult, Tommy. Not you. I don't care what you did. He had no right to throw your mother's things around. No right to shout at you. No right to make you fearful of him."

Tommy nodded and hung his head. "He's only done it one other time."

Blake bit back the words he wanted to say. What good would it do to lecture his son about it? Of course he'd have liked to know back then, but as his momma would say, what was done was done.

"We'll get all of your stuff to our house today," he said. "You'll be okay. We'll move schools. People do it all the time."

Tommy sniffled. "What about Mom?" He kept his head down. "Doesn't she have some legal custody or something?"

"I know lawyers," Blake said. He sat next to Tommy on the bed and took the paper plate from him. Their eyes met, and Blake offered him the most reassuring smile he could. "Tommy, your mother and I have already talked about having you come live with me for high school. We were just in the early stages of talking about it, but she wants what's best for you too."

His eyes widened at that news, and he asked, "Really?"

"Yeah," Blake said. "Now, don't worry. I'm going to take care of everything." A pit had been in his stomach since his son's text yesterday, and he wished with everything inside him that he'd texted Lauren on his way to Carter's Cove. He'd almost done it, and then he hadn't. If she knew he had Tommy that night, she'd insist he go out with them. Or she'd say they could reschedule. Blake hadn't wanted to do either of those, and he'd ended up missing the date completely.

He stood and took a bite of his eggs. After managing to get down as much food as he could, he grabbed his baseball cap and put it on. "Ready?"

Tommy swallowed his last bite of biscuit. "Ready." He shouldered his backpack, shoved his feet in his shoes, and the two of them left the safety of the hotel room.

Gage Sanders pushed away from the wall the moment the elevator opened and he saw Blake, and Blake's relief knew no bounds. "Thank you," he said to his friend, and he hugged Gage right there in the lobby.

"No problem," Gage said. "I've got a private charter, and

we'll get your stuff over there and loaded, and you'll be on the way."

"Great," Blake said. He swallowed, because he wasn't sure if they could get everything of Tommy's into his waiting SUV on the other side. He'd make it work, and Gage would go with him, Blake was sure. They could rent a car right at the ferry station, and he simply had to get off this island with his son.

Now.

So he focused on that, pushing everything else to the back of his mind, where he'd deal with it when it wasn't the closest, hottest fire to him.

Several hours later, he slid into a booth opposite of Tommy. His back ached. His feet. His head. He'd swallowed four pills a half-hour ago, right before he and Tommy had left to come here for dinner.

His son looked at him, then looked down at his hands. "Thanks, Dad," he mumbled.

"Hey." Blake reached across the table as the waitress started to put water glasses down.

"Take a look at the menus," she said. "I'll be right back."

Blake didn't look at her at all. He covered his son's hands with his. They were all about the same size, and Blake had to remind himself again that just because Tommy was tall didn't mean he was a man. He wasn't an adult, and he still very much needed Blake to protect him, care for him, and guide him.

"Hey," he said again. "Look at me, son."

Tommy raised his eyes to Blake, and he wore absolute misery there. "Don't you even think about this for one more second." He raised his eyebrows and hoped he looked stern and fatherly. "Okay? You're my son, and I'm your dad, and I would do anything for you. Anything at all."

A tear slipped out of his right eye, and Tommy pulled his hand away to wipe it. "I've just made such a mess of so many things this summer."

Blake could agree with him, but he didn't need to pile on the kid. "Yeah," he said. He pulled his hands back to his side of the table and picked up his glass of water. "But we haven't been to the hospital once." He grinned at Tommy, who blinked in shock for a moment, and then burst out laughing.

Blake laughed too, and it was exactly what they both needed. "You're right, Dad," Tommy said through the chuckles. "No hospitals this year."

Blake sobered, the love he had for his son overflowing again. "You're almost fourteen," he said. "Your brain has fallen out and is rattling around under your bed. I love you anyway. Okay? So you messed up with a girl this summer. Big deal. You lied to me about where you were going. Okay, we fixed that. Now, we've got this move, and it's going to be A Thing." Blake had no idea how big of a thing, but he knew it wouldn't be easy for Tommy to start at the middle school here, one month into the school year. "But we'll get through it, because you have me, and I have you."

He smiled again, and Tommy nodded. "Thanks, Dad." He flipped over his new phone. "Thanks for this too. Who knew it took so long to set up new phones?"

They'd stood in the cell phone store for upwards of two hours, and Blake was still waiting for his to download the new software and charge before he could get all of his contacts out of the cloud storage. Tommy was too, and they'd decided to go to dinner while all of that happened.

He could only pray that Lauren would understand when he finally got a chance to talk to her. Sandra had given him her number, and Blake had called three times now from various phones. Lauren hadn't answered once. He'd left three messages, but seeing as how he didn't have a permanent phone with him at all times, he wasn't sure how she'd call him back.

It'll be okay, he told himself. Maybe if he said it enough, it would be true.

"You don't want to come?" he asked Tommy. The boy had his eyes glued to his phone, his thumbs moving like lightning over the screen.

"No," he said. "You need to talk to her, not me."

He didn't want to admit that Lauren wouldn't be as angry if Tommy were there, and he faced her house. She had to know he was here, as his headlights had cut through the darkness a full thirty seconds ago. She hadn't come outside, so he headed for the front door.

Her porch light flicked on as he neared, and he stood on her porch and rang the doorbell. In the stillness of this neighborhood, he could hear it outside, and he tucked his hands into his shorts pockets.

He couldn't believe the past couple of days had happened, and he honestly needed a week to recover from all the changes. To absorb them and sort through them.

"Lauren?" he called as he opened her screen door and knocked on the wooden one behind it. "It's Blake."

She didn't answer, and he tilted sideways to look through the window. It was dark inside, and he could only assume that she wasn't home. He removed his phone from his back pocket and called her.

Again.

The line rang and rang, and she didn't answer.

Again.

"Hey, honey," he said, his voice as sugary as he could make it while so much frustration coiled through him. "It's Blake, and this is my new number. You might be wondering why I have a new number, and I can explain it all the next time I see you."

He went down her steps. "I really want to see you Lauren. I'm so sorry about last night." He'd given a version of this apology in each message he'd left, and this was the fourth. "Call me back, okay? Tommy and I are headed home, and you can stop by there too."

He ended the call and pulled open the door to the SUV. Tommy glanced over to him. "She's not home?"

"No, I guess not." Blake looked back to the house, something sad moving through him. He wasn't sure if she was home or not. "She's not answering my calls either."

"I can text her." Tommy raised his eyebrows. "Should I?"

"Sure," Blake said. "Maybe she'll answer you."

"She can't be mad," Tommy said. "You didn't know Cason was going to go crazy."

"Yeah." Blake backed out of Lauren's driveway. "She likes to disappear." His voice came out in a murmur, and a lightbulb went off over his head. Lauren was trying to pull away from him. He wasn't supposed to let her do that, but he didn't know how to keep her close.

Exhaustion filled him, and for once, he wanted someone there to strengthen him. Not someone to take from him. Not someone he had to work so hard to be with. He could really use Lauren's love and support right now, and instead, she wanted him to keep giving, giving, giving to her.

It didn't feel fair, and Blake wasn't sure how much more he had to give anyway.

"Let's go home," he said. "I'm tired, and I need to shower."

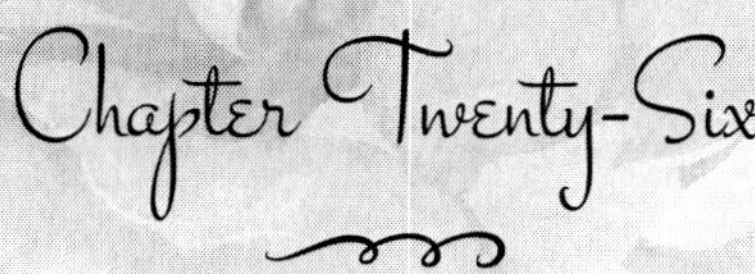

Chapter Twenty-Six

Lauren pushed her cart down the aisle at the hardware store, looking for a new outlet cover. The power had surged yesterday morning, and hers had been fried. She didn't usually make home repairs, but she'd been able to get the ruined one off, and it looked like she could just put a new one on.

She'd done her morning work, and then she'd treated herself to a southwest chicken salad for lunch before stopping here. Once she got home and fixed the light socket, she'd call Blake.

She would.

You will, she told herself as she arrived in front of the socket covers that had a group of four in them. He'd called a few times yesterday, but she'd been busy. She'd met with the printers for Island Sweets, as Bill had approved the final creative designs. She hadn't actually heard her phone ring for the first two phone calls, as she'd been touring their campus and the machines had been running.

The third time he'd called, she'd been driving and hadn't recognized the number. She'd met with Allison Aeyers, and by some miracle, the woman had signed a contract with Lauren, officially becoming her third client. She'd wanted to call Blake then, but he'd not left a number for her to reach him at. She'd called his old number, but it was no longer in use.

Sometimes, her mind ran away from her. She imagined him to have fled the island completely. He'd taken Tommy, and they'd packed up their car, and just started to drive. They'd go until they ran out of gas, then refuel, and go some more. They were running from her, and she had no idea why.

He'd called again last night, when she'd been over at Bea's house. Grant had gone bowling with his new league, and Bea wanted company while she put together a snicker-doodle cheesecake for one of her sons who was coming to visit. He'd arrived today, and Lauren would have to figure out a plan for tonight.

She didn't want to be alone in her house after dark, she knew that. Why, she wasn't sure. It felt too lonely, too easy for her to get lost, too...something.

"Just call Blake," she muttered to herself. He'd come over, and she wouldn't have to be alone. She also really wanted to know what had happened, as Tommy had texted too.

My dad is trying to get in touch with you. This is my

new number, and I know he'd love to hear from you. I would too.

She hadn't known how to answer him. When things got hard for Lauren, she withdrew. That was her default. She'd learned to rely on herself over the years, and she didn't need anyone else.

Except she did, and she knew she did. That was why she didn't know how to respond. She didn't know how to tell someone she loved them, because she wasn't sure how to *show* that love.

"You text back," she told herself, and then she mentally berated herself for talking out loud in the parts aisle. Someone was going to think she was nuts.

"Lauren, hey," a man said, and she turned toward Scott Anderson.

"Scott." She accepted his quick kiss on the cheek and smiled at him. "What are you doing here?"

"Oh, I ran over someone's sprinkler heads mowing today." He wiped one hand down his face. "I have to get over there and fix them, then cross the island for my last job." He looked exhausted, and Lauren felt it all the way to the soles of her feet and back to the top of her head.

She hadn't slept well for two nights now, and she knew it was all because she'd been pulling and pulling to get away from Blake. He hadn't let her go too far, but if she just kept tugging, he might.

After all, everyone else in her life had.

"Then I have to get over to the Lincoln Lightway," he said. "I'm picking someone up for dinner." His smile told her that someone would be a woman, and that he was going on a date.

Lauren's eyebrows went up. "Oh? Is that right? New girlfriend?"

"First date." He chuckled. "I don't think anyone would say she's my girlfriend."

Lauren wondered if he'd been texting Joy. They had each other's numbers, and while Joy had never come out and admitted it, Lauren knew she had a mighty crush on the handsome Scott Anderson.

"Well, have fun." She plucked a socket cover from the display and put it in her cart. Why she had a cart at all, she didn't know. "I have to run too."

"Yep. Good to see you."

Lauren checked out, put her cart away, and drove home. She easily fitted the cover over the outlets and screwed it back into place. She plugged in her phone charger, and then put the right end into her device. It chirped as power started filling the battery, and Lauren knelt on her bedroom floor and stared at the screen on her phone.

She'd said she'd call Blake once she did this task, but she couldn't do it.

She dialed Joy instead. It might be her lunch break at the elementary school where she worked, and she might be able to answer.

"Hey," she said breathlessly. "I just finished eating, and I'm walking the track across the street."

"So healthy," Lauren said. The smile which came to her face felt natural and good.

"What's up?" Joy asked. Wind whipped across the mouthpiece, and that felt like the Coastal Bend of Texas to Lauren.

"I ran into Scott Anderson at the hardware store today," Lauren said instead of telling her anything about the trouble and doubts she was having about Blake. Joy would be able to talk some sense into her, and Lauren didn't want to admit she'd let herself get to this point again. She didn't want to be here, where she expected everyone in her life to leave her. She didn't know when, and she didn't know how long she'd get with them, but she knew they'd eventually leave. Everyone else in her life had.

Not your friends, her mind whispered at her, and Lauren knew she couldn't think in such absolutes.

"Oh?" Joy asked. "What did dear old Scott have to say?"

"He's going out with someone tonight," Lauren said. "First date."

Joy said nothing, and Lauren wasn't sure what that meant. She cocked her head and listened, hoping she could pick up on a feeling though Joy was twelve hundred miles away. "Joy?'

"I'm still here," she said.

"You're upset," Lauren said, catching one tiny hitch in her best friend's voice.

"No," Joy said.

"You are," Lauren said. "Admit it."

"Only if you agree to tell me why you haven't talked to Blake yet."

Lauren pulled in a barbed breath. It hurt her throat as it

went into her lungs, and a stinging vibration radiated through her whole core. "How did you know?"

"Both Bea and Cass have texted me," she said. "Blake's been trying to get in touch with you, and you've sidelined him."

"He missed our three-month anniversary," Lauren said.

"Because his son was in big trouble," Joy said. "Honestly, Lauren, you have no right to give me any relationship advice or assume you know anything about how I feel about Scott Anderson."

"I know." Lauren felt small and insignificant. "I'm going to call him right after we hang up, I swear."

"I miss you so much," Joy said next, all the bite gone from her voice. "I didn't mean to snap."

"I know," she said again. Silence pressed between them, and Lauren didn't mind it. She and Joy had always allowed the silence into their conversations, and if they were sitting across from one another at their favorite Thai place, their eyes would do all the talking.

Over the phone was so much worse, in Lauren's opinion.

"It's okay to admit you like Scott," Lauren said. "To me, at least. I won't tell him or anyone else."

"I know," Joy said this time. She let out a slow, leaky breath. "I do like him..."

Lauren smiled and ducked her head. "Yeah, I know you do."

"I just don't know what to do about it," she said next.

"Now you know how I feel about Blake," Lauren said. "I

can't help who I am, Joy. I can't help that I feel abandoned, even if it makes no sense. Even if he has a really good reason. I just...I needed some time to think."

"Just don't take too much time," Joy said. "That man *really* likes you, Lauren. Just...don't force him to choose between you or his kid. That's not fair, and you already love him too."

Lauren didn't deny it. She didn't know how to say it might be true, but she didn't deny it.

"I'll let you go," Joy said. "You have a phone call to make, and my bell is going to ring in a minute."

"Okay." Lauren pressed her eyes closed. "I love you, Joy."

"I love you too, Lauren."

The call ended, and Lauren let her phone fall to her lap. Why could she tell Joy she loved her, but she couldn't even admit it silently, to herself, about Blake?

She had to do something to make it up to him, and she got to her feet. She went past the office, where she had some work waiting for her, and into the kitchen. The man loved sweets, and she could spend the afternoon baking, then she'd show up at his house with an assortment of apologies and beg him to tell her the story of the past two days.

Yes, that was exactly what she'd do.

Chapter Twenty-Seven

Joy smiled as her last student left her tiny classroom and went down the hall to her regular teacher. The grin slipped away as she faced her empty room again. She pressed the lock on her door and flipped off the lights.

"You don't care that Scott's dating," she told the classroom, which was only big enough to hold a horseshoe table with four chairs around it, and one behind it for her. There were some built-in cabinets behind that, with several feet of windows to let in the light. Between the door and the table, she had a couple of filing cabinets, which held her plants, because Joy believed learning and plants went hand in hand.

A small rug sat on the floor, and she used to get down with the students and play reading games with them. Now, she sat on a chair at the head of the rug to participate. Getting up and down off the floor—especially in a skirt—wasn't exactly easy for her anymore.

She sighed as she rounded the table and sat in the

teacher's chair. She'd been promoted this year. She normally sat at desks outside teacher's classrooms and worked with random students throughout the day.

Now, she had her own room—a mere closet compared to the certified teacher's classrooms, but her own room nonetheless. She worked with the same students every single day, building relationships with them and really having a hand in their progress. The certifications she'd earned over the summer had really helped her.

And there she sat, seriously considering giving it all up.

"For what?" she asked herself. "For a man who's going out with someone else? You can't care about this."

She twisted and grabbed her phone from the basket where it sat during the day. She'd started eating lunch in the faculty lounge, and then she'd been going across the street, where a huge park sat. It had a walking path, and one time around was almost a mile and a half. Because of how the fourth graders staggered their lunch start times, she got a longer lunch than most, and she could eat and walk the loop before she had to be back in her room, ready for her next small group of students.

She worked with twenty children throughout the day, in groups of four. Each group came for forty-five minutes, and then she had fifteen to herself to reset everything and get ready for the next group. Five times a day, she taught the same thing, tailoring the lesson slightly depending on questions, moods, and who needed what help.

They'd only been in school for four weeks, and already Joy could see improvement in every one of her students.

She swiped on her phone and saw she'd missed a few texts from Lauren. *I'm going to make all of his favorite treats to hopefully sweeten him up.*

When you get a minute, can I get that recipe for your raisin-filled cookies?

Joy shook her head, her frustration with Lauren at an all-time high. She loved the woman, but she was astronomically stubborn, so independent, and currently in full-blown self-sabotage mode. Even Bea agreed, and she normally made excuses for Lauren.

Joy knew all the reasons Lauren acted the way she did, probably better than anyone. She shared the feeling of abandonment far too much with Lauren, and she backed out of the texts and went into her cloud storage app, where she kept all of her recipes.

From time to time, one of her sons would ask for one, and she wanted to be able to reply quickly. Her boys were grown, out of the house. Both married and living in the Dallas-Fort-Worth area. Leaving Texas would mean leaving them, and while her boys had lives of their own now, Joy did talk to them and see them fairly regularly.

Wendell had left almost three years ago now, and Joy waited for her throat to close and her chest to hollow. They didn't, at least not to the extent they usually did, and she wondered if perhaps she was ready to move past him.

She'd gone out with Chester McMillan this summer, and it had been fun. Some sparks there, but nothing like the buzz that filled her head when she so much as *thought* about Scott Anderson.

After navigating to his texts, she read through them all again. He'd texted her the very day she'd left Hilton Head with, *Hey, I hope you have a safe trip home. Send me some pictures of your place in Texas. I'd love to see it.*

To Joy's surprise, she'd done as he'd requested, and they'd chatted a little bit about her house there, her kids, and her job. Scott was always—*always*—flirty and witty and fun to talk to, and Joy found herself smiling through the texts for a second time just as she had the first time she'd read them.

Fine, this was at least the sixth or seventh time she'd read through his texts, and they'd made her light up like this every single time.

She'd friend-zoned him near the end of their current conversation, and he'd still flirted with her. He hadn't texted her for about a week now though, and Joy really didn't like the idea of him going out with someone else.

Maybe she didn't want to put him so solidly in the friend zone. Maybe they could flirt and get to know each other across the hundreds of miles that separated them, because with phones and computers and video capabilities these days, was anyone truly that far apart?

She started typing out a message, hated it, and deleted it. How could she say, *So my girlfriend called and we gossiped about you going out with someone else, and I gotta say—I don't like it. I don't like the idea of you going out with anyone but me.*

There was no way she could say that. She wasn't even sure if it was true.

"Oh, it's true," she whispered to herself.

Her heartbeat raced, and she drew in a deep breath. Someone tried to open her door, and Joy looked up. A moment later, a key slid into the lock, and the door opened. The custodian came in, and Joy rose from her chair.

"Oh, good gravy." The man stumbled backward, his hand clutching his chest, clearly surprised to see her there. "I'm sorry, Miss Joy. I didn't know you were still here. You're usually gone by now."

"Yeah," she said. "I'm sorry. I didn't mean to startle you." She turned and opened the bottom drawer in the corner. After dropping her phone into her purse, she straightened and faced Mr. Cutler. "I'm on my way out now. Are you okay?"

He smiled at her, and he had about twenty years on her. "Just got my old ticker fired up again."

She said, "Thanks for taking my trash," and left her classroom. She left the building, and she drove back to her little cottage in a quiet suburb. Bea had lived out in the country, with miles and miles of fields and farmland. Cass had once owned a big, beautiful home on the western border of town, edged with woods. Lauren had lived in an older part of town near the beach, and Joy had loved going to each of their homes for Supper Club.

Her place sat on the smaller end of the scale, but it had a big lot which she enjoyed working in. Her flowers, trees, and bushes always made her smile, and today was no exception.

Bessie lived near the farms on the northwest side of town, and Sage had moved into a condo in downtown Sweet Water Falls after her divorce this past year. With only the three of them left, Joy had grown closer to Bessie and Sage, and they'd started a monthly luncheon outside of Supper Club they hadn't told the others about.

Cherry Forrester had come to the first one, and Joy really was content with her life here.

She was.

She one-hundred-percent was.

Maybe if she told herself that enough, it would become true, because a pinch had started in her stomach, and it would not let go. She got out of her car and went inside, intending to do her afternoon gardening before she started dinner.

Her life was normal. This was what she did every other day of the week.

Somehow, today wasn't just another day of the week. Hilton Head was an hour ahead of them, and Scott might already be getting ready for his date.

Her stomach flipped and churned, and Joy had to do something about it. With a shaking hand, she filled a glass with water and gulped it.

Then, without changing her clothes or taking another moment to think, she started typing out another message to Scott. Either he'd seize onto it and agree, or he'd reject her and go out on his date tonight.

Joy had to know either way, because if she was this skittish right now, she knew she'd never sleep tonight thinking about him having already gone on the date.

No, that couldn't happen, and she had to let him know why he should forget about whoever he'd planned to take to dinner tonight and instead sit home on his couch and text with her.

"Dear Lord," she prayed as she read over the message. It revealed everything. It left her bare and naked for him to see all the way into her heart. He wouldn't have any questions about where she stood once she sent this message. *If* she sent this message.

"If this isn't the right thing to do, stop my finger now." She moved it slowly toward the send button, and all she heard was the pounding of her heart.

So she sent the message.

Chapter Twenty-Eight

Blake looked up from his phone. "The food will be here in thirty minutes," he said to Tommy. "I'm going to run over to Lauren's and see if she'll come eat with us."

"Okay." Tommy didn't look away from his computer.

"You'll be okay here?"

"I'm fine, Dad."

Blake nodded, though his son had his back to him. "Okay." He watched him for another few seconds, then turned and left. Tommy was fine, but that didn't mean he wasn't fighting a battle in his head and his heart.

Blake knew, because he was. He wanted to smooth everything over for the boy, but he couldn't. They'd gone to the middle school here in Hilton Head today, and he'd gotten registered for classes. He wouldn't go until Monday, so he had a three-day weekend ahead of him, and Blake had already called Sandra and told her he wouldn't be in the office tomorrow either.

Things with Tommy had settled. His room was a little fuller, as was Blake's garage, but he was moved in completely. They had groceries, electricity, a school schedule, and a plan. They were cool and safe, and now Blake had to get Lauren back into his life.

It was early for dinner, but that only meant their food would arrive faster and he could spend more time with Lauren once he got her back to the house. He didn't dare think to himself that she might not come. That she might not forgive him for missing their three-month anniversary.

He left the house, his eyes barely seeing if the lights were green as he drove to her house. It didn't take long, and he pulled up only ten minutes later. Another perk of being out before most people left work—less traffic.

His pulse raced in circles, making him-lightheaded. Still, he told himself to get out of the SUV and up to the door, and he did just that. The doorbell rang as the garage door started to lift, and Blake turned back to the driveway.

Lauren's car started; he went down the steps. Then the sidewalk. She didn't back out, and then the slamming of a car door met his ears.

She came out of the garage, and Blake's whole world burst into flames. "Lauren." He jogged to her, not even taking time to absorb the confused expression on her face as he swept her into his arms. "My sweetheart." He held her right against his chest, enthused as she giggled and wrapped her arms around him too.

"I'm so sorry," he whispered. "Things have been so crazy, and you're going to die when you hear everything, but I'm sorry." He pulled away and looked at her, the energy between them vibrant and crackling. "I missed our anniversary. I hated thinking of you here, waiting for me. I know you're mad. But you can't shut me out. Not again. Not when we've come so far already."

"I'm not mad," she said.

Blake knew she was, but he didn't press the issue. She disentangled herself from him, but he wasn't going to let her go very far. She backed up a step. "Come see what I've been doing today."

"I can't wait." He followed her so closely, he nearly hit her when she only went a few paces and then opened the back door of her SUV. He'd been expecting her to go back into the house, and he planted one palm against the back window to keep himself from pitching forward.

She bent inside and then straightened with a huge platter of cookies in her hand. "I've been baking." She looked at him, and he tore his gaze from the delicious-looking and chocolatey scent of the cookies to meet her eye. "For you. These are for you." She handed the platter to him, and it had to hold at least three dozen cookies.

She dove back into the car and emerged with a cheesecake sprinkled with light brown cookie crumbs. "And this is for you too." She gave it to him while he tried to figure out what to say.

She pulled out another bin of treats, and said, "Raisin-filled cookies. You'll die when you have these with coffee. They're *so* good." She put them on the roof of her vehicle. "Lemon bars, because your momma said they're one of your favorites." She held those and gestured to the car with her free hand. "There's more, but..." Tears clung to her eyelashes. "I'm sorry I ran," she whispered.

"You can't get far from me," he whispered.

"I thought maybe if I brought all kinds of sweets, you wouldn't be too sour with me." She swiped at her eyes. "And now here you are, not upset at all." She sniffled and shook her head. "You're so good, Blake Williams. Too good for me."

"No." He put the platter and cheesecake on the top of her car too. "I'm not too good for you." He took the lemon bars and set them aside too. "Do you remember when I said that about you? That you were out of my league?"

She ducked her head and nodded. "That was before you knew how insane I am."

"You're not insane," he said. "You feel things deeply. You've had some past trauma that makes you revert to the little girl who everyone left behind." He reached out and gently put his fingers under her chin and lifted it so she had to look at him. "I'm not going to do that. I had to pick Tommy for a couple of days, because there was suddenly this huge fire consuming both of us, and I had to put it out."

"I would've helped," she whispered.

Blake's whole heart melted, and he gathered her into his arms again. "I know you would've, baby." He would've told her what was going on, but he wouldn't have wanted her mixed up in it, if only to protect her. "Tommy's going to love you when you show up with all these treats. We ordered pizza, and I got the veggie kind you like. Will you come over to our house and have dinner? Stay a while?"

Lauren was smart, and she pulled away. Her eyes brimmed with tears as she nodded. "Our house?"

"Tommy lives with me now." He swallowed. "There's really so much to tell, and I'll start with—Jacinda's boyfriend took my phone the moment I arrived in Carter's Cove to pick up my son, and he smashed it. He'd already crushed Tommy's. We didn't have new phones until last night, and I called you lots of times."

"I got the messages," she said. "I just needed some time to figure out why I hid, and how I could make it up to you."

Blake smiled at her. "I know why you hid."

"Do you? Because I barely do."

"Yeah." Blake ran his hands up and down her bare arms, enjoying the way her soft skin felt against his fingers and palms. "You hid, you retreated, because someone important to you disappointed you. I can't promise I won't do it again. People are disappointing, you know? But I will try so hard not to, because I love you. And you retreated from me, because you love me too, and you don't want to admit it in case I'm going to hurt you."

He raised his eyebrows. "Tell me I'm wrong."

Lauren's deep, dark eyes searched his. "Can we back up to the part where you said you loved me?"

Blake grinned wider and wider and wider. "Yeah, we can." He cradled her face in one palm and brushed away her tears with his other hand. "I love you, Lauren Keller. I love you, and I'm not going to keep it to myself anymore. I love you, and I want *you* to move into my house with me and my son. I want us to be a family." He leaned closer and closer, touching his forehead to hers. "I love you so much, and I want to be your husband even though we haven't talked about marriage. We haven't talked too much about having more kids. I know you want to establish rules for how you can parent Tommy. All of that, but we have time to work through it, and I know we can, because *I love you*."

Lauren's eyes had drifted closed at some point, and her mouth curved upward now. "I love you, too, Blake."

"Mm, I knew it." He touched his lips to hers, the heat exploding between them. He kept the pace slow and the strokes sure, and he sure enjoyed how completely Lauren kissed him back. After several long seconds, he pulled away and said, "I'm going to take that as a yes, you'll come for dinner."

"Yes," she said. She pulled away slightly and added, "I texted you only a few minutes before you were supposed to arrive on Tuesday night," she said. "I said I had some serious things I wanted to talk about. One of them was marriage, and the other was having more kids."

Blake's eyes widened at the same pace as his smile. "I'd love to talk about all of that with you," he said. He reached for the lemon bars. "But I think I want one of these first, and then I want to take you back to my place so you can see Tommy, and we want to tell you everything that's happened in the past couple of days." He peeled back the plastic wrap and took out an ooey gooey lemon bar. "Deal?"

"Deal," she said.

He took a bite of the lemon bar, the sourness making him pucker and smile at the same time. "This is fantastic."

She smiled, her tears gone now. "You're fantastic."

"We can go out tomorrow night," he said. "Celebrate our three-month anniversary just a few days late." He lifted his eyebrows. "Do you want to?"

"Yes," she said, leaning into him again. "I really want to." She kissed him this time, and Blake decided she tasted better than any treat anyone, anywhere, could ever make, and that he was the luckiest man in the world that he got to kiss her.

"Lauren's here, bud," he called as he led her into the house. "She brought cookies." That would get Tommy away from SquareSpaces, though Blake hoped simply having Lauren here would do that.

"Coming!" Tommy yelled from the bedroom. They'd moved his computer in there for now, until Blake could sort through where to put everything permanently. "Two minutes!"

Lauren slid the container of raisin cookies onto the counter and said, "I'll go talk to him if you want to make coffee." She lifted her perfectly sculpted eyebrows at him. She'd put on makeup, and she currently wore a pair of tight yoga pants and a sweater the color of bright Granny Smith apples. It hung low over her backside, and Blake pushed it up until his hand ran along the waistband of her pants and the warm strip of skin atop it.

"Mm, how about you kiss me first, and then I'll make coffee while you go tell him you're madly in love with me and we're going to get married."

Lauren laughed, but when he touched his mouth to hers, she silenced that and kissed him back. She was madly in love with him, and Blake had fallen completely for her too. He forgot about cookies, coffee, and his son until Lauren pulled away and said, "It's been two minutes. Do you want him to catch us making out again?"

No, Blake didn't. But he didn't want to let Lauren get too far from him, physically or emotionally. "All right," he said. "Decaf? Or do you want the original dark roast?"

"Original," she said. "I'll be okay."

"I'm not working tomorrow," he said. "Tommy's not starting at the middle school until Monday." He opened the cupboard where he kept the coffee filters. "So I can handle the original too."

"You're not working tomorrow?" she asked. "Do you want to come over and go over my new client with me?"

He swung his attention toward her. "You got a new client?"

"Just this morning," she said. "Which is why I didn't call you back. I had something going on too." She smiled at him, but it was shy instead of her usual self-confident, gorgeous self. Blake knew her so much better now, and while she didn't intimidate him, she was strong and opinionated. Some of what had scared him before he now knew to be a front Lauren put on so people didn't get too close to her.

"That's amazing, sweetheart." He kissed her quickly

again. "Yes, I'll come over tomorrow to hear about your new client. I just need to figure out what to do with Tommy."

"You don't need to do anything with me, Dad." Tommy walked toward them, and his frowning look of displeasure melted away as Lauren turned toward him. "Lauren."

"My darling boy," she said, and Blake blinked as she left him behind and went to embrace his son. Tommy wasn't the huggy type, even for Blake and Jacinda, but he let Lauren wrap him right up into her arms and hold him tight. He returned the hug too, his smile wide and his face full of bliss as his eyes drifted closed.

Huh, Blake thought. Lauren was obviously more important to Tommy than Blake knew. Gladness overcame him and spread through him as she stepped back and took his face in her hands. "You're okay? Your dad hasn't told me everything, but I was very worried about you two."

Tommy nodded. "Yeah, I'm okay." He looked over to Blake. "My dad took care of everything." Tommy had thanked him for coming previously. He'd apologized for how things had gone. Blake had told him he didn't need to do either of those things, not for him. "I'm glad you're not mad at him. He would've been to your date if he could've been. He would've called if he could've."

Blake turned away then, a vein of humility running through him. Even Tommy could see how much he cared about Lauren, and he remembered he wasn't hiding it anymore. He loved her, and he didn't care who knew. He wasn't going to hold it to himself any longer, and he wanted to climb up onto the roof and shout about his love to the whole island.

"Is the pizza here?" he asked.

"No," Tommy said. "Not that I know of."

Right then, the doorbell rang, and everyone turned toward the front door. "I'll get it," Lauren said, and she strode in that direction. Blake went back to measuring coffee, everything in his life starting to settle again now that Lauren was back where she belonged—with him.

"Blake," she said at the same time Tommy said, "Mom?"

He spun toward the door, beyond surprised to see Jacinda standing on the doorstep. She wasn't crying, but Blake abandoned the coffee anyway, the way she wrung her hands concerning enough for him.

She never came here, and Blake was surprised she knew the address. "What are you doing here?" he asked as he reached Lauren's side. They both looked at Jacinda, waiting for her to say something.

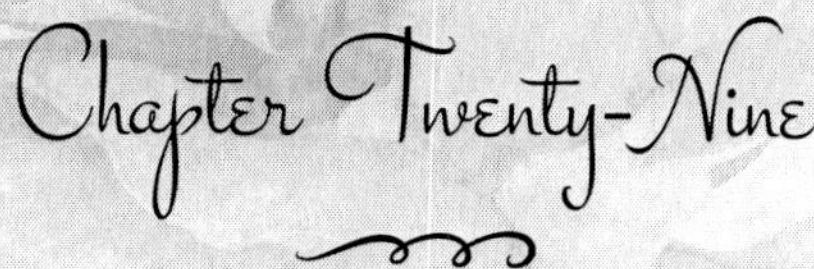

Chapter Twenty-Nine

Lauren threaded her fingers through Blake's as he looked at his ex-wife. "Jacinda," he said, moving forward. Lauren let him go, a sudden wave of self-consciousness moving through her. She hadn't recognized the woman, but how could she? Blake didn't keep pictures of her on his mantle or anything.

It hadn't been until Tommy had said, "Mom?" that Lauren had realized who she was. She'd been upset since the moment Lauren had opened the door, and she'd asked for Blake. That was what Lauren knew. She still didn't know the full story of what had happened on Carter's Cove two days ago, and she honestly wasn't sure she needed to know.

Blake loved her; Tommy had hugged her. They wanted her in their lives, whether they were good, bad, or ugly, and Lauren wanted to be there.

For this too, she told herself.

"What's wrong?" Blake asked. He slid his arm around

his ex and guided her inside. "Come in. I don't need you standing on the porch for the world to see." He checked behind her as she entered, then he closed and locked the door.

"Jacinda," he said smoothly. "This is my girlfriend, Lauren. Lauren, my ex-wife, Jacinda."

"Nice to meet you," Lauren said.

Jacinda's lower lip stopped trembling, and she nodded. "You too."

"Mom." Tommy didn't run to her and hug her the way he had Lauren. "What are you doing here?"

"I just found out you moved out," she said. Her voice pitched up. "I didn't—Cason just told me."

Lauren's eyebrows went up, but it was Blake who asked, "Where have you been, Jacinda? You didn't know your son moved out two days ago?"

"I was in Newark," she said. "I had a meeting there with the people who sell my bath bombs." She barely spared a glance for Blake. "Cason told me your phone broke, and he didn't have your new number." She took a step toward Tommy, and then she hurried to him. He did hug her, and she cried against his shoulder.

She murmured apologies and other things Lauren didn't want to intrude on. She clearly loved her son, and she had some things to work out with Blake, Tommy, and Cason.

They separated, and Jacinda looked at the two of them. Lauren felt like an outsider, because she was one. Her natural instinct told her to leave. Let this family work out their problems without an audience. One look at Blake, and she knew she wouldn't be leaving.

"What are we going to do?" Jacinda asked.

"My son will never live with that man again," Blake said. "Not unless he's an adult and capable of defending himself." He looked at Tommy and then Jacinda again. "I could press charges, Jacinda. Destruction of property. Keeping a minor against his will. Threatening said minor."

Lauren edged closer, shocked to hear him speak like that. Blake caught her eye, and he reached for her.

"He said he'd just gotten bad news." Jacinda's hands went round and round each other again. "You won't really sue him, will you?"

"Everyone gets bad news," Blake said. "Heck, Lauren was questioned by two FBI agents in the middle of the night. She didn't go around smashing cell phones and telling thirteen-year-olds that they weren't good for anything."

Jacinda hissed as she inhaled. "Tommy." She shook her head. "Tom. Tell me he didn't say that."

"He said it, Mom," Tommy mumbled. The doorbell rang again, and he went to get it this time. Lauren looked at Blake, saw the worry there, and followed him.

If Jacinda had come here, Cason could've followed her. They had no guarantee that the person on the other side of the door was indeed the pizza delivery man.

"Tommy, let me." She darted in front of him while Blake and Jacinda continued to talk in hushed voices behind her. She put her foot only inches behind the door and opened it until it met her toe.

A boy not much older than Tommy stood there, three stacked boxes of pizza in his hands. "For Blake?" he asked.

"Yep." She opened the door all the way then and took the boxes. After handing them to Tommy, she signed the receipt and thanked the boy. He left, and Lauren closed and re-locked the door.

"...could've called," Blake said.

"I don't have your new numbers," Jacinda said. "If Cason does, he wouldn't give it to me."

"I didn't call and give your abusive boyfriend our numbers, no." Blake rolled his eyes. Lauren was surprised to see him in such a bad mood, because he'd rarely acted like this. He'd told her he got along with his ex-wife. He opened the top box of pizza, and it was her veggie delight.

She smiled and took the box while he said, "I don't want him to have my number. Or Tommy's. The end. He doesn't need them. Only you do."

"So he won't come stay with me on weekends?" Jacinda asked. "You got him every weekend. All summer. Whenever you wanted him."

"I don't live with someone who's dangerous," Blake said, not unkindly. "Jacinda, I'm not going to give you an ultimatum. I'm not. But he threatened Tommy. He raised his hand to him—now, whether he hit him or not is irrelevant. He—"

"Did he?" she asked.

"No," Blake and Tommy said together. "But he acted like he would," Blake said quickly. "There's a manipulation and fear tactic there, and Tommy won't be around that. You'll have to figure something else out."

She threw her hands up into the air. "Like what?"

"Get a hotel here on the island," Blake said coolly. "You and Tommy can spend weekends on the beach, at the smoothie shop, whatever."

"You need to break up with that jerk," Tommy said, and Lauren ducked away from them so no one would see her smile. She had no voice here, and she was determined not to say anything.

"Tommy," Blake and Jacinda said, making it clear they didn't want his opinion in this conversation.

He rolled his eyes, piled his plate with several pieces of pizza, and said, "I'm going to play SquareSpaces."

Lauren lunged after him. "Can I come?"

He turned and looked at her, his dark eyes wide. "You—yeah, sure."

She nodded, then turned back to the counter to get her pizza. "Thank you, Blake," she said. "Great meeting you, Jacinda. Really." She put three pieces on a plate while she spoke. "I'll just leave you guys to talk."

"Lauren," Blake said.

"Take your time." She met his eye. "Really, I don't mind. This is important." She rounded the corner of the counter and tipped up to kiss him. "The night is young."

He did give her a tiny smile then, nodded, and Lauren hurried to follow Tommy down the hall to his bedroom. Blake had one more on this level, and then another upstairs. There was no bathroom up there, and Lauren wouldn't want to come down in the middle of the night when she needed to go.

His house was quite a bit bigger than hers, and with Tommy living with him full-time now, Lauren had the suspicion that once she and Blake got married, they'd be living here instead of in the charming cottage she'd just purchased.

The thought sat okay with her, and she turned to go into Tommy's room just as he cheered. "Yes, Lauren, come see." He swung toward her in his swiveling chair and then turned back to the screen. "I just got picked on DaringMan's team. This is going to be so epic."

Lauren spotted a folding chair near his desk, and she set down her pizza to set up the chair.

"Oh, they picked DragonCon, shoot," he said next. "Oh, well. At least it'll be interesting." He didn't seem concerned about the conversation his parents were having down the hall in the kitchen. He only stopped smiling so he could take an enormous bite of his pizza, and then he said, "Let the games begin."

"You're kidding." Lauren lay in Blake's arms, the hour at which she should've turned into a pumpkin and gone home long past. Tommy had gone to bed three hours ago, and he'd been up late.

After Jacinda had left, after Tommy had won his heated game of SquareSpaces, after they'd eaten and watched a movie, Blake had changed his clothes and laid on the couch. Once Tommy had gone to bed, Lauren had laid down with him, both of them trying to fit into a tiny space together.

"I'm not kidding," Blake said. "Tommy just wanted to come for the night. He said Cason was really on one, and he didn't want to stay."

Lauren had heard the whole tale now, and it only made her feel more guilty for being upset that Blake hadn't shown up on time for their three-month anniversary date. "I'm glad the two of you are okay."

"Me too," he murmured.

She started to get up, but the pressure of his hand along her back increased. "Stay," he said.

"It's two a.m.," she whispered back. "I have to go. I have to work tomorrow, unlike some of us." She smiled at him, but his eyes were closed. He looked so serene and peaceful, and she balanced herself on one hand and swept her fingers along his forehead with the other.

His eyelashes fluttered, but they didn't open, and Lauren leaned down and kissed him. He responded quickly and eagerly, but Lauren kept the pace slow. She wanted him to know how deep her feelings went, and they were so much more than a fire that burned through its fuel in the first ten seconds.

"I love you," she whispered. "Call me when you're on the way over tomorrow, and I'll make fresh coffee."

"I'll bring pastries," he said.

She wasn't going to argue with that. Harrison had won over Cass by consistently bringing her all her favorite things. In truth, it wasn't about eclairs or raspberry fritters. It was that Harrison took care of her, the same way Blake took care of Lauren.

She got to her feet, and he did too, much groaning and griping in the process. She led him to the door with a smile and asked, "When we get married, do you want to live here?"

That got him to stop complaining, and he took her into his arms again. "I think it would be ideal, yes."

Lauren nodded. "I think so too. Maybe I could...share your office space with you? Could we talk about that?"

His eyebrows went up, but Lauren had been to his office building. He rented the whole thing, and he had at least two rooms that weren't currently in use. She only needed one.

"Of course we can talk about it," he said. "It's a great idea, too."

"I can't believe I'm going to move again," she said, really leaning into his chest.

"Don't worry," he said. "You didn't have much stuff, and I'll help you." He leaned toward her and added, "I love you, Lauren. I'll see you tomorrow, okay?"

"Mm." She accepted his kiss, her way of saying, *Okay. Yes, it's absolutely okay to see me tomorrow and kiss me like this.*

Chapter Thirty

Three Months Later:

Blake looked at the sky, trying to find the horizon where the ocean met the atmosphere. It was all one color of gray, and he couldn't see it. It rarely got too terribly cold on Hilton Head Island, but in the winter, they had plenty of rain and stormy skies.

Today was one such day, and while Blake wanted the sun to shine its brightest on the day he asked Lauren to be his wife, he couldn't wait for the weather to cooperate. He couldn't wait one more day, period.

Another hour felt like torture, but Lauren hadn't come out of her meeting yet. Today was the last day either of them would work this year. The Christmas holidays were almost upon them, and Joy was flying in tomorrow. Blake wanted Lauren to have a shiny new diamond to show off for her friends, and if she'd come out of the country club, he'd be able to get the question asked.

He tucked his hands into his pockets and turned away from the country club. Lauren didn't know he was waiting for her, and staring at the door was like watching a pot of water and willing it to boil. It wouldn't, and when she exited, he'd talk to her.

He wandered down the paved path, his thoughts scattering but his pulse absolutely calm. Lauren had said she wanted a spring wedding, and that she didn't want to be engaged for too long. He figured a Christmas proposal would give her the time she needed to plan the perfect beach wedding, and an engagement of three or four months could hardly be considered long.

In fact, in Carolina, it would be a hurry-up wedding, and he guaranteed his momma would ask if Lauren was pregnant. Blake knew that was an impossibility, but the idea of it made him smile.

They'd talked about marriage, weddings, teenagers, and babies in the past three months, and Tommy had turned fourteen as well. Some days felt like they moved as snails and other days blinked by without Blake knowing what he'd done.

He'd renewed his lease on the building, and this time, he'd added Lauren's name to it as well. She'd be moving her home-based office into his building, and she had two offices off the back door. With the separate entrance, her clients could come in and not have to go past his secretary or down his hallways, and he could still jot over to her office to kiss her whenever he wanted.

He realized then that he'd been wandering, lost inside his

own thoughts, and he turned back to the country club. He'd gone pretty far, and he cursed himself for letting his imagination take control of his life. He'd done that a lot with Lauren, because sometimes he still couldn't believe she'd chosen him. That she loved him.

She said it every day, though, and Blake sure did like hearing it.

He scanned the parking lot as he returned to the big building in the gray light, and to his horror, Lauren's SUV wasn't there anymore. "Stupid," he muttered to himself. "Stupid, stupid, stupid."

He didn't know where she was headed after this, and they hadn't shared their locations with one another. He jogged to his vehicle and got behind the wheel. He waited what felt like an impossibly long time for his phone to connect to the Bluetooth, and then he dialed Lauren.

Taking a deep breath, he told himself to calm down. He didn't need to make a big show for her. He hadn't planned to. The diamond ring sat in his pocket, and he'd been planning to surprise her outside her meeting, drop to both knees, and ask her to be his wife.

Just thinking about it made him cringe. That wasn't a good enough proposal for a woman like Lauren Keller.

"Hey," she said.

"Uh, hey," he said, trying to focus on the conversation and driving and how he could make his proposal better all at the same time. That totally didn't work, and he backed out of the spot without saying anything.

"What's up?" Lauren prompted.

"Where you at?" he asked. "Is your meeting over?" He knew dang well it was, and he might be on her tail.

"Yep," she said. "Finished a few minutes ago. I'm headed to the grocery store to get the meat for the kabobs tonight. Remember we're grilling in Harrison's new outdoor kitchen?"

"Yes," Blake said. "I remember. Are you going to Fresh Mart? Or Shirley's?"

"Shirley's," she said slowly. "Where are you, Mister Williams?"

Great. He'd given himself away. He couldn't think fast enough to come up with a reason, make the left he needed to in order to go to Shirley's instead of Fresh Mart, and berate himself, so he said, "I was hoping to catch you at the country club, but it sounds like I missed you."

"You were? Why?"

"Just wanted to see you," he said innocently.

Lauren didn't buy it for a moment, if her scoff told him anything. "What for?"

Blake didn't hem and haw, because that always gave away more than he intended. "Maybe I just want to kiss you. Maybe I'm anxious to start our Christmas break together. I don't know. I ran out of work to do, and I wanted to see you."

She laughed lightly. "You never run out of work to do."

"Work I *wanted* to do." He smiled and made the left-hand turn. "I'll find you in Shirley's."

"I'm almost there," she said.

He was about five minutes behind, and he once again

couldn't believe he'd walked away from the country club. She had to have come out the moment he turned his back on the place.

Blake wondered if he could dash into Shirley's and grab some roses. "No," he told himself. "Cliché." Lauren didn't want cliché. She wanted special, because she was special.

He arrived at Shirley's, still no plan in mind, and jumped from his SUV. He could get the lemon sorbet she liked and see what floral arrangements they had. He reminded himself that he had a *diamond ring*, and lemon sorbet didn't hold a candle to that. At the same time, he was clearly unprepared to propose, and he toyed with putting it off until he could do a better job of it.

He strode through the automatic doors, his focus singular: sorbet, then flowers.

He certainly didn't expect to come face-to-face with his gorgeous girlfriend two steps into the store.

"You are stalking me," she teased. She wore a somewhat wary look in her eyes, and she hadn't grabbed a cart or anything yet.

"I'm not," he said.

"You look like a man on a mission." She cocked her eyebrows and folded her arms. Another patron tried to come into the store, and Blake moved out of the way.

"I have to use the bathroom," he said, taking her elbow and getting her to move aside so the elderly man could enter too. "Grab a cart, baby. I'll come find you."

Lauren looked like she might protest, and she was downright mouthwatering in her pencil skirt and nearly sheer blouse. It made him look twice, and he leaned down and kissed her. Short, but oh-so-amazing, the kiss revved him up and gave him courage.

An idea popped into his head, and he took a cart from the rows of them and wheeled it around for her. "I want some salmon kebobs if they have them."

"It's on my list," she said.

"Great." He grinned at her. "I'll come find you." He walked away from her and along the front of the store. He ducked into the men's room and took a deep breath. Surely she wouldn't follow him and wait for him. People used the bathroom at the grocery store.

After a minute, he dared to peek out. He didn't see her, and he ducked out of the bathroom and toward the customer service counter. He happened to know Chloe Wiggins, and her father owned Shirley's. Her grandmother *was* Shirley.

"Chloe," he said breathlessly. She looked over to him, her face lighting up when she recognized him.

"Just a sec, Blake," she drawled, turning back to the fax machine.

"Chloe," he said again. "I need to use the PA system."

That got her to turn, her blue eyes wide. "Whatever for?"

"My girlfriend is here, and I want to propose to her." He suddenly remembered the sorbet and the flowers. He pushed them away. The ring and the public address system would have to be enough.

Chloe's surprise melted away. "You always go big, Blake. What if she says no?"

"Not what a man wants to hear," he grumbled.

She abandoned the fax machine and came over to the counter. "All right," she said. "But if I get fired, you have to hire me."

"You're not going to get fired," he said. "I know you let Chief Brownstone use the PA system just last week, to announce to everyone here that his son had just graduated from Georgia Tech with a four-point-oh."

Chloe pealed out a round of laughter and pushed some buttons. "Shirley's does seem to be the place for big news," she said. "Why not a proposal?"

She pressed one more key and held out the receiver. Beeps sounded throughout the store, and Blake drew a big breath.

Now or never.

He took the corded phone, feeling very much like he was back in junior high, calling a girl for the first time. His pulse sprinted now, and he felt like he might throw up. He'd been so calm at the country club, and he didn't know where these nerves had come from.

"Ladies and gentlemen," he said, his voice smooth and bright. "This is Blake Williams, and I have a very important question for one of our shoppers today."

He turned from the customer service desk, and several people had stopped and were looking at him. Women. All women. All smiling.

He smiled back, his shoulders relaxing. "Lauren Keller,

I'm in love with you. You're my sun and my moon, and I want to spend the rest of my life taking care of you, loving you, and raising our family together. I'm up at customer service, and I'd love for you to make your way here and answer one question for me."

Even the checkers had stopped ringing up items. It felt like the entirety of Shirley's had stopped breathing entirely, and Blake basked in that moment.

"Will you marry me?" he practically bellowed into the phone and over the loudspeaker in the grocery store.

He lifted the receiver over his shoulder without turning, and Shirley took it.

Now he just needed Lauren to come up front and answer him. He noticed a couple of women turning toward the back of the store, then another, and another. He watched in their direction, and Lauren appeared at the end of an aisle.

She wore a stunned look on her face, like someone had just thrown a bucket of cold water at her, and she was trying to find air.

He lifted his hand as if she might not recognize him or be able to see him, and she walked toward him in those sexy heels.

He got down on both knees and dug in his pocket for the diamond ring. Praise the heavens, it was still there. He held it up as she arrived in front of him. "Well?" he asked, and it felt strange for his voice to be so quiet. "What do you think? Will you be my wife?"

Lauren looked at the ring and then him. "You're insane, that's what I think."

Chloe twittered behind him, but Blake ignored her. "Is that a no?"

"No," she said, and his heart bounced against his ribs. "I'm not saying no."

"I don't hear a yes." He grinned at her.

Lauren's smile grew by degrees over a few long seconds, and then she said, "Yes," in a loud voice. "Yes, Blake, I'll marry you."

The same series of beeps filled the air as Blake slid the diamond onto Lauren's left ring finger, and then Chloe drawled, "She said yes, folks!"

Applause filled Shirley's, and Blake got to his feet and took Lauren into his arms. He held her tightly, and she did the same to him. He pulled back and gazed into her eyes as Chloe started blasting celebratory music through the store.

"I love you," he said, barely able to hear his own voice. "I hope this gives you enough time to plan your spring wedding."

"It does." She smiled at him and ran her hand down the side of his face. "I love you so much."

He kissed her then, and despite the people still watching, and Chloe catcalling, and all the music around them, he existed inside the slow, sensual touch of the woman he loved. It was just him and Lauren, and that was how Blake always wanted it to be.

Keep reading for a sneak peek at **THE BEACH BLUEPRINT,** the next book in this romance and friendship fiction series. It features Joy Bartlett and how she tries to figure out where she's supposed to be...and with who.

I hope you enjoyed Cass, Harrison, Lauren, Blake, Bea, Grant, and everyone else in *The Seaside Strategy*! **Please leave a review for the book if you did.**

Scan the QR code below to preorder THE BEACH BLUEPRINT, the next book in the series.

Sneak Peek! The Peach Blueprint Chapter One:

Joy Bartlett disembarked from the plane, her heartbeat one giant bass drum. She couldn't believe what she was doing. Still, her step landed smoothly as she navigated the airport in Charleston, as she'd flown in here several times now.

She knew where the rental car counters were, and she knew how to get from there to the cars without even looking at the signs. She could drive from Charleston to Hilton Head easily now, and she couldn't wait to spend Christmas with her besties. Well, some of them, at least.

Bessie had gone to Peachtree to spend the holidays with her daughter. Joy knew they had plans to talk about opening a bakery franchise here in Hilton Head. It wasn't franchised anywhere else yet, and when they'd gone to lunch last week, Joy had told her to simply open her own bakery.

Why should she put money in the hands of her boss?

She was an excellent baker, and with all the tourists here on the island, there was definitely room for another bakery—especially one that only delivered the best Texas sourdough... in South Carolina.

Bessie had started sketching out new plans, and she called Joy almost every day to talk about it.

Joy herself had not started talking to anyone about making a move from Sweet Water Falls, Texas, where she currently lived and worked full-time, to Hilton Head, South Carolina. Half of her Supper Club had made the move now, and the pull for Joy to do so felt like the weight of gravity on her soul.

At the same time, Joy was forty-seven years old, and she couldn't go jump off a cliff—or move halfway across the country—just because all of her friends were doing it.

No, Joy had to have a blueprint first. She needed to be able to see her life here before she could commit to embracing anything that required her packing up almost fifty years of Texas lineage and moving it.

She hadn't mentioned a possible relocation to either of her sons, and she had no husband she had to check off with. Her grandkids pulled at her just as strongly, and they were all in Texas.

"Thank you," she said to the rental car attendant as he lifted her bag into the back of the SUV she'd drive for the next two weeks. She'd packed a big bag and a backpack, but the latter would ride shotgun next to her.

The drive passed quickly, and before Joy knew it, she was turning into the parking lot of a restaurant called Mead's.

She'd not eaten here before, but she'd been told it was amazing, and at three-thirty in the afternoon on a Thursday before Christmas, likely to not be busy.

There weren't very many cars in the lot, and Joy pulled into a spot in the first row next to the building. She had no idea what kind of car Scott drove, as they'd been texting back and forth a lot over the last few months, but their vehicles had not come up once.

"You're insane," she whispered to herself. She met her own gray-blue eyes in the rearview mirror and reached to fix the errant strands of her hair. Her ex-husband had once told her he loved her eyes, because he couldn't quite identify the color of them. Not quite blue, but not quite gray, he'd landed on "slate."

Joy had been describing herself with that adjective ever since. Her hair was blonde, starting to pull in some gray she didn't bother to cover with anything synthetic. She wasn't trying to pretend to be an age she wasn't, and she rather liked her shoulder-length hairdo that waved down even on the worst of hair days.

She wasn't Lauren by any stretch of the imagination. The woman always looked like a million bucks, without a single strand of hair out of place. But Joy had learned not to compare herself to Lauren a long, long time ago.

Joy swallowed and checked the clock on her phone. She'd made good time from the airport, and she'd arrived a bit early. She leaned her head back, a hint of exhaustion pulling through the tight muscles in her shoulders.

She'd have to eventually tell her friends that she'd lied to them. It wasn't really a lie, as she'd had a couple of months to rationalize away this extra day on the island. One, Scott had asked her to come in a day early.

She'd agreed.

No crime in that.

Two, she hadn't wanted anyone to know. Not Bessie. Not Lauren. Not Bea or Cass. If they knew, she'd end up going out with Scott and then staying up all night detailing everything to someone. She didn't want to do that. She wanted a quiet evening to herself after the date so she could determine how she felt about the man.

Right now, as they'd only been texting for the past three months, every cell in her body vibrated in anticipation of seeing him in person. They video chatted often, but there was something different about being in the presence of another human being—especially a man like Scott Anderson.

He'd tickled her interest the very first time they'd met, though she'd tried to put a barrier between them. It helped that he'd barely looked at her, and then the second time they'd "met," he'd come right out and said he couldn't remember her. Constructing that wall had been easier then. Keeping him out of her thoughts had proven nearly impossible, and Joy really only achieved it when she slept.

"He canceled his date to stay home and talk to you," she reminded herself. Every time she thought about that evening back in September, she grew warm. Then immediately cold, for now she had to live up to the reputation of a woman who could make a man cancel his date to stay home and talk to someone who lived over a thousand miles away.

Someone knocked on the window, and Joy jumped a Texas mile in her seat. A strangled yelp came from her throat, and she threw up both hands as if she'd ward off the unwanted evil trying to get to her through the glass.

Scott stood there, and he laughed right out loud. The rental car window didn't mute it so much that she couldn't hear it, and while her adrenaline poured through her, she also calmed. She grinned at him, all that nervous energy joining the hum already in her veins until it became a roaring buzz.

She reached for the door handle and popped the seal there. "Hey," he said, grabbing onto the door and opening it the rest of the way. "Sorry. I realize how creepy that was."

Joy slid from the SUV and had to look up at Scott as he stood about eight inches taller than her. His golden hair shone with that red she'd been dreaming about, and she had the strangest urge to run her fingers through it.

"Hello." Awkwardly, she reached for him and sort of stutter stepped into him while she grabbed onto him to hug. "It's good to see you."

"In person," he said. "In the flesh." He held her easily, effortlessly, and Joy told herself to calm down.

She moved out of the way and closed the door. Only then did she remember her purse. "Oh, I need my purse." She retrieved it and smiled at him again.

"Can I hold your hand?" He grinned at her and looked at her out of the side of his eye. "I mean, I feel like we've been together for months, but I've never actually held your hand."

Joy stepped with him, and on the next forward movement, her fingers slid into his. She smiled and said, "Yeah, this is nice."

"Mm." Scott took her into the restaurant. "You've never been here?"

"No, sir," she said.

"Chester didn't bring you to Mead's?" He acted scandalized, his grin playful and full of teasing. She'd talked to him via video where he did this too, and she found him so adorable. "I'm shocked by that."

"Really?" She flirted right back, the action easier in person than she'd anticipated. "Why's that? Do they serve... questionable meats here?" She glanced around like she'd see a horse or a dog on its way to the kitchen.

Scott laughed, the sound as delicious in person as Joy had heard through her phone. "No," he said. "But it's definitely some of the best food in all of Carolina." He spoke like a lifelong Southern boy, and Joy had to admit she sure did like that.

"When you come to Texas," she said. "I'll take you to my favorite barbecue place."

Scott's lighter blue eyes lit up. "You want me to come to Texas?"

Joy grinned at him. "I just invited you, so yes." She turned toward him as they approached the hostess station. "What do you think? Can you ever take time off?" He owned a huge landscaping company, and he worked outside seemingly day and night.

"Yeah," he said slowly. "For you, Joy, I think I can take some time off." He spoke in his slow, sexy, Southern drawl, and Joy swore the ground vanished beneath her feet for a few seconds.

The earth swooped and trembled, and then Scott was right there to hold her steady. "All right," she said simply. "We'll work that out later."

"Two," Scott said to the hostess. "And we want a booth away from all the noise, if possible." He knocked on the top of the podium. "Thanks, Sam."

"You got it, Scott." She plucked two menus from the side of her stand and smiled at the pair of them. "This way."

Joy's phone rang, which sent her heart into another somersault. She plucked it from her purse, pausing as Scott started after Sam. The number was unfamiliar, but something inside Joy's mind recognized the number, and she needed to answer it.

"I need to grab this," she said.

"Sure." He looked to Sam and back to her. "I'll get the table and come back for you."

She nodded and swiped on her phone, turning her back on the rest of the restaurant at the same time. "Hello?"

"Miss Bartlett?" a cool female voice asked.

"Yes, ma'am."

"This is Sophie from The Island Sand Bar."

"Oh, sure," Joy said. She'd booked a room at the seaside

hotel for tonight. Tomorrow, she'd be staying with Lauren in her cute cottage house.

"I'm so sorry, but we won't be able to have you stay with us tonight."

Joy's stomach dropped to her feet, where it wobbled and hung there for a moment. "I'm sorry?"

"Our kitchen flooded, and that sparked a fire. We have no electricity." She sounded truly sorry. "I've already called our sister site, but unfortunately, they're full."

"Okay," Joy said, really drawing out the word. "So...I just have nowhere to stay tonight?"

"I can provide a list of hotels in the area, and you can make some phone calls." Something banged and then zapped. Sophie shrieked, and Joy pulled the phone away from her ear. The screen darkened, and alarm stitched through her.

She turned in a full circle, her mind doing the same thing.

"Joy?" Scott asked. "You okay?"

She faced him and shook her head. "Uh, maybe? That was my hotel, and they had a flood that killed their electricity. I don't have a room tonight." She looked up at him like he'd know what to do.

Call Bea, she thought. *Or Cass. She has a huge house.*

But that would require her to tell them she'd come into town early—just to see Scott. She'd have to tell more than Lauren that she'd been texting him for the past three months. She wasn't sure she wanted to do that quite yet, and the longer she searched Scott's face, the more she thought she didn't want to call one of her friends.

"Let's go sit down," he said, taking her arm in his. "We'll figure something out, okay?"

She nodded and let him lead her to a table in the far corner of the restaurant, with big windows that looked out over a pond. She had no idea what possessed her, but the moment she slid into the booth, she looked at Scott doing the same and blurted out, "Maybe I could stay with you?"

Sneak Peek! The Beach Blueprint Chapter Two:

Scott Anderson had a big laugh, and he used it a lot. His first instinct after Joy—the gorgeous blonde he'd been crushing on for a solid six months—asked if she could stay with him was to laugh.

Hard.

He managed to pull back on that before anything escaped his mouth. Thankfully. He did need a few moments to stare and blink while he tried to come up with what he should say or do instead.

Joy Bartlett waved her hand like she was swatting away errant flies. "Never mind. That was so stupid. There are like, fifteen thousand hotels here. I'll find another one."

Scott's face did relax into a smile then. The woman had just asked to stay with him. He hadn't known where they'd be when he saw her. Flirting and texting and even calling a woman was something Scott excelled at. He could talk to anyone—literally anyone—but he didn't tell Joy that. He wanted her to feel special, and she was.

He enjoyed talking to her more than anyone else in his life right now, that was for dang sure. He couldn't wait to finish with his lawns, bushes, shrubs, trees, and pools to get home, shower, and then talk to Joy. She evened out all the odd things inside him, and Scott liked her far more than any other woman he'd dated in oh, at least five years.

"I totally want you to stay with me," he said, leaning forward and ignoring the waitress as she approached. In the end, he decided he better not be so open and flirtatious and...scandalous in front of a stranger.

He looked up at the woman—not a stranger—and his face split into a grin. "Kate," he said. He slid out of the booth and hugged the woman. "This is a secret," he murmured in her ear, and then he faced Joy.

She also stood and Scott put his arm around Kate, who he hoped looked enough like him to assure Joy they were related. Kate stared at the side of his face too, but Scott ignored her. "Joy, this is my cousin, Kate Arnold. Kate, this is Joy Bartlett."

No qualifier, though Scott knew which one he wanted to use. He'd been talking to Joy for three months. They hadn't seen each other in person once, until today. He shouldn't have brought her to Mead's. Instead, he should've insisted on meeting her in Charleston and taking her somewhere there so they could be alone.

Everywhere Scott looked, he saw people he knew. It wouldn't be long before Grant, Harrison, Blake, Oliver, and

Ty knew about this date. And that meant Joy's Supper Club friends would know too.

His pulse blipped in his chest as Joy put that stunning smile on her face and leaned forward to shake Kate's hand. "So great to meet you," she said in that sexy drawl that was so much like his, but so different too.

"Oh, where are you from, honey?" Kate asked.

"Texas," Joy said. She smiled and met Scott's eye.

"Let's sit," he said. "We don't need to stand." He slid back into the booth. "I want the smothered potato skins, Katie. And the strawberry lemonade sweet tea." He picked up his menu and looked over it to Joy. "It's incredible. It's why I wanted to bring you here." She'd talked about her sweet tea, which was her grandmother's recipe, as well as several other varieties around her small town in Texas

Her face lit up. "That's this place?"

"Yes, ma'am." He grinned at her and didn't look at the menu again. He didn't need it.

She looked up at Kate. "Do you have peach?"

"Absolutely. Peach it is." She didn't write anything down. "Any other apps?"

"I haven't even looked," Joy said.

"I know what you want, baby," he said, and he swore he didn't mean to sound all sultry. His voice just came out that way with Joy. He looked up at Kate, his face heating when his cousin smiled so wide, those drawn-on eyebrows so dang high. "She'll like the artichoke dip, please. And bring us an order of the bar pretzels—double the hot mustard sauce."

"You got it, Scotty." Kate turned and walked away before

Scott could growl at her for using his childhood nickname. He hadn't been Scotty for decades, and blast her for embarrassing him on his first real date with Joy.

He cleared his throat and turned his attention back to the woman across from him. "Everyone on the island is going to know about us by nightfall." He shifted in his seat. "I sort of forgot she works here."

Joy's surprise hit him straight in the throat. "So my friends..."

"They live on the island," he said. "And they all have husbands or boyfriends who are well-connected locals." Scott shook his head, his chin dipping down in regret. "Sorry, Joy. I know you wanted to keep this a secret."

She picked up her phone calmly, and Scott loved this aloof side of her. She'd shown it to him plenty of times this past summer, when he'd been blatant in his feelings and asked her out to her face. Twice. Maybe three times, even when she had a boyfriend.

"Not exactly a secret," she said quietly. "I'm just...I don't want the pressure of talking about us yet." She looked at him. "You get that, right?"

"Yes," he said, but he wasn't sure if he did or not. Kate would razz him about Joy, and that didn't bother Scott. He could admit he liked her—he wasn't trying to keep that a secret. It almost felt like Joy wasn't sure of her feelings for him, and that thought rang so true, he knew it was.

Take the flirting down a notch, he told himself. He could. For her, he would.

"One problem at a time," she said. "I need a hotel tonight."

"You could tell your friends and then stay with Lauren," he suggested, but Joy shook her head before he even finished the sentence. "I was going to say...before Kate came over." He swallowed and wished he had his strawberry lemonade sweet tea. "I totally want you to stay over, but I'm not in my place right now, remember? I've got a studio apartment on the edge of the ocean, and that might be a little...intimate for our first date."

Joy's face turned a delicious shade of pink, and that satisfied Scott greatly. "You're right," she said. "I forgot."

"That said." He leaned back in the booth and folded his arms. "I want you to, for the official record and all that. But, I also have someone you can call about a hotel room. In fact, I'll text him now."

He took his phone from his pocket and started tapping. "I stayed there for a few nights before I got into this studio. Ty's great, and if he has anything, he'll give it to you, I'm sure."

"I know Ty," she said. Scott looked at her, surprised. "I mean, sort of. He's the real estate agent who helped Lauren buy her house."

"Oh, of course." Scott had forgotten about that too. He couldn't hold things in his head the way he used to, and he let extraneous details flow through his mind without holding onto them. This skill normally served him without a problem, but his ability to forget anything and everything sometimes got him into trouble—like when he hadn't remembered meeting Joy the first time.

He hadn't had a day go by where he hadn't thought about her since seeing her sunbathing on Harrison Tate's deck, months and months ago. Even after she'd turned him down. Even after she'd been sassy with him, and he figured he had no chance with her. She'd burrowed into his skull, and his brain wasn't letting her go.

Of course, then she'd texted him out of nowhere in September. He could scroll all the way to the top of their messaging thread and re-read the message, but he didn't need to. He had it memorized.

Hey, it's Joy Bartlett, and I just heard you're going out with someone tonight. I don't want you to. That's bold, I know, but as I thought about you going out with anyone but me...I didn't like it. Call me. Or text back. Or don't and enjoy your date.

He'd never gotten a bigger shock in his life than that text, and he could still see himself coming to a complete standing halt as he read it. The mowers and edgers had continued around him, and he'd laughed and laughed and laughed.

Then, he'd promptly messaged her back, saying he was finishing up one last lawn for the day, and then he'd call her that night. He'd canceled his date with a woman who's name he'd already forgotten, and he'd been talking to Joy every day since.

Ty's message popped up, and Scott smiled. "He says he's got a room at Beach Beauty, and that's a nice property."

"Can I afford it?" Joy wore a worried look, and Scott had

learned over the months that her default was worry. She worried about everything, from how her sons were doing—a legitimate concern—to her students, to if her cat was lonely at home during the day while she worked. She worried over him too, and Scott sure did like that, because he knew Joy only worried about things she really cared about.

He reached across the table and took her hands in his. Touching her...there was nothing like it. Phone calls, video chats, and texting were one thing. Being with her, holding her, touching her, seeing her only a few feet away...that was magic.

"Yeah," he said. "You can afford it, because he said it's free."

She shook her head, her expression turning hard. "I don't need his charity. I can pay something."

Scott grinned and shook his head. "This isn't a contest, Joy. Are you going to insist on paying for dinner tonight?"

"No," she said, the set of her jaw a tad on the stubborn side.

He cocked his head and pulled his hands back to his side of the table. "Why not?"

"We're on a date."

"He's doing you a favor."

"I don't need a favor."

"Then the hotel is part of the date," Scott said. "Dinner and a place to stay." He smiled at her, and Joy finally cracked.

"You're impossible," she said.

"You like impossible," he threw back at her.

She laughed then, and that sound while they were in

close proximity could never be replicated over the phone. He joined her, and then as they quieted, he said, "I'm so glad you're here."

"Strawberry lemonade sweet tea," Katie practically yelled. "Peach sweet tea." She set both glass mugs down with loud clunks. "Do y'all know what you want to eat?" She looked back and forth between Scott and Joy, her auburn ponytail swinging as she did, as if she hadn't just interrupted something sweet and tender and intimate.

Scott gestured for Joy to go first, because he needed another moment inside the feeling streaming through him and he didn't want to speak and ruin it. He wanted to keep Joy in his life for a while, and that meant he had to figure out how to hide all of his flaws until she was madly in love with him.

However long that took. However much time she needed to figure out that he was the one for her. Only then would he allow some of the...less great things about himself be known.

"THIS PLACE IS TOO NICE," JOY COMPLAINED AS SHE entered the room Ty had gotten for her. "Oh my word, Scott, look at that view!" She hurried over to the bank of windows across the room while he towed one of her suitcases across the threshold and into the room.

She sighed; the door closed; Scott left her large suitcase

by her small one and went to join her at the windows. "I told you this was a beautiful property."

"I can't believe it's available."

"You're a few days before the Christmas crowds." He lifted his arm around her, and Joy sank into his side. The sun outside had started to set, as it was December, and that meant they got less daylight house. They stood there and watched it sink lower and lower, the reflection on the water almost gone before Joy said, "This was the perfect day."

"Was it?" he asked. "Flying for most of it, then driving here, and then me scaring you in the parking lot?" He chuckled and adjusted his hand lower on her arm to keep her close.

"Everything after three-thirty," she amended.

"Hmm." He pressed his lips to her temple. "That sounds like everything with me, sweetheart."

She didn't deny it, and instead said, "Yeah."

Scott needed to leave right now, or he wasn't sure he'd be able to bring himself to do it. He dropped his arm and turned away from the view, from Joy. His eyes landed on the big, puffy, king-sized bed, and everything inside him tightened. "Well, I better get going." He swallowed and walked on wooden legs toward the exit.

"You're not working tomorrow, are you?" she asked, following him.

"No, sweetheart. We're going on that alligator thing in the morning, remember?"

"Yeah, I was just checking."

He turned back to her at the door, and she came within inches of him. Too close, but not close enough at the same time. "I'll bring breakfast, because this place doesn't have it." He gave her a smile. "And we have reservations at Lighthouse Point for lunch. Then, I guess I'll have to let you go see Lauren."

Joy returned his smile and put one palm against his chest, branding him. Sealing him as hers. "Thank you, Scott." She tipped up onto her toes, and Scott easily took her into his arms. Did she want him to kiss her? Could he do that and then walk away? He honestly wasn't sure.

She smelled like peaches and vanilla, and he couldn't wait to taste it on her lips. He leaned down, giving her plenty of time to stop him. She didn't.

Scott touched his lips to hers, expecting heat, and getting burned instantly. He held for a moment, took a breath, and then stroked a better kiss across her lips. She responded eagerly, and Scott couldn't help but wonder if she'd thought about him every day since last summer, despite going out with another man.

She sure kissed him like she had, and that was just fine with him.

Oh, boy. Kissing already? Joy is going to be in so much trouble....

Preorder THE BEACH BLUEPRINT now! Scan the QR code to get it on any retailer.

Books in the Hilton Head Romance series

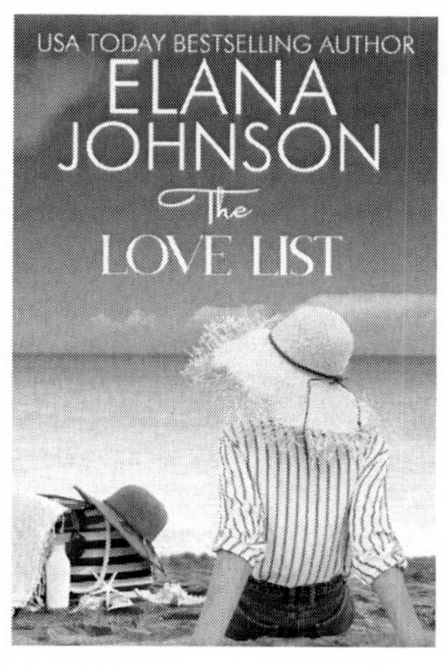

The Love List (Hilton Head Romance, Book 1): Bea turns to her lists when things get confusing and her love list morphs once again... Can she add *fall in love at age 45* to the list and check it off?

The Paradise Plan (Hilton Head Romance, Book 2): When Harrison keeps showing up unannounced at her construction site, sometimes with her favorite pastries, Cass starts to wonder if she should add him to her daily routine... If she does, will her perfectly laid out plans fall short of paradise? Or could she find her new life *and* a new love, all without any plans at all?

The Seaside Strategy (Hilton Head Romance, Book 3): Lauren doesn't want to work for Blake, especially not in strategic investments. She's had enough of the high-profile, corporate life. **Can she strategically insert herself into Blake's life without compromising her seaside strategy and finally get what she really wants...love and a lasting relationship?**

The Beach Blueprint (Hilton Head Romance, Book 4): Joy Bartlett needs a blueprint before she takes a single step in any direction. She loves seeing what she's getting into before committing, and moving 1200 miles from Texas to South Carolina just because half of her Supper Club has doesn't mean she's going to start packing boxes. Can she figure out how to arrange all of the pieces in her life in a way that makes sense? Or will she find herself cut off from everyone who's ever been important to her?

Books in the Sweet Water Falls Farm Romance series

Cross Cowboy, Book 1: He's been accused of being far too blunt. Like that time he accused her of stealing her company from her best friend... Can Travis and Shayla overcome their differences and find a happily-ever-after together?

Grumpy Cowboy

Grumpy Cowboy, Book 2: He can find the negative in any situation. Like that time he got upset with the woman who brought him a free chocolate-and-caramel-covered apple because it had melted in his truck... Can William and Gretchen start over and make a healthy relationship after it's started to wilt?

Surly Cowboy

Surly Cowboy, Book 3: He's got a reputation to uphold and he's not all that amused the way regular people are. Like that time he stood there straight-faced and silent while everyone else in the audience cheered and clapped for that educational demo... Can Lee and Rosalie let bygones be bygones and make a family filled with joy?

Salty Cowboy

Salty Cowboy, Book 4: The last Cooper sibling is looking for love...she just wishes it wouldn't be in her hometown, or with the saltiest cowboy on the planet. But something about Jed Forrester has Cherry all a-flutter, and he'll be darned if he's going to let her get away. But Jed may have met his match when it comes to his quick tongue and salty attitude...

Books in the Hope Eternal Ranch Romance series

Hopeful Cowboy, Book 1: Can Ginger and Nate find their happily-ever-after, keep up their duties on the ranch, and build a family? Or will the risk be too great for them both?

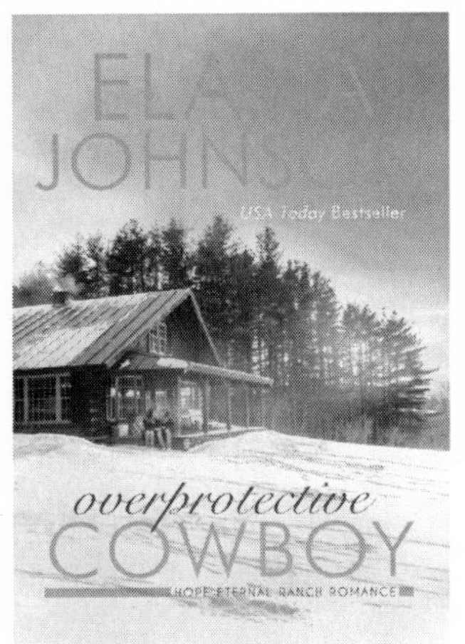

Overprotective Cowboy, Book 2: Can Ted and Emma face their pasts so they can truly be ready to step into the future together? Or will everything between them fall apart once the truth comes out?

Rugged Cowboy, Book 3: He's a cowboy mechanic with two kids and an ex-wife on the run. She connects better to horses than humans. Can Dallas and Jess find their way to each other at Hope Eternal Ranch?

Christmas Cowboy, Book 4: He needs to start a new story for his life. She's dealing with a lot of family issues. This Christmas, can Slate and Jill find solace in each other at Hope Eternal Ranch?

Wishful Cowboy, Book 5: He needs somewhere to belong. She has a heart as wide as the Texas sky. Can Luke and Hannah find their one true love in each other?

Risky Cowboy, Book 6: She's tired of making cheese and ice cream on her family's dairy farm, but when the cowboy hired to replace her turns out to be an ex-boyfriend, Clarissa suddenly isn't so sure about leaving town... Will Spencer risk it all to convince Clarissa to stay and give him a second chance?

Books in the Hawthorne Harbor Romance series

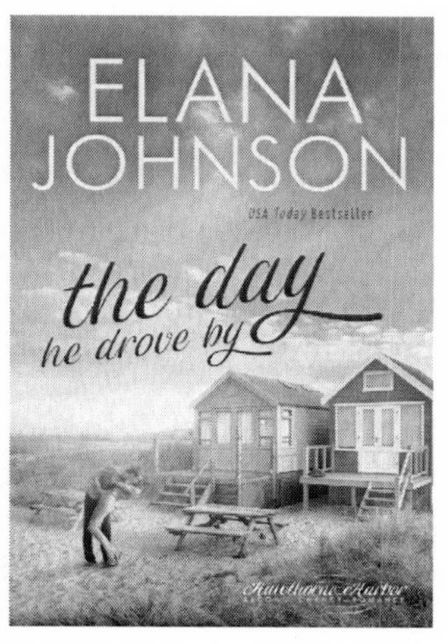

The Day He Drove By (Hawthorne Harbor Second Chance Romance, Book 1): A widowed florist, her ten-year-old daughter, and the paramedic who delivered the girl a decade earlier...

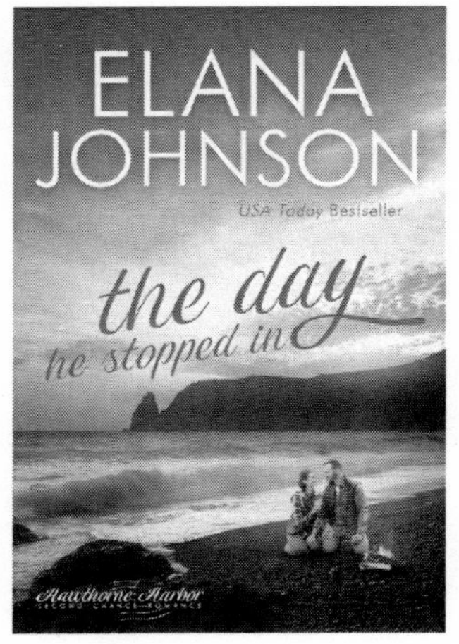

The Day He Stopped In (Hawthorne Harbor Second Chance Romance, Book 2): Janey Germaine is tired of entertaining tourists in Olympic National Park all day and trying to keep her twelve-year-old son occupied at night. When longtime friend and the Chief of Police, Adam Herrin, offers to take the boy on a ride-along one fall evening, Janey starts to see him in a different light. Do they have the courage to take their relationship out of the friend zone?

The Day He Said Hello (Hawthorne Harbor Second Chance Romance, Book 3): Bennett Patterson is content with his boring firefighting job and his big great dane...until he comes face-to-face with his high school girlfriend, Jennie Zimmerman, who swore she'd never return to Hawthorne Harbor. Can they rekindle their old flame? Or will their opposite personalities keep them apart?

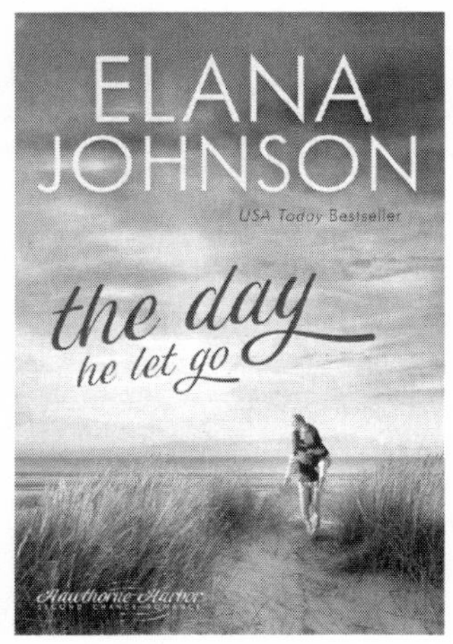

The Day He Let Go (Hawthorne Harbor Second Chance Romance, Book 4): Trent Baker is ready for another relationship, and he's hopeful he can find someone who wants him and to be a mother to his son. Lauren Michaels runs her own general contract company, and she's never thought she has a maternal bone in her body. But when she gets a second chance with the handsome K9 cop who blew her off when she first came to town, she can't say no… Can Trent and Lauren make their differences into strengths and build a family?

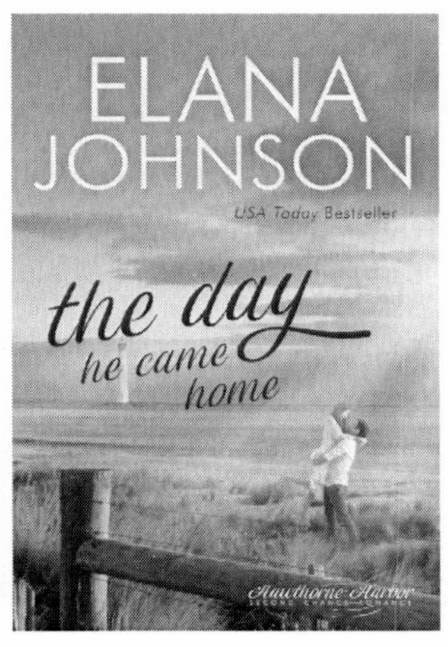

The Day He Came Home (Hawthorne Harbor Second Chance Romance, Book 5): A wounded Marine returns to Hawthorne Harbor years after the woman he was married to for exactly one week before she got an annulment...and then a baby nine months later. Can Hunter and Alice make a family out of past heartache?

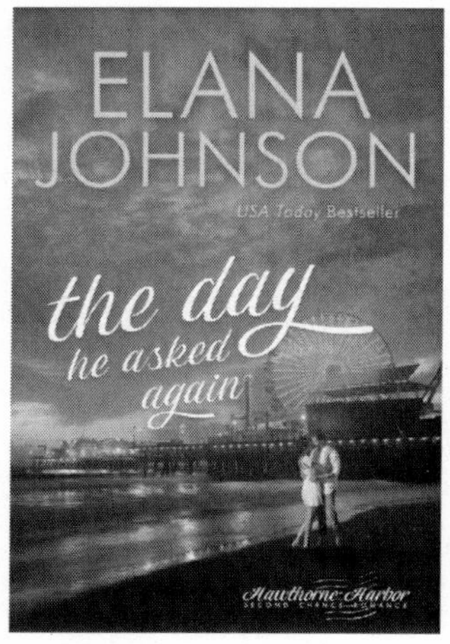

The Day He Asked Again (Hawthorne Harbor Second Chance Romance, Book 6): A Coast Guard captain would rather spend his time on the sea...unless he's with the woman he's been crushing on for months. Can Brooklynn and Dave make their second chance stick?

About Elana

Elana Johnson is the USA Today bestselling and Kindle All-Star author of dozens of clean and wholesome contemporary romance novels. She lives in Utah, where she mothers two fur babies, works with her husband full-time, and eats a lot of veggies while writing. Find her on her website at feelgoodfictionbooks.com.

Made in United States
North Haven, CT
06 November 2022